"Don't talk to me about love," she challenged.

"Right." Impatience put an edge to his light, careless words. "Because what would a frivolous, reckless cowboy like me know about something as consequential and enduring as love?"

She was only saying what needed to be said. What they both already knew. Couldn't he see that? She whispered, "I can't be who you need."

"Funny." One corner of his mouth lifted. There was nothing easy or indifferent about his half grin. "I only ever wanted you to be you."

"This is me." She thrust her arm at the closed hospital room door. "I'm a mother. A deputy. I live to serve and protect. That's who I am."

"You really don't see yourself, do you?" he asked.

She raked her fingers through her hair. "You want a happy-go-lucky cowgirl, Caleb. And that's not me anymore."

Dear Reader,

I relocated often growing up, and that trend continues. It doesn't matter whether you're moving from one apartment to another in the same building or venturing across country, relocating is hard work. It's also exciting, exhausting, fun and frustrating. But that's change—a bundle of mixed emotions that are best when acknowledged and trouble when ignored.

In *A Proposal for Her Cowboy*, Lacey Nash returns home and finds herself boots deep in change. Lacey wants to prove herself at her new job and with her family, no matter how challenging. When Lacey runs into a cowboy from her past, she realizes the biggest change might be heart-sized. If this adventure-first cowboy and strong-minded cowgirl can trust their hearts, they might find love is a journey best taken together.

It's summer in Three Springs, Texas, where swimming isn't reserved only for the townsfolk, the social calendars are full, and there's always room on the porch. So grab a glass of lemonade and join the fun.

Happy Reading!

Cari Lynn Webb

A PROPOSAL FOR HER COWBOY

CARI LYNN WEBB

H Harlequin

HEARTWARMING

 Harlequin®
HEARTWARMING™

Recycling programs
for this product may
not exist in your area.

ISBN-13: 978-1-335-05119-6

A Proposal for Her Cowboy

Harlequin Enterprises ULC
22 Adelaide St. West, 41st Floor
Toronto, Ontario M5H 4E3, Canada
www.Harlequin.com

Printed in Lithuania

MIX
Paper | Supporting
responsible forestry
FSC® C021394

Cari Lynn Webb lives in South Carolina with her husband, daughters and assorted four-legged family members. She's been blessed to see the power of true love in her grandparents' seventy-year marriage and her parents' marriage of over fifty years. She knows love isn't always sweet and perfect—it can be challenging, complicated and risky. But she believes happily-ever-afters are worth fighting for. She loves to connect with readers.

Books by Cari Lynn Webb

Harlequin Heartwarming

Three Springs, Texas

The Rancher's Secret Crush
Falling for the Cowboy Doc
Her Cowboy Wedding Date
Trusting the Rancher with Christmas
The Texas SEAL's Surprise
His Christmas Cowgirl

Return of the Blackwell Brothers

The Rancher's Rescue

The Blackwell Sisters

Montana Wedding

The Blackwells of Eagle Springs

Her Favorite Wyoming Sheriff

Visit the Author Profile page
at Harlequin.com for more titles.

To my grandparents,
whose love story continues to inspire me.
I miss you.

Special thanks to my editor, Kathryn Lye.
To my husband and daughters for always being
ready with a hug and a laugh. To my writing gang,
who doesn't hesitate to answer my calls and texts.
My stories are better thanks to all of you.

CHAPTER ONE

BABYMOON. BEFORE LACEY NASH could translate her ex-husband's early-morning text, the two-way radio clipped to her shoulder chirped.

Static scratched across the speaker, followed by the timid but sweetly high-pitched voice of Gertie Tiller. The long-time dispatcher for Three Springs County Sheriff's Department. "Deputy Nash. You copy? C-o-p-y."

Lacey waited for Gertie to finish stretching out the *y* in *copy* like the final note in a solo stage performance. Silence was her cue. She pressed the button on her radio and said, "Ten-two." Then a quick, "Copy."

"Copy that," Gertie singsonged. "Over."

Lacey grabbed her newly issued camel-colored deputy's hat from the hook in the mudroom and walked outside.

More static. A distinct throat clearing, then Gertie said, "Code ten-fifty-three at Clearwind Lake."

The road was blocked at Clearwind Lake. Lacey locked the door to her stepdad and late mom's ranch house, which was serving as Lacey's residence, and reached for her radio.

But Gertie was back. Her words expanded her vocal range into a squeaky high pitch. "Correction. Code ten-ninety-two at Clearwind Lake."

Parking complaint. Lacey unlocked the dark blue SUV parked in the driveway and climbed inside the latest addition to the fleet of vehicles for the Three Springs County Sheriff's Department.

Another throat clearing crossed the speaker and Gertie's overly excited words peeled out. "Code ten-fifty-four. Clearwind Lake. That's the one."

Livestock on the roadway. Lacey buckled her seat belt, started the SUV, and pulled out of the driveway. Given the continued stretch of silence across the two-way, Lacey finally took her chance. She activated the radio speaker and said, "I'm en route to Clearwind Lake."

A long sigh pushed across the two-way. Censure filled Gertie's suddenly bland words. "I know you are new, Deputy Nash, but we prefer to use codes on this frequency."

Lacey laughed, then sobered before she spoke. Gertie was part of her team now, and Lacey wanted the woman to like her. She pressed the radio button for a succinct "ten-four."

Sunglasses on, Lacey watched a hawk soar above the endless open plains of the Texas Panhandle that stretched out on either side of the road. The land was broken only by fence lines marking off ranches, cattle farms, and recently harvested wheat fields. Not another person was in sight. Only her and the hawk. Her shoulders loosened as they'd been steadily doing since her arrival stateside six months earlier. Now she was back home for good. No more active-duty deployments overseas. No more putting service before family. She'd made promises, and it was past time to keep them.

Her phone chimed a new text alert. No doubt from her ex-husband. *Again.* He was one of a handful of people who had her personal phone number and used it regularly. Lacey ignored it. She had time to deal with her ex-husband and his baby-moon situation—whatever that was—after her shift ended.

She might have moved home to reconnect with family, but she still had a job to do. One she took quite seriously, even if she was patrolling sleepy country roads, instead of being part of an active military police force stationed on a massive base in South Korea or Germany.

Lacey turned onto the road leading to Clearwind Lake and pulled in behind a familiar deep blue Three Springs County Sheriff's Department truck. Her stepdad, Sheriff Wells Hopson, was already on the scene. No surprise there. *Swells*, as she'd affectionately called him when she was a kid, was more dedicated to his job than anyone Lacey knew. Her superstep—her other nickname for him—was the reason she'd chosen a career in law enforcement.

But right now, he was Sheriff Hopson, her superior and her boss. He stood in the middle of the road with his back to her. Two men stood beside him. The taller was a classic cowboy, from his worn brown hat and his plaid shirt and fit-just-right jeans to his dust-covered boots.

Oversize camo-colored waders swallowed the shorter man. Still, she recognized the shock of white in the man's otherwise short dark hair. Mayor Paul Molina had been at her swearing-in ceremony for Three Springs County Sheriff's Department. Mayor Molina had a firm handshake, a thick accent, and a rumbling, good-natured laugh not easily forgotten.

"Gentlemen." Lacey approached the trio, followed the direction of their focus, and finally got to the source of their standoff. *A turtle.* Albeit a very large one. And if she wasn't mistaken, a turtle of the snapping breed. No wonder Gertie had trouble with the correct code. Lacey shook her head. "Don't tell me you three are scared of a turtle."

"It's not exactly little," Mayor Molina mused and switched his fishing pole to his other hand.

Lacey eyed the turtle, guesstimating he weighed in at close to forty pounds.

"And they aren't called snapping turtles for nothing," Sheriff Hopson offered.

"Remember when Gus Ranford lost his toe to a snapper?" Mayor Molina rocked in his rubber boots as if checking that his toes were still attached.

Lacey winced. Her gaze tracked to the cowboy, and her own toes curled in her black patrol boots. Her heart snapped to full attention. *Caleb Sloan.* The cowboy was no stranger. *And* he was no longer a boy she'd once known in high school. He was inches taller than her towering stepdad, unfairly handsome, and watching her like he knew the secret to life and wasn't willing to share.

One corner of his mouth tipped into his cheek, and he touched the brim of his hat. Just a flick of his fingers in acknowledgment. Amusement washed through his slow Texas drawl. "Where exactly was Gus when this snapper got him?"

Lacey knew exactly where she was when she'd first been hooked by Caleb Sloan, his daredevil charisma, and thrill-seeking ways. On a date with one of his best friends. That hadn't stopped her from recklessly accepting Caleb's dare that night and the many others that soon followed.

But the days of carefree nights, reckless abandon, and teenage adrenaline rushes were long gone. Her mother's cancer diagnosis had reined Lacey into being responsible and pragmatic. Later, an unexpected pregnancy had extinguished the last of the impulsive nature still kindling inside Lacey. She'd outgrown cowboys like Caleb Sloan and was surely better for it.

"Gus was walking barefoot in Eagle Run River." Sheriff Hopson rubbed his fingers across his upper lip hidden inside his well-groomed beard. "Got him good. Wouldn't let go until he'd gotten what he wanted."

"Never did find that turtle." Mayor Molina eyed the turtle blocking the road as if he might be the toe-snatching culprit.

"I'm sure Gus always put his boots on before going into the river after that incident," Lacey said.

"Don't reckon that he did." Mayor Molina chuckled. "Rather, he walked on the other bank of the river. Used to say if he lost his other little toe, he'd be back in balance."

Caleb's laughter spilled out, unchecked and unabashed.

And entirely too distracting. Lacey's lips twitched. She tugged her attention from the much-too-good-looking cowboy and focused on the issue at hand. "Well, this turtle can't be left here. Someone will run him over."

"How do you tell a male from a female turtle?" Mayor Molina knocked his bucket hat askew.

"Tail size." Lacey waved toward the turtle. "Males have longer tails than the females." The guys blinked blandly at her. She shrugged. "Aspen got an A on her school project about turtles and sent it to me."

Caleb stuck his hands in the back pockets of his jeans and considered her. "Then you know the proper way to handle a turtle, Deputy."

She knew the proper way to handle more than a turtle, including how to handle a disarming cowboy like him. *Don't.* She added a challenge to her words. "Do you?"

His close-lipped grin and his hooded gaze were pure mischief, as if riling her was the only game he wanted to play. But Lacey dealt with lawbreakers and avoided heartbreakers at all costs.

He nodded.

She set her hands on her hips. "Then why haven't you moved the turtle?"

"We like our toes and our fingers." Sheriff Hopson held his arms out in front of him and wiggled his fingers.

"We can't stand here all day, watching this turtle to make sure he crosses safely." Lacey didn't try to hide her exasperation.

"I suppose we could draw straws," her stepdad offered. "Shortest one moves the turtle."

Lacey glanced at her watch. Thirty minutes until the park officially opened. They could be sorting straws for the next hour. She walked to her vehicle and grabbed a pair of gloves from the passenger seat. Passing by the men, she tossed over her shoulder, "Watch and learn, boys."

Lacey circled the turtle from the back and picked him up. Quick and efficient. She wasted no time releasing him into the grass and backing away with her hands up. Like most wild animals, turtles preferred not to be handled. The turtle poked his head out, considered her for a brief second, then started ambling through the grass. Lacey turned to gloat, but the men were focused on Sheriff Hopson. *Huh?*

Her stepdad tapped his phone screen, cleared his throat, and announced the time.

A triumphant grin spread across Caleb's face, and he extended his hand, palm up. "Pay up. I called that one almost to the minute."

"She always had a big soft spot for wildlife."

Her stepdad passed Caleb a twenty-dollar bill and added, "Even the mean ones."

Mayor Molina placed another twenty dollars on Caleb's palm and said, "I suppose you knew that little fact too, Caleb Sloan."

"I used to know that." Caleb smiled and stuffed the cash in his back pocket. "But it has been years since Lacey and I have seen each other. People change."

Caleb had changed. His shoulders were broader. The beginning of a dark beard covered his cheeks as if he'd woken up eager to take on the day and skipped shaving. And there was a confidence in the well-built man before her that she found more than a little appealing.

But clearly the boy she'd known hadn't grown up. *The devil-may-care is rooted deep in that boy, Lace. Take care not to get tangled up too.* Those had been her mother's words after meeting a teenage Caleb Sloan.

Lacey hooked her thumbs on her utility belt, jabbed her elbows out to expand her space, and bumped her unwanted thoughts about the handsome cowboy aside. "This was a bet? Don't you have real work to be doing somewhere else?"

"It's my day off." Mayor Molina snapped the suspenders on his waders and waggled his eyebrows. "Only work I intend to do today is fish."

"Well, now that the livestock is no longer blocking the roadway—" Lacey peeled off her gloves and turned toward her vehicle "—I think I'll get back to work."

"The turtle isn't the livestock, Deputy Nash," Caleb drawled and then chuckled. His gaze gleamed before he pointed to the lake nearby. "Walter is."

Lacey gasped, then sputtered, "That's a bull."

CHAPTER TWO

ONE OF THE largest bulls Lacey had ever seen was standing serenely in the lake, within splashing distance of the area roped off for public swimming. The same area families would soon be arriving to use while they enjoyed their last days of summer vacation. She'd been so focused on the snapping turtle she'd never even glanced at the water. Not exactly the attention to detail she prided herself on in her line of work.

"That's a Beefmaster bull to be exact," her stepdad offered mildly.

"What's he doing here?" Lacey asked.

"Don't look at me." Caleb held up both hands, grinning. "I didn't invite him."

"Clearly, Walter believes the lake is his own personal watering hole." Mayor Molina waved his arms and brandished his fishing pole as if preparing for a joust. "He charged me something good earlier. I dropped my tackle box, and now my best lures are scattered all over the shore."

Lacey spun and eyed the rust-colored bull. "Who does Walter belong to?"

"Murphy." That reply came in unison from the trio.

"Where's Murphy?" Lacey prodded.

"Boise." Again, the reply came in unison.

"As in Boise, Idaho?" Lacey clarified.

The trio nodded.

"Well, Walter can't stay here." Lacey crossed her arms over her chest. "Allyson Loret is having her tenth birthday party here in just over an hour." Gertie had shown Lacey the parks and rec calendar yesterday after they'd gone through the fish and game handbook.

"Sort of takes pin-the-tail-on-the-bull to a whole other level, doesn't it?" Caleb quipped.

Her stepdad and the mayor chuckled.

"This isn't really a time for jokes," Lacey said. "Walter needs to be moved. We can't very well throw a rope around him and walk him home."

"Why not?" Caleb dusted his hands on his jeans. "You said it yourself, Deputy Nash, we can't have Walter crashing the birthday party, even though he's quite tame."

Tame. "That's a two-thousand-pound animal," Lacey said. With a battering ram for a head, amazing agility, and nothing meek in his massive, muscular body. She glanced at Caleb. "What? Are you going to stroll over there and just lasso Walter?"

"Something like that." Caleb lifted one shoulder.

"Be serious, Caleb." Lacey moved to block him. "This isn't a game."

Caleb eyed her from beneath the brim of his cowboy hat. "This isn't my first rodeo, Deputy."

Lacey shot him a look. "This isn't a rodeo either." There was no arena. No fences. No precautions. No first aid. Nothing but him and a bull. The odds heavily favored the bull.

A teasing tone matched his broad grin. "Why, Deputy Nash, I do believe you might be worried about me."

"Of course I am." Lacey leaned toward him. "It's my second day on the job, Caleb Sloan. I can't have a citizen I'm supposed to protect be trampled by a bull. Not. On. My. Second. Day."

"No one is getting trampled today." Caleb knocked his cowboy hat lower on his head. "Your record will remain unblemished."

He sounded disappointed in her, as if she'd somehow let him down. Lacey narrowed her eyes and searched his face. *Impossible.* This was Caleb here-for-the-entertainment-only Sloan.

"Relax, Deputy." Caleb's smile thinned. "Reinforcements have arrived."

The reinforcements were two trucks with attached trailers and a pair of tall cowboys. After handshakes with the newcomers, Lacey was introduced to Evan Bishop, one of the largest local cattle ranchers in the area. The other cowboy was none other than Ryan Sloan, Caleb's champion bronc-riding older brother.

Lacey's stepdad and the mayor jumped into the sheriff's truck and drove it to block the park entrance until Walter was contained.

"What's the plan?" Ryan opened the doors of the

horse trailer hitched to his truck. Evan went inside and guided a sleek bay out.

"I figure I'm going in." Caleb handed his cell phone to his brother. "Unless either of you want to test the waters?"

"My Mischief doesn't appreciate the water like your horse." Ryan led a gray-dun mustang into the parking lot, then worked on saddling the powerful horse. Evan seconded Ryan's claims.

"You aren't seriously going into the water, are you?" Lacey watched Caleb head inside the trailer. "That's your plan? Swim with Walter?"

"There's a little more to it than that." Caleb guided a stunning dark gold Palomino horse out of the trailer.

"A cowboy, a bull, and a lake." Lacey shifted her gaze from one cowboy to the next. "Does anyone else think that sounds like the start of a bad joke?"

Evan ducked his head, hiding his grin, and escaped inside the trailer.

"We need to stop and think." Lacey squeezed her fingers to her temple. She was known for being levelheaded in any situation, even the most stressful. She was also notoriously hard to ruffle, according to her former captain. Yet she felt flustered. And wasn't that more irritating than a swarm of horseflies? She widened her stance as if to prove her cowboy couldn't knock her completely off-balance. "We need to talk this through."

"There's no time. The kids are coming soon. Walter has got to go." Caleb tapped his wrist. "Tick. Tock. Tick. Tock."

Still, she hesitated and rounded on Caleb's older brother for backup. "You have to agree there's nothing reasonable about swimming with a bull."

"There's nothing particularly sensible about Walter preferring this lake," Ryan countered.

"But here we are." Caleb motioned toward the bull still standing hip-high in the water, seemingly bored by the commotion he was causing.

Lacey knew better than to believe a bull had found his inner zen in a public lake. Even one with a fetching white mottled face and a sleepy look about him.

"My daughter is coming to the birthday party." Evan carried a saddle from the trailer and set it on his bay horse. "Riley will be more than mad if Walter ruins her afternoon swim with her friends."

"Nothing for it, Lacey." Caleb laughed, easy and upbeat. "Walter's pool time is up." He paused and tipped his head at her. His grin came slowly. "Now, Deputy, as luck would have it, we have an extra horse who appreciates the water. You're welcome to join me for a morning dip."

Join him.

Lacey blinked and watched his smile lift into his cheeks, all white teeth, charm, and challenge.

"I seem to recall a time when you couldn't stay out of the water. Always goading me and our horses to join you for a swim." He leaned toward her. "Think of it like old times." With that, he walked away, whistling a happy tune, and then disappeared inside the trailer.

Oh, her cowboy wasn't wrong. That was back when they were teens and she spent endless summer days doing exactly what she wanted. Indulging her love of horses, the water, and whatever brought her joy. But this wasn't a vacation. And one persuasive yet provoking cowboy wasn't going to make her forget herself or her duty. Lacey crossed her arms over her chest.

Ryan said quietly, "Believe it or not, Caleb knows what he's doing even if he seems less than serious."

Serious. Caleb looked absolutely thrilled. Lacey muttered and reached down to untie her boot. "He looks like he's headed to a water balloon fight with the birthday party kids."

"Caleb treats everything like a good time." Ryan met her gaze over his horse's back. "This should not surprise you. Didn't you two spend a lot of time together in high school?"

"That was high school." Lacey loosened the shoelaces on her other boot. "It was all about having a good time back then."

"True." Ryan made a final adjustment to his horse's saddle. "Gran Claire always admired what she called Caleb's extra ounce of giddyup in his get-up-and-go."

"I'm also certain your gran Claire wished for a little less giddyup more than once," Lacey countered.

"It's good to have you back, Lacey." Ryan laughed. "Maybe you could hang out with my little brother more. Your down-to-earth sensibilities might rub off on him."

Hang out with Caleb Sloan? Not happening. Lacey wasn't a teen looking for adventure. These days she was looking for routine and stability. Things Caleb wasn't known for. Her gaze landed on her barefooted cowboy. Caleb had swapped his jeans for swim trunks and ditched his plaid shirt for a plain T-shirt. But his cowboy hat remained firmly in place along with his confidence.

He watched her slide her boots off and headed toward her. "Change your mind, Deputy?"

About being tempted by a certain daredevil cowboy? Not likely. Lacey shook her head.

"Are you scared you might enjoy this, Deputy?" Caleb rubbed his chin, his words casual.

"There's nothing to enjoy here. And you certainly shouldn't be treating it like some big game either." Lacey unfastened her utility belt and walked to her car. She dropped the belt, two-way radio, and her cell phone onto the seat and rearmed the vehicle. Then she went back to Caleb. "And I'm not scared."

"I don't believe you," he challenged.

"I'm a mom now, Caleb." She stripped off her socks and tossed them on her boots. "I don't have time for fear or fun."

He tapped the rim of his hat higher and eyed her. "Then what are you doing?"

"My duty." Lacey took the reins of the chestnut Arabian horse with four white socks from Ryan.

She led the horse toward a rock, stepped on the stone, and mounted bareback in one fluid motion.

Admiration flashed across Caleb's face before he turned and mounted his horse bareback.

Lacey guided the horse to stand beside Caleb's, close enough that her knee brushed his bare leg, and her words reached his ears only. "Seems not much has changed. You still need a cowgirl to protect you from yourself, don't you?"

"A lot has changed since high school, Deputy. That I can promise you." There was a glint in his blue eyes. "But one thing remains the same."

"What's that?" She adjusted her horse's reins.

His lips twitched. "Once a cowboy, always a cowboy."

And once a fool… But she promised herself never again. Her failed marriage had taught her the perils of losing her heart to the wrong man. And this cowboy was all kinds of wrong for her.

"Time to wrangle Walter," Caleb announced and handed Lacey a rope. "Do you remember what I taught you about roping a steer?"

"Some lessons are hard to forget." Lacey coiled the rope to her liking and gripped it in one hand.

"That's good to know." Caleb chuckled. "And if you have fun, Deputy, I promise not to say: *I told you so.*" He winked and turned for the shoreline.

Lacey followed him. He looked relaxed, his horse equally untroubled by the bull staring them down.

Walter appeared unimpressed by their arrival and, more important, not the least bit riled. But even

Lacey knew that could all turn on a dime. She kept Walter in her sight line.

"Fortunately for us, Walter is motivated by food," Caleb explained. "This will help get him into the trailer once he's out of the water. Unfortunately, Walter has indulged his love of wandering during his retirement at the farm. When he gets out beyond the dock, like he is now, he gets stuck and freezes on the sandbar."

"This has happened before." Lacey considered the supposedly scared bull.

"Took us a while last time as I was the only one in the water." Caleb adjusted his position on his horse. "Now I have you to assist."

"What are we doing exactly?" Lacey asked.

"Wading into the water, roping Walter, and encouraging him to leave the sandbar." Caleb worked his rope through his fingers. "When we get him to shore, we bribe him with a trail of his favorite snacks that will lead him right into the trailer."

Lacey twisted around and saw Ryan scattering carrots and potatoes on the ground. "Can't we throw apples to Walter to get him to move?"

"Tried that. Walter didn't appreciate bobbing for snacks. Can't say I blame him." Caleb rolled his shoulders. "Now we leave the apples inside the trailer as his final reward."

"You make it sound simple." Lacey flexed her fingers around her rope.

"What could go wrong?" Caleb smiled. At her

frown, he reached over and touched her leg. "You don't have to do this," he said and clearly meant it.

Lacey lifted her chin. She meant to pull her own weight, professionally at the sheriff's department and personally as a parent. She would settle for nothing less. And if it meant wrangling a bull out of a lake, so be it. "Here's hoping Walter is famished from his swim and wants his snacks more than he wants to trample us."

"I'm willing to bet on it," Caleb replied.

Lacey wasn't taking that bet.

"Follow my directions from Walter's other side." Caleb pointed to where he wanted Lacey.

Lacey and her horse splashed into the lake. When the water swirled around her calves, Caleb halted her. His rope glided around Walter's neck on the first try. Lacey finally hit her mark on her fourth attempt.

Turned out the roping was the easiest part. Coaxing Walter off the sandbar took patience and persistence and a bit of a soaking.

There was an ongoing loosening and tightening of the slack in their ropes in tandem with the backward and forward movement of their tolerant and well-trained horses. It was a war of wills until Walter shook his massive head, gave in with a snort, and stepped forward. Lacey cheered and called encouragement to the bull, promising him all sorts of delicious delights if he just came to shore.

Finally, Walter reached his first onshore snacks, devoured them quickly, and lumbered along the makeshift path of tasty goodness. Lacey and Caleb kept pace beside the bull, guiding him gently toward the open trailer.

Ryan and Evan waited on their horses, their ropes ready in case Walter decided on a detour. In the end, Walter's appetite won out, and the fresh produce captured the old bull's full attention. Soon, Walter was inside Evan's trailer, noshing on a bushel of fresh apples, none the worse for his swim.

The horses were praised, rubbed down, and in Ryan's trailer in no time. Minutes later, Ryan and Evan jumped back in their trucks and pulled out of the parking lot. Lacey waved goodbye and headed to her vehicle.

"It's only you and me." Caleb followed her. "You can admit it now, Deputy."

"Admit what?" Lacey unrolled her pant legs and squeezed more water out of her uniform.

Caleb lifted his cowboy hat and brushed his hand through his thick brown hair. His damp T-shirt stuck to his chest. He still wore his shorts, but he'd slipped on his cowboy boots. His wide grin suggested he'd been mastering the art of the proper cannonball at the lake all day, not roping a bull. "You can admit you had fun just now. I promise not to tell."

And I promise not to be charmed. By him or the diversions he lived for. The same ones she used to crave. Once upon a lifetime ago. Lacey opened her car door and glanced at him. "There's nothing to tell. I was doing my job."

"Fine, Deputy Nash, welcome home," he drawled,

his eyebrows lifted. "If you change your mind and decide to start chasing fun like you used to, come and find me."

"I can't," she said simply but decisively. "I'm a mom now."

"Last I checked moms aren't exempt from enjoying life," Caleb said, amusement in his words.

"And cowboys aren't exempt from growing up," she countered.

His smile never wavered. He touched the brim of his hat and dipped his chin. "Hope to see you around, Deputy."

Lacey watched Caleb walk over to her stepdad and the mayor near the shore where the pair had been collecting the mayor's lost fishing lures. Laughter soon erupted from the men. Lacey shook her head and got into her vehicle.

Fun wasn't her priority. Her eight-year-old daughter was. She'd missed the last five years of Aspen's life while serving overseas. Now she was home to rebuild their relationship. To do that, Lacey had to become as perfect a mom as her ex-husband's current wife. Aspen's stepmom quite possibly held the title for best mom ever. At the very least, the woman had set a very high parenting standard.

Chasing after adventure with a handsome, heartbreaker cowboy like Caleb Sloan would be misguided and unwise. Nothing about that sounded the least bit perfect.

CHAPTER THREE

CALEB SLOAN WAS the last Sloan brother still single. His older brothers had all found love with their life partners and a golden future. Caleb had never given the future much consideration. He preferred to live in the moment, never tied down to anything or anyone.

But he couldn't deny the restlessness he felt recently or the nagging suspicion that his current lifestyle wasn't sustainable. Maybe "the moment" wasn't everything it was cracked up to be.

Not to mention, he wanted to be his family's first call in a crisis, not the one they called only for a fun time. Case in point, Josh had contacted their oldest brother for help after his recent wedding setback, leaving Caleb, Josh's very own twin, to find out last.

Now, Josh and his fiancée were headed to Alaska to help Vivian's parents, who'd been in a rafting accident, and the rest of the family had rallied, thanks to Carter, and kept the couple's nuptials on track in their absence. Everyone except Caleb.

Worse, a pretty cowgirl Caleb hadn't seen since high school had accused him of not yet growing up.

Just that morning. As if Caleb hadn't changed since their teenage years. But Lacey Nash only knew the boy Caleb had been, not the person he was today. Proving the bold deputy wrong was going to be immensely amusing and extremely satisfying.

Caleb parked his truck in front of Misty Grove Distillery and climbed out. He ran his palms over his clean button-down dress shirt and newest pair of jeans. He waved a greeting to the distillery's maintenance manager driving a UTV through the parking lot and headed toward the most recent addition to the property: a two-story building that housed a tasting room on the first floor and the main offices on the second.

No, Caleb wasn't satisfied any longer. And it was clearly time for a change. He walked into his oldest brother's corner office and handed a folder to Carter.

Carter opened the folder and scanned the paperwork inside. "What's this?"

"Job application for Misty Grove." Caleb sat in one of the twin high-back chairs in front of his brother's massive desk.

"I know that." Carter dropped the folder and frowned. "Why is your name on it?"

Caleb met his brother's unflinching stare and aimed for a serious and professional tone. "I'm applying to work here."

"You already work here." Carter crossed his arms over his chest and rocked back in his leather office chair. "We all work here. We own the business."

"No. I fill in here," Caleb corrected. He helped out whenever Carter was short-staffed in the warehouse or when he needed a last-minute tour guide. Caleb leaned forward and tapped the papers. "This is for the marketing director position."

"That's a full-time job, little brother." Carter arched an eyebrow.

Carter had skipped over the unqualified argument and struck right at the perceived problem. Caleb's work history was rooted in part-time. More often seasonal and temporary.

Caleb notched his chin higher. "I know what it is."

"You don't do anything full-time," Carter said and quickly held up his hand when Caleb opened his mouth to argue. "Those were your words, not mine. That's just the way you are, little brother. The way you've always been."

But not the way he intended to continue being. The problem was proving he could change—to himself and his family. He eyed his older brother. "I want the rehearsal dinner and the reception."

Carter scrubbed his hands over his cheeks. He hadn't shaved in days, and his eyes were red-rimmed. He wore the look of a sleep-deprived new father well, thanks to the arrival of his twins. Carter sighed. "What?"

"Give me Josh's rehearsal dinner and reception to organize," Caleb jumped in as was often his way. All in and no second thoughts. "Give me full control.

We'll host the reception here at the distillery. No interference from anyone else."

Carter closed his mouth and studied Caleb.

Not receiving an outright refusal, Caleb rushed on, "It'll be a preview of the types of events we could hold here. And it will provide a glimpse into what I can do in terms of marketing as well." He paused, then added, "Also, it's one less thing you have to deal with."

Carter steepled his fingers under his chin, seemingly unmoved by the weight of what he had to deal with. He asked carefully, "What about the firehouse? The rodeo?"

Caleb volunteered at the fire station and worked as a pickup rider at the rodeo for the local stock contractor. He mostly picked up shifts when he wanted, where he wanted. He argued, "That won't get in the way."

"What happens when a more tempting offer catches your attention?" Carter pressed.

Caleb wasn't offended. The old Caleb lived by such whims. But not now. "Come on, Carter. Josh is my twin. I'm his best man. I will get this done." He inhaled. *If you want something different, Caleb, you have to do something different. Otherwise, all you've got is the same.* This strategy was certainly different enough to make his late gran Claire cheer. "Everyone is going to love both events. I guarantee it. And you will want to hire me."

"But will you be happy, little brother?" Carter asked and waved his arm at the stacks of documents and the open laptop on his desk. "Committing to an office forty hours a week. Tied to a chair and desk day in and day out."

Caleb blocked out the image of riding beside his deputy at the lake that morning. Like old times and yet somehow better. More appealing in a new sort of way. His interest in Lacey Nash was not the point though. He countered, "You're happy. In fact, this is the happiest you've ever been, big brother. Your words, not mine."

"I am happy. More than I thought possible." Carter twisted the wedding ring on his finger and smiled. "But that's more to do with Tess, the life we're building together, and now our kids." Affection softened his features as if he still hadn't quite adjusted to having his own children.

Caleb was impressed by his brother's easy acceptance of his new parental role. And he still marveled at watching Carter turn from tough-as-nails into a soft marshmallow whenever he held his daughter and son.

While Caleb loved his niece and nephew, that wasn't the change he wanted.

"Let's be clear, big brother," Caleb said. "I'm thrilled for you and Tess. I'm delighted my twin is getting married. And that Ryan and Grant are both hopelessly in love. I even love each of my sisters-in-law."

"*But,*" Carter pressed. Amusement flashed in his gaze.

"But I'm more than happy with my current relationship status set to single," he explained. A certain fiery-haired, brown-eyed deputy notwithstanding. Still, falling in love was one adventure too far for him. After all, hearts were not to be trusted.

Carter arched an eyebrow at him.

Caleb straightened in the chair and refused to back down. "This is about you recognizing me as more than filler around here." Not Caleb recognizing his heart.

"You got it." Carter nodded. "The rehearsal dinner and reception are all yours. Show me what you've got, then we'll talk about marketing director."

"You won't regret this." Caleb pushed out of the chair and headed for the door.

"Just make sure you won't regret this." Carter's words stopped Caleb in his tracks. There was a hint of caution in his tone and expression. "You have to be certain this is really what you want, little brother."

"I wouldn't be here otherwise." Caleb walked out of the office, confident that a career pivot was all he needed to bring his life back into balance.

CHAPTER FOUR

LACEY HAD BEEN stateside for only six months and living in Three Springs for less than a week. She'd been meticulous about her transition from active duty to civilian life. She'd worked with a counselor at the army's VA office to transfer her skill set from the military police to a deputy sheriff's role. Not once, while completing her classes and the sheriff training academy, did she second-guess her decision. Not once did she question her abilities.

Yet standing on the quaint front porch of her ex-husband's newly built house in Belleridge, she was doubting herself. Was she too late? Too late to make up for the years she'd missed with her daughter.

How she'd love to drive to her stepdad's ranch and claim one of her mother's encouraging hugs. Unfortunately, her mom had passed away five years ago. Lacey was on her own, with her regrets and her decisions and her promises. She inhaled and pressed the doorbell.

Her ex-husband opened the door, wearing a polo shirt, slacks, and his typical half smile. The one that softened the calculation in his gaze and enhanced his features. Jeffrey Furth was one of the youngest partners at his law firm, dedicated to his career in contract law while always managing to look after his family.

Jeffrey folded Lacey into a quick hug and said, "You never answered my texts."

Her ex-husband had a talent for wrapping any criticism inside kindness, as if to soften the rebuke. Still, Lacey had always sensed she fell short with him when they were together, and it seemed she felt the same even now. She released him and stepped inside. "Sorry, I was working."

"Well, there's no time to explain that now." Jeffrey shut the front door and touched his ear. "I can hear the oven timer going off in the kitchen."

As if on cue, Sarah-Beth, Jeffrey's wife of four years, appeared in the great room with an enthusiastic welcome. Her smile was as sunshine-bright as her sunflower-yellow dress that fell delicately over her pregnant belly. Her embrace was all-encompassing despite her petite stature. Sarah-Beth was polite, warmhearted, and impossible not to like.

"Dinner is ready. It's best while hot." Sarah-Beth turned without releasing Lacey's arm and called up the stairs for Aspen, then added, "Aspen, your mom is here."

Mom. That was Lacey. A simple word over text and quick video chats. But to *be* a mom. Not so easy. Lacey hadn't been hands-on in five years. And she'd misstepped a time or two when she'd had the role full-time. But tonight wasn't about dwelling on the past.

Footsteps sounded on the hidden staircase, and her daughter appeared. Taller, as expected. She was a burst of color in a lilac cotton tank dress and floral-print platform high-tops—just like her step-mom. Lacey ran her hand over her neutral-colored T-shirt and plain jeans. She'd never been one for bold colors. She and her daughter were different that way.

Aspen's dark blond hair was the exact shade of her dad's. One more difference. Lacey tucked her red hair behind her ear. Anyone would think Aspen was Sarah-Beth and Jeffrey's daughter, not Lacey's. Until they looked into Aspen's deep brown eyes. Those were an exact match to Lacey's. The hesitancy—the wariness—in Aspen's gaze mirrored how Lacey felt.

Lacey forced a smile around her uncertainty and held out a paper shopping bag. "I brought banana pudding from Lemon Moon Diner for dessert."

Delight filled Aspen's face. "That's my favorite."

Lacey gave Aspen a slightly awkward one-armed hug and slanted a grateful glance to Sarah-Beth for the dessert suggestion. There was so much to learn about her daughter, but it wasn't a race.

"Aspen, please put the banana pudding in the refrigerator." Sarah-Beth led Lacey into a modern country kitchen with butcher-block countertops, white Shaker cabinets, and just the right number of vintage knickknacks to be whimsical, not over-the-top. A scented candle invited guests to breathe deeply, relax, and stay for a spell.

Lacey inhaled and lowered her shoulders. This was the first of many evenings. The awkwardness would fade in time. *Practice patience.* Apt advice from her transition adviser.

"Lacey, what would you like to drink? We have wine and beer." Sarah-Beth motioned to the built-in wine refrigerator. "As well as sparkling water and pink lemonade."

"Pink lemonade please." Lacey took in the wall of framed artwork. Each piece was signed in block letters by Aspen and provided a visual timeline of kindergarten through third grade. Studio portraits and vacation snapshots filled the adjoining wall. The imprint of a happy family was stamped in every corner, shelf, and niche in the homey house. She added absently, "Pink lemonade is my favorite."

Aspen shut the refrigerator and spun around. There was accusation and wonder in her words. "It's my favorite too."

Common ground. That was a good start. Lacey exhaled. They would find even more.

"Mama-Beth puts strawberries in hers to make it pink," Aspen explained. "And she uses secret ingredients to make it sparkly like a unicorn's magic."

Lacey used the artificial pink lemonade mix from a can. She wasn't surprised Sarah-Beth leveled up simple lemonade and stirred it into something magical. Lacey smiled. "I can't wait to try it."

"It's nothing but a splash of cranberry juice and sparkling water," Sarah-Beth whispered and pressed a tall glass into Lacey's hand. Her expression was compassionate, her words understanding. "I'll text you the recipe. Comes together in a snap."

Nothing for the talented Sarah-Beth who seemed to excel at culinary endeavors and family management. Lacey lived to protect and serve. But kitchens needed to be protected from her.

"I've been craving cranberry juice since I found out I was pregnant." Sarah-Beth laughed, scooped a heaping serving of pasta from the casserole dish on the stovetop, and handed the plate to Lacey. "This is my three-cheese chicken parmesan pasta." Sarah-Beth served Jeffrey and earned a sweet kiss from her husband.

Lacey and Jeffrey had never shared such easy affection. Lacey's mom and Swells had. Lacey had always wanted that. Back when she still wanted a life partner and a relationship. Now the only relationship that mattered was the one with her daughter.

"This is my favorite meal." Aspen took her plate from Sarah-Beth, headed to the rustic kitchen table, and tipped her head. "Guests sit there."

Lacey slid into the chair at one end of the table. Jeffrey sat at the other end.

Aspen settled on the left side of her dad and smiled. "Mama-Beth lets me help make the noodles."

"We've been experimenting and making our own homemade pasta." Sarah-Beth took the chair on

Jeffrey's right and smoothed a napkin over her lap. "Tonight is our first attempt at bow tie noodles."

"I think they're perfect." Jeffrey speared a noodle on his fork and grinned at Aspen, then his wife. "Just like you two."

The perfect family. The trio was that. With their homemade pasta, homemade lemonade, and home-grown connection. Lacey didn't begrudge them any of it. She would be forever grateful Jeffrey and Sarah-Beth were there for Aspen when Lacey wasn't. Lacey simply wanted her own special connection with her daughter. She just wasn't certain how to build one. Or even where to start. Still, she'd never backed away from a difficult mission before. And this was the most important one yet. "So, Aspen, when does school start?"

"In two weeks. Then I'll be an official fourth grader." Aspen sprinkled more parmesan cheese over her pasta. "There's lots to do before my first day. Lots."

Her daughter stretched out *lots* into several syllables. Lacey detected a hint of warning. As if Aspen was cautioning Lacey that she might be too busy to spend time with her. But Lacey wasn't there to interfere. *Patience.*

"Speaking of a lot going on." Jeffrey set his fork down, wiped his napkin across his mouth, and revealed a wide grin. "I have an announcement now that we're all together. It's a surprise really."

Aspen rubbed her hands together. "Dad always has the best surprises, right, Mama-Beth?"

"He's certainly surprised us more than a time or two." Sarah-Beth chuckled. "We've enjoyed every one so far."

That her ex-husband had never organized a good surprise of the birthday sort or any other for Lacey during their time together was not the point. Although, getting served divorce papers while Lacey had been deployed overseas had been quite surprising. That was part of the past Lacey wasn't here to revisit. She held on to her smile.

"Surprise, honey," Jeffrey announced. "We're going on a babymoon."

"A babymoon. Really?" Sara-Beth pressed her fingers against her cheeks. "But I thought there wasn't time. That we couldn't…" Her words drifted off as her tears slipped free.

"You're happy, right?" Worry stretched across Jeffrey's face. He reached for his wife. "This is what you wanted."

"I'm thrilled." Sarah-Beth accepted the napkin Lacey handed her and patted her damp cheeks. "When is this happening?"

"That's the thing," Jeffrey cast a quick glance at Lacey before smiling at his wife. "We leave this weekend. Saturday actually. I know it's soon."

Two days soon. The surprises kept coming. Lacey sat back. She should not be shocked. This was her ex-husband's way. He did things his way. He was usually well-intentioned, not purposely inconsiderate. He simply assumed he knew best. As for fallout, that was for everyone else to clean up.

"Where am I staying?" Aspen asked quietly.

There was that fallout. Written all over her daughter's pale face.

Jeffrey reached across the table and squeezed Aspen's arm. "With your mom at the ranch, of course."

Lacey was speechless. She really should've answered his text this morning.

"It'll be good for you two. To reconnect." There was an insistence in Jeffrey's words. "That's what you want, isn't it, Lace?"

Absolutely, but on her terms and Aspen's. Not his. Lacey figured Aspen and she would get to know each other at their own pace. No rush. No forcing. No pushing. Lacey inhaled, searching for the serenity Sarah-Beth's scented candle promised. "How long will you be gone?"

"Three weeks." Jeffrey eyed her, not looking the least bit apologetic.

Three weeks. Twenty-one days. Just her and Aspen. Lacey kept her expression neutral, despite her racing thoughts outpacing her racing pulse.

Aspen had been three years old when Lacey was last on full-time parenting duty. She'd been scribbling outside the lines and playing in the sandbox. That was a far cry from the almost nine-year-old girl seated at the table. The girl with stronger opinions and more complex feelings. Lacey and Aspen knew nothing about each other on the daily. What did Aspen like for breakfast? Or lunch? Was she early to bed and late to rise like her mother? Or smiling at the sunrise like her father?

"I've got a client in Florida," Jeffrey explained. "The timing worked out brilliantly where I'll be able to combine work and pleasure in the Florida Keys. It just aligned and came together seamlessly."

For you. Lacey nodded.

"What about the Junior Royal Rodeo Contest?" Aspen looked at her stepmom. Her words were imploring. "We were supposed to go shopping, Mama-Beth." Aspen aimed her displeasure at her dad. "You promised me I could enter this year."

"I promised I'd think about it," Jeffrey corrected. "It's not really a good time."

How many times had Lacey heard that in their brief marriage? *It's not a good time, Lace. I've got to concentrate on law school. Or my internship. Or anything else. Can't we talk about this later?*

"Maybe next year, honey," Jeffrey offered.

"That's what you said last year." Aspen's eyebrows smashed together. "What about my riding lessons? I only just started."

"I put those on hold." Jeffrey's words were calm yet resolved. "With the baby coming soon and the new school year, and now your mom is finally home. This is for the best."

Lacey slipped her hands under her legs to keep from raising her arm and asking who it was best for. But she'd been home less than a week. Surely it was too soon to toss her mom-card on the table. It wouldn't be fair to anyone. But the defeated expression on her daughter's face made her chest ache.

"When school begins in two weeks, you'll be too

busy for horses and all that anyway," Jeffrey stated. "Surely you'll want to take piano lessons this year and more art classes."

"Until you change your mind on that too." Aspen frowned and eyed Lacey. "I suppose you don't want me to have any fun either."

I want you to like me. Not look at me like I'm the enemy. I never wanted to be that. Lacey opened her mouth.

Jeffrey cut her off, "Aspen Carole Furth, we do not use that tone in this house." Jeffrey's frown matched Aspen's. "You need to apologize."

"I'm not sorry." Aspen shoved her chair back and shouted, "You are all ruining my life." Then she raced across the great room and up the stairs.

Definitely not the reunion Lacey had imagined. She started to stand. Jeffrey touched her arm. "Let Sarah-Beth go check on her. Sarah-Beth has a way with Aspen's unfortunate outbursts."

Unfortunate outbursts. He'd accused Lacey of having similar reactions. *Lace, there's no need for so much emotion. This is solving nothing.* At that time, her mother had been battling cancer again. Her husband had been withdrawn and distant, except when he was with their daughter. Lacey had been struggling to balance the demands of work and parenting and a marriage that was unraveling. Then she'd gotten notice about her deployment. There'd been every need for emotion.

Jeffrey pressed on, "We have things to discuss, and now is a good time."

Lacey sat back down. Sarah-Beth gave Lacey's shoulder an encouraging squeeze and slipped out of the kitchen.

Lacey watched Sarah-Beth until she disappeared up the stairs and glanced at her ex-husband. "Don't you think this news warranted a phone call?"

"You wouldn't have answered," he countered. "You were working."

Lacey started to argue.

"Don't deny it, Lace. Your job has your full focus. As it should, by the way," he said. "I'm not blaming you. It is what it is. Besides, I did text, if you will recall."

He stopped short of blaming her for being unprepared. If only she'd replied to his text. Too late now for if only's.

"I won't apologize. My wife wants a babymoon." Jeffrey pushed away from the table and refilled his plate with more pasta, clearly undisturbed by the commotion he'd caused. "The timing works, and I'm taking full advantage. I'm doing this for Sarah-Beth."

Lacey had seen how much it meant to Sarah-Beth. But she'd also seen the devastation on her daughter's face. That was difficult to overlook. "I'm happy to have Aspen even if she's less than thrilled to stay with me."

"Aspen will come around," he said gently. "Give her time."

That was exactly what Lacey was trying to do. "I'll need her doctor's contact information and every detail about school." What was the protocol for the first day of school? Were moms still cool in the fourth grade? Did she drop off and leave or walk her in?

"Sarah-Beth has everything organized. School supplies are already bought." Jeffrey returned to his chair. "She'll fill you in on everything you need to know for the first day of school and anything else in regard to Aspen's care."

Ready or not, Lacey needed to get her mom act together. Yet Lacey had no idea how she would ever measure up to Sarah-Beth's practically perfect step-mom status. Lacey knew she was far from flawless; still that wouldn't stop her. "Aspen will stay with me." Lacey paused, then added, "And it's going to be wonderful." She'd make it so.

"That's good to know." Jeffrey polished off his second helping and leaned his elbows on the table. "Now that you're home permanently, it might be time to revisit our custody agreement."

"Seriously?" Lacey searched Jeffrey's face. She'd considered it but only in passing. It was nothing she had wanted to hope too hard for, especially this soon.

"You've got three weeks to prove that you can be the parent you need to be with our daughter." He eyed her.

"I came home for Aspen." Lacey had no intention of leaving and letting her daughter down again. She picked up her lemonade and kept her words casual. "What's this about the Junior Royal Rodeo Contest?"

"Let it alone, Lace." Jeffrey waved his hand. "It's better this way. Don't take on more than you can handle."

"But Aspen seemed pretty upset," Lacey said.

"It won't be the last time she's disappointed in not getting what she wants." Jeffrey sighed. "Besides, the decision has been made."

"You already decided not to let her enter before you even booked the babymoon," she guessed.

"Does it matter when I decided?" He frowned. "Horses and all that, it's just a phase. She'll move on in a month anyway. That's the way kids are."

"What if she doesn't?" Lacey pressed.

"She will," he insisted. "Besides, we aren't exactly horse people."

Lacey hadn't been either. Until her mom had married Swells and her new stepdad had taken her riding. She'd fallen in love with the sweet mare and never looked back. And today at the lake, on Caleb's horse, she'd felt a rush of those feelings all over again. "I wasn't either, but I learned and loved it."

"And you were reckless and careless when you rode." He arched an eyebrow at her. "I remember the stories you told me."

True, she'd ridden too fast, jumped things she shouldn't have, in hindsight. Been fearless. But she'd never purposefully put a horse in danger. The horses had been well trained, well-conditioned, and

Lacey had trusted them completely. As if her horses had understood that riding had been her escape. In those daring moments, she'd been truly free. Truly happy. It was hard to explain. Even harder for people who didn't ride to understand.

"Aspen and horses aren't a good fit." There was a decisiveness to his words. "Trust me."

Lacey trusted that her ex was a good father and meant well. But she wanted to talk to Aspen. Hear from her daughter what she wanted. And perhaps be the one to make it happen for her.

Jeffrey paused. "I know that look."

Lacey blinked at him.

"Promise me you'll let it go, Lace." Jeffrey held her stare. "One reformed daredevil in the family is more than enough. Aspen isn't like you."

"What does that mean?" Lacey asked.

"Nothing." Jeffrey pulled back. "Just promise me you won't encourage her. Aspen is talented at the piano and art. That suits her."

"She could do all that and ride horses too," Lacey argued.

"To what gain?" he asked.

"Why can't it simply be for the pure joy of it?" Despite the bull and her claims about duty, Lacey had felt a bit of that former joy at the lake. And she'd welcomed it.

"That's not the lifestyle we've built for our family." Jeffrey stacked the empty plates and stood up. "Rodeos and horses are not the world Aspen is being raised in. It's not for her."

It wasn't for him. Never had been. But that didn't mean Aspen should be excluded.

"It's not what you do anymore either." Jeffrey walked into the kitchen and set the dishes in the sink. "You're a deputy now and a mom. What more could you need?"

An image of a certain cowboy with mischievously tempting blue eyes and an unshakable smile came to mind. Quickly, Lacey tried to regain her focus. "We aren't talking about me. We're discussing our daughter."

"Horse riding lessons. The Junior Royal Rodeo Contest. Where does it end?" Jeffrey asked. "We've got college to fund, not a horse to buy and a stable to build."

"Isn't being a kid about being exposed to all sorts of things? Trying new things?" Lacey carried over the last of the dinner dishes. "Shouldn't we encourage that as her parents?"

"Parenting is also about guiding our kids in the direction we know is best for them." Jeffrey dried his hands. "Same as our parents did for us."

Lacey crossed her arms over her chest.

"You gave up horses, Lace," he said. "And haven't suffered."

There hadn't been a choice. Her mother had been diagnosed with cancer. Her parents had sold her horses to cover the mounting medical bills. Lacey had gotten an after-school job and wanted to keep her parents from worrying about her. But she'd suffered. They all had. "The situation is entirely different."

"No." Jeffrey set his hands on her shoulders and looked into her eyes. "If we're going to coparent, we need to be on the same page, Lace. Same as our parents were."

"What that means is, I need to be on the same page as you," she clarified.

"I know our daughter." There was absolute certainty in his expression and words.

Lacey met his gaze. "I'm still going to talk to her about it."

"Go right ahead." His eyes softened at the corners. "Then you'll see I'm right."

"What happens if you're wrong?"

"We can discuss it when I get back." He squeezed her shoulders, then chuckled. "But you know better than anyone I don't change my mind."

Lacey's mind was set too. Her daughter's opinion mattered. She wanted to listen to Aspen's side. But honoring her daughter's wishes could throw a wrench in Jeffrey's vision of ideal coparenting. And like it or not, her ex-husband was in control of their custody arrangement.

But Lacey could tread softly. After all, her daughter's happiness was at stake. And if it edged Lacey out of enemy territory in her daughter's mind wasn't that worth it?

CHAPTER FIVE

"Last call!" Caleb shouted to the few remaining customers inside The Feisty Owl Bar and Grill, where he was filling in as bartender. The main dining room and kitchen had closed several hours ago. The staff were most likely already asleep in their beds. Caleb had sent Wes Tanner, the bar owner, home earlier to check on his wife, Abby, who was pregnant with their third child.

He placed several used wineglasses into the mini dishwasher below the counter and glanced up when the front doors opened. Surprise shot through him at the late arrival. But his smile spread slowly as if he wanted to keep the happiness to himself.

The intriguing woman walking toward the bar had always stirred something inside him. Back when he first met her, she'd been willowy and tall for her age. He'd never minded much when she looked him in the eye with her bold gaze and accepted his dares. Same as she hadn't backed down at the lake just that morning.

If he'd been of a mind to challenge for hearts, he'd consider hers a worthy prize. Even though his own heart had never been up for the taking. Still, he couldn't deny that the cowboy who claimed her heart would be the luckiest person around. And Caleb hated him already.

He scrubbed at a stain on the bar and tried to rescue his suddenly deflating smile. "Evening, Deputy Nash."

"I'm off the clock." She dropped her purse on a barstool. "I'm just Lacey right now."

There was nothing *just* about this particular cowgirl, even now with her chin-length red hair, striking dark brown eyes, and a certain poise that came from losing and winning life's battles. Not that he was noticing as anything more than an impartial former-friend-turned-temporary-bartender. "Well, *Just Lacey*, what can I get you?"

"There's no root beer at the ranch house." She sat on a stool. "And everything is closed."

"We've got you covered." It looked like he had something to offer her after all. Caleb grinned. "Want a scoop of ice cream in it? We've got that too."

"Don't make fun of my root beer craving." Lacey rested her elbows on the bar top. "Weren't animal crackers your late-night go-to snack?"

"Still are." And he refused to feel anything about the fact that she remembered such an insignificant detail about him. He filled a tall glass with ice and soda and considered the troubled glint in her gaze. "I was serious about the ice cream. Gran Claire always told me a scoop made everything sweeter, even your worries."

"Your gran Claire made everything sweeter," Lacey mused. "And better."

"That she did." Caleb set the root beer on a coaster in front of Lacey, then leaned down to brace his arms on the bar. He'd been the last Sloan sibling to find his height. In college, he'd finally topped out at six feet five inches, making him the tallest Sloan brother by a good inch and a half. Gran Claire had called him a special sort of late bloomer.

Late bloomer or not, Caleb had always been compelled to meet this cowgirl eye to eye. "I'm not even in the same league as Gran Claire when it comes to dealing with problems, but I'm here. What's keeping you awake tonight, Just Lacey?"

"I don't think you can help with this one." She dropped a straw into her glass and chuckled. Yet the sound lacked any real pleasure.

"Try me. I might surprise you." He spread his arms wide as if to prove he had nothing to hide. "If it's relationship advice you need, I've got that. I'm practically a wedding coordinator now. Although wedding consultant has a certain ring to it."

Whatever the title, wedding and Caleb Sloan were more apt to clash than harmonize. Lacey gaped at him. "You? A wedding coordinator?"

"Technically, I'm not coordinating the ceremony. My brother Josh and his fiancée, Vivian, have that handled." Caleb watched closely for her reaction to his next admission. "I'm organizing the rehearsal dinner and the reception."

"But you know nothing about romance." Lacey

leaned in as if imparting a long-held secret. "Word around town is that you haven't even been on a second date. Just a series of first dates."

She'd been asking around town about him? He liked that idea more than was prudent, even if she was pointing out his flaws. "My dating history doesn't mean I don't know about romance." *I could show you.* He straightened before that thought took root and quickly said, "Besides, I've been to my fair share of weddings."

"As a guest." Lacey pinched her straw and stirred her soda. The ice swirled around in her glass like the amusement curving across her face. "I bet you spent most of your time at the bar too."

"Don't forget the dance floor." Caleb lifted his eyebrows. "Can't resist a line dance." Or a slow dance with the right partner. Someone like her if he was choosing.

Her hair slipped from behind her ear, swept forward, and brushed against her jawline. Right where he wanted to slide his fingers to test for himself just how smooth her skin really was. If she was in his arms, he could do exactly that. Yeah, he would definitely pause for a dance-floor slowdown with Deputy Nash. Not that he would be asking her anytime soon.

Lacey straightened and secured her hair back behind her ear. "Caleb, be serious."

He was serious. He'd dance with her. Just about anywhere, he supposed. He grabbed the bar towel from under the counter and got a firm hold on his foolish thoughts. This was supposed to be about her troubles, not his.

"What do you remember about the food at those weddings you attended?" Lacey ticked reception details off on her fingers. "What about the theme? The colors. The decor. The centerpieces. The table favors."

"I do remember the cake at Jodie Hayes and Harris Newton's wedding last summer." Caleb shrugged and frowned. "For the record, I don't recommend a kiwi and matcha cake. Unless you like the taste of freshly mowed lawn."

Lacey shook her head and stared at him. Amazement filled her words. "You really intend to put together an entire wedding reception for your brother."

"I do." Caleb crumpled a paper napkin and shot it into the wastebasket. He raised his arms in victory and said, "Just wait. You're going to be speechless when you see it."

"I don't think I'm on the guest list." She sipped her soda.

"You are now." Did the wedding coordinator have guest list privileges? Too late now. He wasn't rescinding the invitation. Still, he rushed on, "That means you'll need a plus-one of course."

Her eyebrows pulled together. "Why?"

"Because you need romance in your life, Just Lacey." And if she was dating someone, then he wouldn't want to dance with her. Wouldn't be tempted to sweep her off her feet himself. As if he was suddenly into things like that. But the only thing he was into was his career change idea and securing that full-time job at the distillery.

"How do you know I don't have a life of romance already?" she countered.

"Simple." Caleb gestured toward the unoccupied barstools on either side of her. "You're sitting all alone on a fine evening like tonight."

"I'm here because I wanted root beer." Lacey toasted him with her glass and finished her drink. "And if you'll recall, this is the only place open at this hour."

"If you had romance, you wouldn't be thinking about root beer at this hour." Even more, she wouldn't be here with him. And he wouldn't be thinking about slow dances and impractical entanglements either.

"Romance is the furthest thing from my mind," she countered.

He wanted it out of his mind too, immediately, in fact. Dating led to a relationship, and what followed were expectations like forever love and long-term commitment. And that, for him, was where things fell apart and hearts got permanently bruised. He refilled her glass. "What is on your mind then?"

She took another deep sip, then tipped her head at him, sending her hair swaying against her cheek again.

He refilled the straws to keep from securing her hair behind her ear himself.

She asked, "Have you ever heard of a babymoon?"

Definitely not the conversation detour he'd expected. "That's what parents-to-be go on for a few days before their baby arrives."

She looked startled. "How do you know that?"

"My sister-in-law, Tess, had twins this past June," Caleb explained. "Carter took Tess on a babymoon to a luxury resort in Sedona. Apparently, the spa specializes in mother-to-be wellness. But both Tess and Carter got a weekend of private pampering."

They'd both returned blissful and practically glowing, prompting Caleb to do a quick internet search on the resort and their offerings. But a cowboy like him didn't need to glow. As for bliss, he would find that on his own terms.

Lacey's smile was soft. "A spa in Sedona sounds romantic and relaxing."

"That's what I hear." Caleb folded his arms and went back to leaning on the bar top. "Now Tess is convincing Maggie that she needs to take a babymoon. Maggie married Grant last year."

"Have all your brothers married?" Lacey smeared the water droplets on the outside of her glass.

Caleb lifted his hand, waving good night to Trey Ramsey and Keith Bauer, the last of the late-night bar patrons. And then there were two. He returned his attention to Lacey. "Once Josh and Vivian exchange their wedding vows, I'll be the last single Sloan brother in the family."

She considered him. "That doesn't bother you?"

"Not even a little." There was pride and conviction in his words. Once more, they'd detoured back to him. He aimed his grin at her and flipped the conversation. "But back to this babymoon—are you organizing one?"

"My ex-husband and his wife are going on one," she explained. "So Aspen is coming to live with me for the next three weeks."

One more reason Lacey Nash was all wrong for him. She was part of a package deal. There were two hearts at stake, not one. That was double the heartbreak...and nothing Caleb wanted to be responsible for. He took in Lacey's less-than-delighted expression. "That should be a good thing, right?"

"Aspen isn't exactly happy about it." She wrinkled her nose. "She even claimed her dad and I were ruining her life."

Caleb winced. "Ouch."

"But I didn't even know about the Junior Royal Rodeo Contest until this evening. Jeffrey had already decided not to let Aspen enter. He only just told her at dinner." Lacey lifted her hands. Irritation crossed her face. "My ex-husband can take all the credit for ruining his daughter's life this round."

"Are you talking about the contest that's part of Three Springs's Rodeo Reunion over Labor Day weekend?" Here was ground he knew quite well. He'd spent a large portion of his time growing up inside a rodeo arena competing with his brothers and now as part of the rodeo's auxiliary staff. He loved every part of the rodeo, considered it a second home.

"What are you, Caleb Sloan? Like the town busybody or something?" Lacey stabbed her straw into the ice in her glass. "How do you know about that too?"

"Maggie, my sister-in-law, is the rodeo director. I guess you could say I have an inside scoop." He laughed and shrugged. "You do remember that this is a small town, right?"

Lacey's laughter blended with his. "Where everyone knows everything."

"More than that, everyone shares everything they think they know with everyone else." He leaned toward her and pressed his finger against the bar top. "Fortunately for me, most of that sharing goes on right here."

"Do you work here full-time?" She glanced around the empty bar.

He shook his head. "Only when needed." And lucky for Caleb, Wes Tanner, the owner and his oldest brother's best friend, had needed Caleb's bartending skills tonight, or Caleb would have missed Lacey. He rubbed his chin. "You know, I can talk to Maggie. I'm sure it's not too late to enter Aspen in the Junior Royal Rodeo Contest."

Lacey was silent.

"You would definitely earn points with your daughter," Caleb suggested.

"Tempting," she admitted and set her palms flat on the bar top. "But it doesn't matter. I know nothing about rodeo contests like that. I wouldn't even have the first clue to help her get ready."

"Well, the offer stands," he said.

"Thanks." She sipped her root beer and seemed

to be studying him over the rim of the glass. "So, you're a volunteer firefighter and EMT. Bartender. Rodeo pickup rider. Wedding coordinator. Have I missed anything?" Before he could respond, she added, "I make sure to listen well when those locals share what they know."

Soon he'd be down to one job. One job title. Once he impressed his older brother. As for his deputy, he wondered what it would take to impress her.

Not the direction he wanted to go. He rinsed his hands off in the sink and tossed that idle thought aside. "The locals forgot tour guide at the distillery."

"When do you sleep?" She chuckled.

He liked the carefree sound. A bit too much. He plucked up an empty bin and stepped from behind the bar before he decided to make her laugh more. Just for his enjoyment. "Why would I sleep? I might miss something good."

"You've been on the go since we met." She slipped off her stool and followed him over to the section of tall round tables. "When are you going to slow down?"

Now that teetered very close to a common topic among his family. Their questions, however casual, always circled around the same theme. Caleb frowned. "Do you mean settle down?" Same as his family.

She hesitated, not fully committing.

"I'm working on a few things for the future." He stacked empty beer glasses inside the tub.

"Care to share what exactly?" She picked up two wineglasses from a nearby table and placed them into the bin.

"Not quite yet," he hedged and avoided meeting her gaze, not wanting to see the same doubt in her expression that his own family had been unable to hide earlier. After he'd announced his decision to work full-time at the distillery.

"Tell me about your plus-one for the wedding." She trailed after him, collecting more empty bottles and glasses from nearby tables. "Is she urging you to slow down too?"

"I don't have a plus-one." He couldn't quite pull the bewilderment from his words. "I'm the event coordinator. I'm exempt." That sounded reasonable enough to him.

Yet her frown indicated her displeasure. "But you need a date. As the wedding consultant, you should have a plus-one to prove you know all about romance."

"I don't need a plus-one to prove anything." Caleb lifted the tub and headed toward the kitchen.

"Wait. You've already dated all the single women in the county, haven't you? And at the rodeo." Amazement and amusement blended around her words. "You can't get a date, can you?"

"Of course I can get a date, if I choose to." Which he did not. Thank you very much. There'd been a time he'd gone on those first dates she'd accused him of. But recently, he'd given up those as well, preferring to avoid that trouble entirely.

"Prove it," she charged.

Oh, he recognized that forthright tone. The one that challenged and always intrigued him. He turned around, not surprised to find her less than a step behind him. "This is starting to feel like a wager."

Her smile turned knowing. "You never could turn one down."

"You never did back away." Then again, neither had he. And now he stayed right where he was. Close enough to tuck her hair behind her ear if he was of a mind to test the strength of those friendship bonds.

"Admit it, Caleb. You don't know what you want in a woman, same as you don't know what you want out of life. I do know what you need and that's a woman as dedicated to freedom as you." She stepped closer and braced her hands on the bin he held. "I bet I could find that woman quicker than you ever could."

"That's as confused as me saying I could help your daughter win the Junior Royal Rodeo Contest because I know cowgirls so well." He spun toward the kitchen before he was tempted to set the bin down and reach for her instead to prove what sort of cowgirl he could want. Needing the last word, he added, "Which I do, by the way. Know cowgirls well." With that, he let the door swing shut behind him.

"Like I said, prove it, cowboy." She pushed through the door right after him and stood in the kitchen, hands on hips. "Coach my daughter to win the contest, and I'll find you the perfect wedding date."

He set the tub on the stainless steel counter and opened the large commercial dishwasher. "What happens when you don't find my perfect date?"

She crossed her arms over her chest and lifted her chin. "I'll… I'll…get onstage and sing."

He glanced over his shoulder and considered her. "You vowed never to get on another stage after that one audition in ninth grade." Afterward he'd found her crying outside the auditorium, inconsolable. Lacey Nash, for all her bravado, had a serious case of stage fright. But she also had a voice that could soothe the crankiest infant or the most fly-by-night cowboy like him.

She eyed him. "I confess. I haven't been onstage since the day of that horrible audition."

He nodded. "So if you find my ideal date, what do you get?"

"You crochet three scarves and donate them to Three Springs's Rodeo Reunion silent auction." Her satisfied smile spread wide. "I know your gran Claire taught you. Remember when I caught you in the yarn aisle at the old craft store in Belleridge after school?"

Caleb nodded. He remembered more about her than was probably wise. That afternoon he'd been testing the gauge of different crochet needles for a difficult stitch he'd been trying to master to surprise his gran Claire. It had been impossible to pretend he was in the wrong aisle when Lacey had ambushed him, then refused to leave. Still, Lacey was the only one outside his family who knew about his favorite hobby. He'd been surprised she'd kept his confidence. Then again, he'd kept hers.

He'd kept other confidences too. Like how much he'd missed her when she ended things with his friend and they stopped hanging out so often in high school.

Lacey watched him. Her expression was thoughtful. "You aren't scared to accept this bet, are you?"

"Not exactly."

"Then we're doing this," she said.

"Unless you'd rather admit defeat now and skip straight to the singing." He hitched his thumb over his shoulder. "There's a microphone already set up on the stage out there. All we need to decide is whether it's a slow or fast song."

She laughed and flexed her fingers. "Maybe instead you should start warming up your hands for all that crocheting you're going to be doing."

Caleb grinned. He'd always liked that about her. She gave as good as she got. "I'm partial to an old-school country song."

"Remember neutral colors tend to be very calming for babies." One eyebrow flexed. Her tone was patient and knowing as if they were standing in the paint aisle at Rivers Family Hardware. "Think pale yellow. Or soft gray or even sage green."

"Are those your favorite colors?" he asked.

"Pale lavender," she said. "Wisteria are my favorite flowers."

That was information he might consider useful if he ever wanted to gather a list of his deputy's likes and dislikes. He dried his hands and headed for the swinging door. "Country classics are my favorite."

"Noted." She never hesitated. Her retort was far too cheerful. "I'll make you a playlist, and you can listen to it while you crochet."

"Do you prefer traditional or infinity for a style of scarf?" He watched the confusion register on her face. His smile stretched wider. He held the front door of the bar open for her. "I thought you might want a scarf to keep your vocal cords warm before your performance."

She stopped in the doorway and considered him. Her gaze was steady. "You know I always play to win. That hasn't changed."

But his awareness of her *had* changed. It was deeper. Stronger. It tugged on those elusive heart-strings. Good thing he'd clipped those years ago. "I'd be disappointed if you just gave in." Same as he would be hurt if he gave in to what his heart was saying. He skimmed a gaze over her face. "About that scarf..."

"Save it for the auction." She laughed and pulled her car keys from her purse. "My vocal cords won't be needing it. That much I can assure you."

He stepped back, watched her make her way to an old compact truck and climb inside. The truck's engine rumbled in the silent night.

One thing was certain. She was going to lose their bet. Because he feared he was watching his ideal cowgirl drive away right now. The cowgirl he could want if he was a different sort of cowboy.

Lacey Nash was made for settling down and the long-haul kind of love that only strengthened over time. She deserved a cowboy built for the same. Caleb lived only for the moment. And the only long haul for him was the lockdown on his heart. After all, love would surely trip him up if he stuck around to let it.

So he would keep his cowboy boots in motion like always and his destination in sight. And let nothing tempt him to change direction, not even his bold, brown-eyed deputy and her unwavering affinity for wagers.

Caleb turned, pointing his cowboy boots toward the bar and away from Lacey's fading taillights.

Less than an hour later, his checklist for closing was complete, the cash register receipts balanced, and the money secured in the safe. One more circuit through the main dining room and perimeter of the bar ensured the patio doors and windows were locked. He switched off the LED Open sign in the front window, armed the security system, and walked outside to his truck. The only place to go now was home.

He should be tired, worn out from the long day that had started at sunrise. But that restlessness rolled through him. It'd become something of a norm recently, like a chatty shotgun passenger he couldn't quite ignore. Only with Lacey, he'd felt a different sort of energy. A caring, more welcome kind. But still, they had shared nothing more than a friendly chat between a bartender and a customer.

As for their wager, well, he wasn't certain what that was other than a bout of nostalgia and an easy slide back to their old friendship. There'd been no official handshake to finalize the wager like they'd always done before.

Just as well because taking Lacey's hand in his tonight would've been a temptation too far.

Back on Sloan land, Caleb parked outside the detached garage beside the large farmhouse. The same one generations of Sloans had grown up in. The same one Caleb and his brothers had called home since they were little kids. What was supposed to be a short summer visit with their grandparents became something long-term and permanent. Thanks to his parents' divorce and his mom choosing to pursue her medical degree over raising her kids.

Now Carter and Caleb were the only two Sloan brothers left living on the property along with their grandpa Sam and uncle Roy. Although his other brothers and their wives hadn't gone far. Their properties each connected to the original Sloan land by way of an adjacent pasture, a patch of forest, and a stream.

Caleb climbed out and frowned at the brand-new ice-blue convertible angled a short distance away.

A movement near the stables caught his attention. He shifted as the owner of the stylish, statement-making sports car stepped from the shadows.

Lilian Sloan.

What was his mother doing here? She lived all the way over in Belleridge. Caleb checked his surprise.

She lifted a hand in greeting, her smile tentative.

That was to be expected. Mother and sons had been estranged until recently, when Lilian had abruptly shown up in town, intent on making up for past mistakes. Caleb supposed he was the last holdout with respect to forging a new relationship with his mom, same as he was the last single Sloan brother. But that common ground his older brothers seemed to have found with Lilian Sloan seemed to be just out of reach for him.

He shut his truck door and approached her, noticing she held a swaddled bundle in her arms. That the renowned heart surgeon had turned into a doting grandmother was almost unfathomable, given Lilian Sloan had skipped the parental stage for the most part with her sons. Caleb's frown deepened. "Mom."

"You're thinking it must really be desperate times if your brother and Tess called me to babysit Beck." Her words were hushed and lulling.

He was thinking he seriously needed to reconsider his night-owl tendencies. If he'd gone to bed at a reasonable hour like a normal person, he wouldn't have run into the only two women who seemed to possess the unique ability to stir up feelings inside him. As if he hadn't spent his entire life figuring out how not to free-fall into those so-called *feels*. "Mom, what are you doing here?"

"Giving the new parents some much-needed sleep." She made a cooing sound against his nephew's forehead.

"Where's Sadie?" he asked, referring to his niece and Beck's fraternal twin.

"Sleeping like an angel." His mom tapped the baby monitor clipped at her waist. "I've been listening. Not a peep out of her. But Beck seems to be having an out-of-sorts evening. Neither Tess nor Carter could get him to settle down after he ate."

Settle down. There was that phrase again. Caleb knew how his nephew felt. Out-of-sorts was his personal theme of late. Except when he'd been with Lacey, then he'd felt... He cut off that thought before it gained traction. Definitely not the time for that. He wanted to keep his head clear for this conversation.

"Your gran told me she used to walk you outside when you were fussy. She claimed she clocked several miles walking circles around the barns holding you at night." A pensive hopefulness circled through his mom's words. "Thought I'd try that with Beck."

Did you ever do the same for me? Caleb knocked that aside. He already knew the answer.

Caleb had barely passed his first birthday when his mother had dropped him and his brothers at their grandparents' ranch and never looked back. Her professional goals were noble perhaps to an outsider, but to someone who'd counted on her and trusted her to be there when he needed her, she'd failed badly at the time. He'd been too little to remember whether his mother had held him or his twin, Josh. But Caleb had decided somewhere along the way that she most likely hadn't. Certainly mothers who held and comforted their kids didn't turn their backs on them like she had. But that was the past. Nothing to see there. He crossed his arms over his chest. "Is it working?"

Beck's face pinched. His tiny body squirmed.

His mom's sigh held no heat. "It seemed to be. I think we might need another brisk walk around the barns." His mom peered at him. Her expression and tone were neutral. "Care to join us?"

So he could see even more how comfortable she looked holding his three-month-old nephew? How her caring seemed natural and genuine? It made no sense. This wasn't the woman he believed her to be. Yet watching her now made him reconsider. And that set him back. It was unexpected. Yet not in the let's-dive-right-in-and-explore sort of way he liked.

Caleb tucked the blanket under his nephew's chin. "You two seemed to be doing fine before I interrupted."

"I believe it has more to do with the lack of motion than your presence." She swayed from side to side.

"All the same, I'm going to call it a night." He watched Beck's face release. At least his nephew seemed to be relaxing. Caleb felt even more on edge now. "I've got to be up early for work."

His mother's eyebrows lifted. "I would've thought

this late night would earn you a morning to sleep in and relax."

"Lazy mornings aren't really my thing," he said. Downtime offered more opportunities to think than Caleb cared for.

Reflecting is not something you avoid, Caleb. It's something you cherish.

But, Gran, if I don't go do things, I'll have nothing to reflect on.

Caleb would've sworn he heard his gran Claire's laugher in the rustle of the trees lining the driveway. He glanced at his mom. "There's no time. I'm taking over Vivian and Josh's reception and rehearsal dinner. And soon, the marketing job at the distillery."

She looked puzzled as she kept up the slow rocking motion. "And that's what you want?"

Her reservation about his announcement was not a surprise. His family hadn't hidden their doubt or skepticism. "Why does it feel like you don't agree?"

"If you're happy, that's all that matters." She swayed on.

Beck pouted as if he too doubted all that would lead to Caleb's happiness. His mother quickly adjusted her hold on Beck.

Lilian barely knew her youngest son. Caleb hardly wanted her to worry about him now. Besides, he was fine. He cleared his throat. "I know what I'm doing. What I want."

"That's good to hear." She cradled Beck up against her shoulder and cooed at him again, a series of *there-there*'s and gibberish. Her grin was wry. "Now I need to give my grandson what he wants."

For the first time since his mother's return, he wondered what she wanted. Caleb tugged the cotton hat decorated with teddy bears lower on Beck's forehead, then touched Beck's cheek. "Let your dreams take flight, little one."

His mother added quietly, "And tomorrow you can wake up and chase them."

Startled, Caleb lifted his gaze, took in his mom's wistful smile and tender expression. Searched again for that calculating career-minded stranger who'd left her family behind, but he came up blank. Again. He tucked his hands into his jeans pockets. "Gran Claire told me that when she tucked me in."

"That was my favorite good-night wish," his mom whispered and pressed her cheek against Beck's head. "She said it to me every night growing up too. She was a wise woman."

Caleb nodded and noted Beck's nose wrinkling. "Beck however is looking less than pleased with such sage advice."

"He certainly is." His mother chuckled. "We'd best get moving. Good night, Caleb."

"Night." He started for the spacious two-bedroom apartment over the garage. The one he'd moved into after Josh and Vivian had moved into the farmhouse that had once belonged to Gran Claire's family on the adjacent property.

"Oh, Caleb, if you need help with the reception or rehearsal dinner, please don't hesitate to ask," his mother offered before she disappeared around the barn.

Caleb rubbed his forehead, made his way upstairs, and skipped turning on the lamp. Light certainly wasn't going to chase away his confusion. Not an hour ago, he would've dismissed his mother's offer out of hand. Now he appreciated her for making it. Not that he was accepting it.

It was certainly a night full of curveballs. Those never bothered him much. Just hit 'em out of the park had been Grandpa Sam's long-standing advice. But for the first time ever, Caleb hesitated.

His phone screen lit up in the dark. Caleb opened the new text from his deputy. It was a crocheting tutorial video that she'd captioned with one word: Inspiration.

His smile slipped slowly into place. Followed by that familiar rush of energy.

He knew he had to win their wager. How could he not? Otherwise, he feared he just might lose a lot more than having to crochet a few colorful scarves.

CHAPTER SIX

LILIAN SLOAN EYED the dark apartment windows over the garage and cuddled her grandson closer. She picked up her pace. "It's you and me, Beck. Surely, we can figure this out together."

Beck yawned against her shoulder.

"We need to get back to deciding on a name for me," Lilian murmured.

She hadn't quite adjusted to her new status as grandmother. Having passed on most of the "mothering" part, now she seemed to have jumped feet-first into the "grand" part of parenting, intent on not missing this phase. She was retired, starting a new life chapter, and terrified.

Still, she was determined not to let the fear stop her. She'd been scared before—alone after her divorce from her sons' father. She'd pulled herself together then, graduated from medical school, and built quite a career for herself. A career she had been determined would mend her broken heart and outshine the memory of her cheating ex-husband.

As the years passed, the hurt and anger from the divorce faded. Fortunately, she'd excelled in the operating room and discovered who she was meant to be. Now she was adrift again, no longer holding a scalpel but instead an infant.

She fixed the blanket around Beck's tiny chin. "I will find my footing with you and my family." She'd made good progress so far and was committed to going the distance this time. She kept her steps brisk. "It all needs to start with a name. I do believe we've tossed out the standard Grandma, Grams, Granny."

Beck yawned again.

"Right, uninspiring." Lilian circled the stables. "Do we consider Gigi or Glamma or GamGam then?"

Beck sighed, his little body going lax in her arms.

"Right. Nothing worth waking for." She stroked his cheek, then reached to tuck his hand under the blanket. "How about Nana or Nan?"

Beck's tiny fingers curled around her finger and squeezed.

"I think we're getting close," Lilian whispered, trying to swallow the emotion from her words. "But if it's all the same to you, let's not decide tonight. We both know I'm still finding my footing. I don't want to trip myself up."

Three loops around the barns complete, Lilian made her way back inside the silent farmhouse. She tucked her soundly sleeping grandson in his crib beside his twin sister's crib and mentally congratulated herself. She crept out of the second-floor nursery, tiptoed downstairs, and felt her grin expanding.

The last time she'd sneaked down these stairs she'd been a teenager, trying to meet her boyfriend for a late-night swim at the Sloan family pond. She'd been celebrating how stealthy she was when she reached the mudroom undetected. Then the light had switched on in the kitchen, revealing her mother and highlighting Lilian's failed escape. She vowed that night that she'd be leaving Three Springs after graduation with no intention of ever looking back. She'd mostly stuck to that vow.

She turned the corner and pulled up short at the soft glow of the kitchen light. Only it wasn't her mother waiting for her. It was her oldest son, Carter. He was setting clean bottles and formula containers out on the kitchen island.

"Carter, you should be sleeping," she chided quietly.

"As should you." He opened the refrigerator, pulled out a bowl of grapes, and offered her some. "And I just slept four hours straight thanks to you. I feel ready to take on the world."

She noted the exhaustion under his eyes but refrained from challenging him. "I predict Beck will sleep for another few hours before he wakes up hungry and ready to alert the world."

"He doesn't seem to enjoy sleeping, but he certainly likes eating." Carter's shoulders shook with laughter.

"If you scoot back to bed, you can have a few more hours of sleep too." Lilian took the fruit bowl from her son and set it back inside the refrigerator. "Imagine how you'll feel then."

"You might be right." Carter covered his yawn

and grinned. "Tess made sure the guest room is all prepared for you."

"I told her not to do that." Lilian picked up her purse from the side counter and searched for her car keys in the outside pocket. "But I appreciate it."

"You're not staying?" He frowned through another yawn.

"I want to drive my new convertible with the top down at night." She peered at her son. "Silly, isn't it?"

Carter's expression softened. "Not even a little bit."

"I sound like a teenager." Perhaps it was being back in her family home. Wistfulness or something like that. When she left New York, her medical degrees packed into moving boxes and her hospital badge deactivated, she'd decided to free her emotions. She would feel what she felt and work through it all on her terms. Right now, she was feeling like a midnight drive.

"Be careful, okay? No speeding and watch out for other cars." Carter paused and rubbed his jaw. "And I sound like an overprotective father."

"That's not a bad thing. Your children will be better for it." She walked toward the mudroom, Carter following her. "Besides, driving home in the morning, there won't be any stars to appreciate."

"Text me when you get home." Carter held open the back door for her, stepped onto the porch, and pulled her into his affectionate embrace.

An unsolicited hug from her son, who insisted on watching over her. There was surprise and gratitude. Regret too. Regret for all that she had missed of her sons growing up. *Stay in the moment, Lilian.*

She reached up and touched Carter's cheek. "Get some sleep. My grandchildren will need you wide awake and ready in the morning."

Once again, she was thankful for her parents. They'd raised her sons to become honorable men. She couldn't have asked for anything more.

Fifteen minutes into her drive back to her small cottage in Belleridge, Lilian eased her car over to the side of the deserted bypass and stepped out. She walked to the hood of her car, sat on top, and fixed her gaze on the stars lighting the entire sky. It was a view she hadn't realized she missed until now.

She spotted the truck approaching from the opposite direction, noted the law enforcement lights on the roof, and read the bold white Three Springs County Sheriff's Department lettering on the door when the vehicle slowed to idle beside her.

The window rolled down and revealed a weathered yet very handsome face beneath a buckskin hat. "Evening, ma'am. I'm Sheriff Hopson."

"Evening, Sheriff," Lilian said and introduced herself.

Sheriff Hopson cut the truck engine. "Do you need help?"

"I do." She took in the silver tinting his well-groomed beard and the laugh lines fanning around his eyes. Felt a quick hit of attraction when he stepped from his truck, revealing a lean, fit frame and a height she appreciated. She pointed toward the sky. "I can't seem to find the Big Dipper or the Little One for that matter." She slanted her gaze back toward him.

His eyebrows notched into his forehead. "If it's stargazing you're wanting to do, ma'am, the best place for that is at Silent Rise Canyon. There's a bluff out there."

"Is that so?" She shifted on the hood and considered him. "This spot right here doesn't seem so bad."

He scratched his cheek. Those laugh lines deepened. "But out at Silent Rise, you can almost touch the stars."

"Now you've captured my interest." In more ways than one. She slipped off the hood of her car and skimmed her hands over her pants. "How do I get there?"

"Afraid I can't tell you that." His expression was reserved, but there was a noticeable glint in his gaze.

Lilian frowned.

"But I could show you," he offered. "If you had a mind to spend the evening with an old-time cowboy."

There was nothing old about the man. He looked fine from his shoulders to his boots. Oh, she noticed the cowboy in his stance and in his confidence. She smiled. "Only if you have a mind to spend time with a retired doctor past her prime."

"Well, Doc, if you don't mind my saying, I happen to think experience looks quite fetching on you."

Lilian's cheeks warmed. No, she didn't mind in the least.

He opened her car door for her and tipped his hat. "How's Saturday night work for you?"

"That'll be fine." She slid into the leather seat and glanced up at him. "Where should I meet you?"

"Oh no, Doc, we're gonna do this proper." He shut her door and kept his attention fixed on her. "Dinner, stargazin', and maybe even a kiss on the cheek good night under the porch light, if we're both of a similar mindset."

"That sounds like a date, Sheriff Hopson." She buckled her seat belt and tried to clip her sudden excitement. She was a renowned heart surgeon, known for her steady resolve and even stricter discipline.

"Got something against a date?" he asked, sending those laugh lines crinkling.

"I'm a grandparent," she blurted.

"Welcome to the club. Between you and me, it's one of the best titles you can have." Amusement and pride flashed in his gaze. "But we're more than a title, aren't we? And we've certainly earned the right to have our own brand of excitement."

"What brand of excitement is that exactly?" she asked.

"You will have to join me for our date to find out." He tapped the brim of his sheriff's hat. "See you Saturday night, Doc."

Just like that, Dr. Lilian Sloan felt all those free, fanciful emotions from her teenage years spilling through her. And instantly, Lilian was knocked off-balance but in a perfectly good, perfectly wonderful way.

CHAPTER SEVEN

GAME ON.

Lacey closed the email confirming that Aspen's application to enter the Junior Royal Rodeo Contest had been received. The very one she'd filled out and submitted while sipping her morning iced expresso, thanks to Caleb's sunrise text. He'd forwarded the Junior Royal Rodeo Contest website link and a last-chance offer for her to concede.

An offer Lacey had not accepted. She started her truck and put it in Drive.

It was purely selfish, but Lacey wanted the next three weeks to start with a check mark in the win column. That meant giving her daughter something she wanted and going against her ex-husband's wishes. There would be fallout, but Lacey hoped to deal with that after Jeffrey and Sarah-Beth returned from their babymoon.

In the meantime, Lacey intended to do everything to help her daughter succeed in the Junior Royal Rodeo Contest. That included accepting Caleb Sloan's assistance and taking advantage of his connections.

Lacey had researched Caleb's very talented sisters-in-law last night after sleep eluded her. She was hopeful that with their rodeo background and achievements in the arena, they could offer some much-needed guidance and advice. After all, she wasn't going to leave her daughter's chances in the Junior Royal Rodeo Contest solely in the hands of one unpredictable cowboy and a spur-of-the-moment wager.

Her phone chimed as she stood outside the headquarters for Three Springs County Sheriff's Department. She opened a new text from Caleb and chuckled at the attached country music video links and his caption: Inspiration. The cheerful emojis he'd added confirmed her suspicion that her cowboy might be one of those exasperatingly chipper morning types.

She tapped on her phone screen. One quick internet search, and she texted her response to Caleb, complete with her own collection of emojis and hashtag: #cowboycrochet.

Smiling, Lacey entered the two-story office building that housed the department, a small jail, and the courthouse. She was early for her shift, and she had a cowboy match to make. Apparently, one of her favorite things was still besting Caleb Sloan. Time to get started.

"Good morning, Gertie." Lacey walked over to the modern curved desk that served as reception and dispatch. Lacey hoped her words sounded conversationally casual as she asked, "You wouldn't happen to have any single relatives living in the area, would you?"

"Only ones here are several decades outside your age bracket." Gertie lowered the microphone on her headset and revealed her slow blooming grin. "If you're wanting a hookup, it's Breezy and Gayle Baker we need to be calling."

Hookup? For me? Definitely not what Lacey wanted. "No." That word came out with unintended force. Lacey flapped her hands, trying to lower Gertie's indoor voice.

"Well, you can't turn your eye on the married ones," Gertie whispered. Disapproval punctuated her hushed tone. "That's frowned upon around here."

"I'm not turning my eye on anyone, married or otherwise," Lacey argued and lessened the urgency from her words. "I only just moved here."

"No time like the present to get started." Gertie's attitude gained more gusto.

"What are we starting?" asked Lacey's stepdad as he crossed the threshold, his sheriff's hat propped on his gray-tinged hair and his uniform precisely pressed.

"Lacey's social life, Sheriff Hopson," Gertie supplied, with even more zeal. "Seems she's getting it going."

"Nothing like jumping right in with both feet." Her stepdad stopped at the end of the long reception desk. Approval creased the edges of his smile. "I've been telling Lacey for months it's past time she gets back out there."

Gertie nodded sagely, like she'd been offering the same advice to Lacey for even longer. Her shrewd gaze fell on Lacey. "Can't let a divorce sour your enjoyment of life."

"It didn't," Lacey said weakly. "I was working overseas." And feeling a lot of satisfaction with her career as a military police officer.

"Can't let work interfere either." Her stepdad rubbed his beard. "It's all about balance."

Gertie gave another sage dip of her chin. "My first marriage only lasted three years. I worked hard, and he played even harder. I never much cared for the seesaw on the playground, and my marriage felt the same. Second marriage was just as teeter-tottery."

Lacey was feeling slightly off-kilter herself…and uncertain how to veer the conversation away from her personal life. That there was no "social" in her personal life was entirely on purpose. A preference she had no interest in changing anytime soon.

Gertie shook herself as if dusting off that sand from the playground. "But the third time, well now, it has sure proven to be the charm." Gertie twitched her penciled-in eyebrows at Lacey. "My Joe and I been married going on twenty-three years. Finding the right partner is the key."

Her stepdad nodded. "Gertie, I take it you have leads on a partner for our Lacey."

"Already connected with my network." Gertie tapped a nail on her phone screen and plucked at her spiky platinum blond hair. "I'm proficient in multitasking."

Lacey smoothed the wince from her expression.

Gertie's phone chimed. "Look at that Gayle Baker's fast response time. She's especially spry when it comes to our bowling league and matters of the heart."

There were more of them. Women like Gertie. Right in town. Lacey grimaced and mentally flipped through a list of excuses that might halt this runaway train. *My single-mom plate is full. I've only just recently got back to town. I'm fine just as I am, on my own two feet.* Lacey rocked in her black lace-up boots. *Look. Steady. No fixing or mending required.*

Gertie's phone chimed again. Then again.

Lacey swayed.

Her stepdad set his arm around Lacey's shoulders and squeezed. Amusement threaded through his words. "Looks like the news is spreading about you, Deputy Nash."

"Best buckle up, dear." At the sixth chime, Gertie cackled. "Your social life is on speed dial now."

Speed dial. Lacey swallowed her groan. No one to blame but herself for this snag. Nothing to do now except retreat. Lacey pointed toward the clock on the wall. "Looks like my shift is starting. Better get to work."

Gertie set her phone down and scooted her chair along her desk like a train on its tracks. "Deputy Nash, I've got a ten-ninety-two on Fortune Street outside Three Springs's town hall."

Lacey nodded. "Improperly parked car."

Gertie glanced at her, and her glossy lips pursed.

"Ten-four," Lacey added.

Gertie's mouth relaxed. Yet a challenge glinted in her sharp gaze. "And we've got a ten-forty-nine at 412 Wildflower Court."

"That's Harvey Engell's house." Her stepdad frowned.

Lacey was confused. "Drag racing?" Wildflower Court was a cul-de-sac less than a mile from downtown Three Springs.

Gertie frowned. "Sheriff, you certain you don't want me to take that constable training after all?"

A sworn position would grant Gertie the right to carry a badge and a gun and arrest folks. The woman was already a force to be reckoned with.

"You're needed too much right here, Gertie." Her stepdad nudged Lacey in the ribs. "Keeping our deputies in line."

Gertie's shoulders straightened. She opened a drawer, took out a booklet, and slid it across the desk. "Deputy Nash, I'll be charging for your next codebook. See that you don't misplace this one. Paper isn't cheap."

Lacey accepted the booklet and tucked it into the wide pocket on her cargo pants. "About that ten-forty-nine."

"That's a barking dog," her stepdad offered and held open the door for her that led to the deputy's desk and his corner office. His eyebrows raised. "Drag racing is ten-ninety-four, Deputy."

Gertie beamed at him. "That's why he's been elected sheriff for four straight terms. Follow his lead, Deputy."

"I will," Lacey promised. Although in truth, she'd been following her stepdad's lead for years now. Ever since her mother's cancer diagnosis days before Lacey's sixteenth birthday. She had no intention of stopping now.

Her stepdad turned in the open doorway of his office. "Deputy Nash, that dispute between the Buckner family and the Engells on Wildflower Court started before I was born. Stick to today's dispute only and try not to get sideswiped by their age-old feud."

"Understood." Lacey pulled her keys from her pocket and stopped at her desk to pick up a court summons and the wage garnishment documents she needed to serve on her way to Wildflower Court.

"Don't forget, I'll be over to the house with the new toilet and showerhead for Aspen's bathroom," her stepdad called out. "We can replace them both tonight."

"You didn't have to do that." Lacey tucked her lunch into a desk drawer. "Aspen and I could've shared the master bathroom."

"You both need your space," her stepdad said. "That's what your mom told me when you were living with us. That's why we put in that second bathroom."

That was Wells's doing. He'd gone above and beyond to make sure Lacey had felt at home in the large ranch house. He hadn't stopped at a bathroom installation. He'd taught her to ride a horse as well as any cowboy. And he'd taught her to drive both on the road and off in everything from a riding lawnmower to a tractor to a truck. But mostly Wells had taught her what it meant to serve and protect. "Thanks. I'm sure Aspen will appreciate it."

"Once we get the toilet and shower working again, she will appreciate it," he corrected. "Has to be perfect for my granddaughter."

Comments like that explained why Wells had a piece of Lacey's heart. She'd been his daughter from the beginning. Never a step-anything. Never an inconvenience. Never a bother. Despite already having three biological children to call his own. And Aspen, well, she'd been his granddaughter from the first call Lacey had made to tell her mom and Wells of her surprise pregnancy. When Lacey had emailed about moving back stateside, Wells let her know he'd meet her at the airport with the keys to the ranch house, claiming he'd been ready to welcome her home for far too long.

Her mom and Wells had bought the ranch house and land together as their wedding present to each other. The fifteen-acre property had been a dream realized for Lacey's mom and the foundation for the couple's retirement goals. But after Lacey's mom passed and that future collapsed, the dream had become more of an upkeep nightmare for Wells. He'd moved to a town house in Belleridge but hadn't sold the ranch. He claimed it was Lacey's legacy and hers to keep or sell.

Lacey headed out. "Well, I've got my tool belt

ready and White Olive Pizza Shop saved to my contact list. Dinner is on me."

"Looking forward to it." He glanced at his phone and laughed. "And, Deputy, you might want to avoid checking your phone."

Lacey frowned, already reaching for her cell. "Why?"

"Seems Gertie included the rest of the team in your social life start-up." Her stepdad's deep laugh spilled free. "Deputy Frew and Deputy Byatt already have suggestions. And Deputy Trevino wants to know if you would consider dating navy or air force? He's got cousins serving in both military branches."

Lacey left her phone untouched and jammed her hat lower on her forehead. No choice now. She was going *no reply*. To her stepdad and her peers. And avoiding Gertie for the foreseeable future. She beelined for the door, lengthening her strides to outpace her stepdad's laughter.

All because she'd challenged a charismatic cowboy, then refused to back down. Surely one day she'd learn to curb her impulses around her cowboy and walk away before trouble found her. If only for her own peace of mind.

CHAPTER EIGHT

CALEB FLIPPED A pancake on the griddle in the Sloan farmhouse kitchen, then placed it on the growing stack filling a plate nearby. More salt and pepper for the scrambled eggs cooking in the large frying pan on the stove. Followed by a quick check of the bacon sizzling in the oven. Caleb wiped his hands on the dish towel he'd tucked into his waistband, satisfied all was as it should be.

It was Friday morning. His day to cook breakfast for his family. Even though three of his brothers and their wives lived in different houses now, the Sloan farmhouse remained the gathering place for family meals. If they were in town, the Sloans made it to the farmhouse dining table for breakfast and dinner.

It was precisely how Caleb envisioned the entire day proceeding: as usual.

Not a curveball in sight.

Today he intended to get back to his normal routine. No wrangling a bull with a pretty and tenacious cowgirl at his side. No late-night root beer chats that tempted him to slow down and linger with said cowgirl. And most definitely no *feels* today.

Today was all about focusing. He had things to prove after all. And standing around accomplished nothing.

Carter wandered into the kitchen, cradling baby Sadie in his arms. His hair was uncombed, his T-shirt wrinkled, yet his gaze was clear and alert.

"You look rested." Caleb slipped on an oven mitt, pulled the pan of bacon from the oven, and set it on the cool side of the eight-burner stove.

"Thanks to Mom." Carter handed Sadie to Caleb, then went to work preparing two baby bottles.

Caleb tucked the pink blanket around the baby and swayed like his mother had in the driveway. Sadie sighed contentedly, and Caleb offered his mom silent kudos. "I thought Mom would be here for breakfast, but her car is gone."

"She left last night." Carter filled a bowl with hot water and dropped both filled bottles inside to warm. "With her top down for some late-night stargazing."

"And you let her go?" Caleb turned off the burner for the eggs and returned to his slow side-to-side sway. "That hardly seems safe."

"How was I supposed to stop her?" Carter fixed two cups of coffee and set them on the table where he and Tess usually sat. He frowned at Caleb. "I can't take her keys. She's an adult."

Caleb said, "Doesn't mean we shouldn't look out for her."

"What is happening here?" Carter scooped Sadie back into his arms and eyed Caleb. His words were as bemused as his expression. "We are talking about Lilian Sloan."

"Our mom," Caleb corrected and grabbed shredded cheese from the refrigerator.

"Exactly." Carter stayed close by, following Caleb back to the stove. "This is the same person you've treated with less warmth than an ice bath since she moved back permanently."

"Can you *not* make this a thing please?" Caleb scooped scrambled eggs into a folded pancake to assemble his popular pancake breakfast tacos.

"But it is a thing," Carter stressed. "You and Mom don't..." Carter's face pulled in. "You two just don't."

His brother wasn't wrong. But today wasn't about reflecting on his messed-up dynamic with his mother. "Look, Mom and I ran into each other last night when she was here taking care of Beck." Caleb crumbled bacon over his pancake tacos. "We talked. Not a big deal."

"And the next time Mom wants to go stargazing alone after midnight..." Carter said.

"Call me. I'll go with her," Caleb said. "I'm usually up late anyway."

"You're right." Carter ran his hand through his hair, tousling it even more. "This is *so* not a big deal."

Caleb couldn't let it *be* a big deal. Otherwise, he might be tripping too close to those *feels* he wanted to avoid. Caleb ignored the heavy sarcasm in his older brother's words and thrust the plate at him. "That's the last of the maple pork sausage. If you want it, you better eat now before Ryan gets here."

"I'm already here." Ryan strolled inside, leaned around Carter, swiped a piece of sausage off Carter's plate, and plopped it in his mouth.

Caleb laughed. "I warned you."

"No more. The rest is mine." Carter lifted his plate out of Ryan's reach and frowned at his brother. "I thought Elsie would've taught you manners by now, Ryan."

"My wife loves me with or without manners. Besides, I thought you were greeting me with that plate like a good host, big brother." Ryan motioned toward Carter. "In fact, you look like you've got your hands full, I can take it for you."

Carter grinned and transferred baby Sadie into Ryan's arms. "My daughter wants to see her uncle."

"Favorite uncle." Ryan gathered Sadie close against his chest and cooed at her. "Isn't that right, little Sadie?"

"You can't be the favorite." Caleb went back to assembling his pancake tacos with the precision of a short-order cook filling a backlog of open tickets. "You didn't bring any gifts."

Ryan picked up a piece of bacon from the cookie sheet and took a bite. "And you did?"

Caleb aimed his spatula at the collection of large plush stuffed animals propped up on the couch in the family room. "There's even one for Maggie and my unborn niece or nephew she's currently carrying."

"I'll give you this round, little brother." Ryan

fist-bumped Caleb. "But we've got years to settle the score for favorite uncle."

"Caleb, you really need to stop buying things for the twins." Tess walked in carrying baby Beck, picked up a blue-eared stuffed cow, and snuggled it tight. "But this is seriously cute and super soft, so thank you."

"Anything for my niece and nephew." Caleb set a plate on the table for Tess and motioned her to sit.

"Sure smells good in here." Grandpa Sam touched his stomach and paused in the archway. "Caleb, I'm glad you're here. Thought maybe you'd be too busy for sitting down with us."

"Breakfast is the most important meal of the day." And not letting down his family was even more important. That started by not skipping out on his usual responsibilities, even the simple ones like cooking family breakfast. Caleb fixed another plate for his grandpa.

Uncle Roy came in, finished tucking in his button-down shirt into his jeans, and greeted Caleb with a request for double the bacon.

The back door opened and slammed, then Maggie hurried in. "Please tell me I didn't miss breakfast. The hospital called early. They needed Grant for an emergency surgery on an incoming patient, and I fell back to sleep."

"You're right on time." Caleb piled pancakes onto a plate for his sister-in-law. "Plain pancakes. No eggs. And everything your stomach and the baby likes."

"Caleb, move in with Grant and me please." Maggie wrapped her arm around his waist and squeezed. "Our new place is less than a ten-minute drive away. It's even faster on horseback since Grant and Ryan carved out that new trail through the woods."

"He can't move in with you guys," Tess called out and lifted her coffee cup in a toast. "We need him here at the farmhouse more. No one makes coffee like Caleb does."

"And everyone needs their coffee in this house," Grandpa Sam chimed in. "Puts us in the right frame of mind to start our day."

"And deal appropriately with each other." Ryan grinned and tapped his glass against Carter's.

"That's why I perfected the art of coffee years ago." Caleb fixed his own plate and joined his family at the table. "Otherwise, mornings would have been unbearable around here."

"That's because Caleb is a morning person." Ryan waved his fork at everyone around the table. "And the rest of us are not."

"Just doing what I need to for my family." Caleb polished off his breakfast taco.

"Speaking of helping out family." Ryan stood up, piled more bacon on his plate, then added several slices to Uncle Roy's plate. "Caleb, Elsie had to bring her nieces to camp this morning. But my wife wanted me to tell you that she can help you with the rehearsal dinner and reception. Just call her."

He thought of his mother's very same offer. Caleb set his fork on his plate and sat back.

"Count me in." Maggie brushed her hand over her pregnant belly. "I just need a little advance notice. I'm ironing out a few hiccups with the Rodeo Reunion schedule."

"I can help you, Maggie," Caleb offered. "Just say the word."

"Caleb, your plate is already spilling over," Maggie chided.

That was intentional. His choice. Downtime had never been much to his liking.

Tess picked up a bottle from the bowl of water, tested the temperature on her arm, then returned to the table. Her words were gentle. "It's okay to say no once in a while, Caleb."

And risk letting someone down? Not happening if Caleb could help it.

"Tess isn't wrong." Carter accepted a bottle from Tess and repositioned baby Sadie for her breakfast. "Remember, I've got the event tent ready as a backup for the reception if you need it."

"Nothing wrong with a solid backup plan," Grandpa Sam mused.

"I appreciate it, but I've got it handled." Or he would soon enough. He couldn't afford to doubt himself if everyone around him already was. Before anyone else could offer their assistance, Caleb continued, "In the interest of taking Tess's advice, I'm going to say no to everyone here. Thank you, but I don't need your help." He couldn't very well take them to work with him when he got the full-time marketing job, so he needed to start as he meant to go on: on his own.

"That settles that." Tess laughed and pointed toward the hallway. "This is the last thing I'll say about it. Vivian mailed her wedding notebook overnight to the house. It's in the office for you, Caleb."

Caleb lowered his shoulders slightly, yet his suspicions lingered. It wasn't like his family to back off so swiftly. "I'll be sure to grab it before I leave."

Ryan dropped his hand on Caleb's shoulder and squeezed. "If you won't accept our help, then let's talk about something else interesting that I heard about a certain deputy."

Deputy. Caleb worked to remain relaxed. Any flinch, and his brother would pounce.

"Is this about Lacey Nash being at the bar late last night with Caleb?" Maggie took a bite of her pancakes and grinned around the mouthful. "I heard about that."

Uncle Roy gave a murmur of agreement and a head bob.

Grandpa Sam refilled his mug with the coffee carafe Caleb had placed on the table earlier, then tapped a heaping spoonful of sugar in. His words were as slow as the spoon he swished in the dark steaming liquid. "Seems we've all heard something about Caleb and a certain deputy."

Except it was nothing. Even if Caleb had lain awake entirely too long last night wondering about his deputy. But that was what happened when Caleb was idle too long. His mind ventured places his heart wished him to go. But that only led to bruised hearts. And that took the joy out of everything. No one wanted that, least of all Caleb, who prided himself on sticking to a life of fun and adventure.

"I was bartending." Caleb braced his elbows on the table, kept his words indifferent. "Should I tell you who else was at the bar with me last night?"

Ryan scoffed. "But Lacey was one of the last to leave."

"I'm not sure what that has to do with anything," Caleb said. Other than how having his deputy entirely to himself had been energizing and refreshing and not the least bit disagreeable.

"It's more like an observation," Ryan mused. "To do with what you will."

"In that case, I'll clear the table and tidy up the kitchen." Caleb gathered the empty plates around him. "I've got a meeting with the caterer later this morning."

"Come on, Caleb." Ryan jumped up and chased after him. "I'm sure everyone would like to know what you thought about Lacey in action yesterday at the lake. She never hesitated with Walter. It was quite incredible."

He thought his deputy had looked magnificent riding bareback on Denny, his Arabian. Lacey always had a natural affinity and grace on a horse. And she hadn't lost that, not even a little. He'd been impressed by her absolute steadiness and control, as if she'd been riding every single day since high school. He shrugged. "You already said it. She did well yesterday."

"Better than that." Ryan huffed. He accepted the empty plates from Grandpa Sam and Uncle Roy and paused for the round of goodbyes from the older cowboys. Then Ryan came right back to the conversation. "I would want Lacey riding with me in any situation. Any day."

You can't have her. She's... Caleb clenched his jaw hard and beelined for the kitchen sink. He could end his brother's prying by announcing that Lacey was setting him up with his perfect match. Thus proving there was nothing between him and Lacey.

Why had he even agreed to that?

"Ryan, leave your brother alone," Maggie scolded, then nudged Ryan back toward the dining table.

"Thanks, Mags." Caleb poured soap over the dishes in the sink.

"I owed you for the pancakes." Maggie chuckled and pulled a clean towel out of the drawer. "Which were excellent by the way. That offer to move in still stands."

Caleb laughed and handed her the frying pan to dry. "Hey, Mags, what can you tell me about the Junior Royal Rodeo Contest?"

"Not much," Maggie admitted. "I only ever competed in the arena."

"But you're the director for Three Springs's Rodeo Reunion," Caleb argued. "The contest falls under your jurisdiction."

"Isn't that like a conflict of interest if Mags tells

you insider secrets about the contest?" Ryan suddenly reappeared, took the frying pan from Maggie, and put it away. "And why do you want to know?"

"Lacey mentioned it last night," Caleb hedged. "I was curious." Mostly about how to win the bet with Lacey. That part he left out. His family most likely wouldn't consider the wager the most responsible thing, and he was trying to prove he could change.

"I do know there's a lot involved for each contestant," Maggie said.

Caleb thought she was exaggerating but refrained from calling his sister-in-law out. Then he'd have to admit he was helping Aspen prepare for the contest. And his family would surely read too much into that. Those inevitable questions he didn't know how to answer would surely follow. "Okay, if you think of anything I can pass on to Lacey, let me know."

Maggie tipped her head and considered him. "Are you sure there's nothing going on between you and Lacey?"

Nothing he would ever admit to. "I thought we already went over this."

"Right." Maggie smiled and leaned in close. "If I tell you how to win the contest, will you tell me the truth?"

"You really are relentless, Mags." Caleb's shoulders shook. "The truth is we're friends."

Maggie's lips formed a fake pout before she grinned. "It was worth a try. I can't tell you how to win other than to get the highest scores from the judges."

Caleb nodded and concentrated on washing the dishes. One more thing he'd figure out for himself.

Thanks to Ryan and Maggie's assistance, the kitchen was back to rights in record time. He was just thankful the conversation never veered back to a certain deputy.

Caleb gently rubbed Beck's back and kissed Sadie's forehead, then picked up Vivian's wedding notebook from the home office. He skimmed the pages on his walk to his apartment.

Unfortunately, there were few notes and a rather excessive number of cutout magazine pictures. The photos featured everything from color choices to flowers to bridal gowns. There was enough to fill several bridal magazines in fact. The random collection of images and uplifting quotes was a bit dizzying. Caleb carefully closed the notebook to keep the pictures contained and left it on his kitchen table.

He was rinsing the shampoo from his hair in the shower when his phone started ringing. No sooner had he turned off the water than his voicemail chimed and his text message alert sounded.

Caleb dressed quickly, toweled off his hair, and skimmed his half dozen new text messages.

Maggie had sent the links to several websites on how best to prepare your junior cowgirls and cowboys for competition. Those would be very useful.

The caterer from The Jamming Fig texted to confirm Caleb's late-morning tasting. He checked his watch and grinned. He would be right on time.

The organizer of Belleridge's Last Dog Day of Summer, happening the following week, wanted to run through his emcee responsibilities at his earliest convenience. The dog event was one of his favorites. He looked forward to it every year.

And Wes Tanner wanted to know about his availability to bartend through the end of the month. Well, that depended on his success as a wedding coordinator and his pending full-time job offer. He kept his response to a simple I'll get back to you. Still, he might be able to fill in on the weekends and an occasional evening.

Lots to do. Even more to consider. Just the way Caleb liked it. On-the-go was his preferred setting. Had been since he was a child.

The voicemail came from the head of Three Springs County Fire Department. Chief Franson needed Caleb on call that afternoon. Kellie Pratt, one of the full-time firefighters, had to take her seven-year-old son to the ER for a possible broken wrist after he fell that morning. Caleb texted Kellie to check on her son and then responded to the fire chief before quickly changing into his fire-department-issued navy pants, navy short-sleeved shirt, and steel-toed boots. He grabbed his go bag with extra clothes and supplies, then headed out the door, humming the whole way.

It was shaping up to be a good day indeed.

CHAPTER NINE

FEET AWAY FROM his truck, the first curveball of the day hit Caleb.

He stopped humming mid-verse and took in the two older cowboys already seated inside his vehicle. He opened the rear passenger door and tossed his bag on the floor mat. Then he climbed into the driver's seat and glanced over at his front-seat passenger. "Grandpa Sam." A quick tilt of his head, and Caleb met the alert gaze of his uncle from the bench in the back. "Uncle Roy. Who wants to explain what you two are doing?"

"What does it look like?" Uncle Roy grumbled and buckled his seat belt with a decided click. "We are going to the tasting with you."

Click. Caleb shifted and regarded his grandfather.

Grandpa Sam snapped his seat belt strap against his chest. "Listen here, Caleb Sloan. We were invited to the tasting by Vivian and Josh."

"And you're not stopping us," Uncle Roy stated.

"Fine." Caleb started his truck, turned around in the driveway, and drove down the long private road. "But let's go over the ground rules."

"There's only one rule we need to cover." Grandpa Sam tapped his finger against the console. "Roy and I have got opinions about food. We'll be voicing them to you and the chef. Like it or not."

Roy leaned between the front seats and shook his head. "We did not like those fancy finger foods and gourmet dinner choices at Carter and Tess's wedding. No, siree."

"My stomach ached for days after that so-called fish and vegetable burger," Grandpa Sam lamented and rubbed his stomach. "I want Josh and Vivian's guests to talk about the wedding, not suffer some form of food poisoning."

Caleb wiped his hand over his mouth and caught his laughter. His grandpa and uncle's antics made it impossible to hold on to his irritation. Not that he was surprised. Grandpa Sam had always spun the sour from Caleb's mood since Caleb was a child. The two older cowboys had hearts dipped in gold and intentions just as pure, even if their methods could be problematic at times.

Caleb straightened and cleared his throat. "Okay, my turn. We are only going to the restaurant and home. No detours of any kind." He paused for a beat, then continued, "I'm on call this afternoon and need to get you home."

"Kellie Pratt's son broke his wrist something good." Grandpa Sam stroked his beard, his words pensive.

"Got his foot caught on the last step off the school bus," Uncle Roy added.

"How do you know about that?" Caleb slanted his gaze toward his grandpa. "I only just heard."

"We've got our sources." Grandpa Sam's fingers sank into his thick beard, and his chin lifted. "Don't ask who either. We like to keep things confidential."

Uncle Roy warned, "Good ones too."

"I've nothing to hide," Caleb announced, aside from a bet with a pretty deputy and feelings he didn't want to encourage. "So your sources have nothing to report about me."

"You'd be surprised," Grandpa Sam mused, then swiftly diverted the conversation. "Now, what's on the menu? I'm getting hungry."

"You just ate breakfast a little while ago," Caleb said. "I made it. I watched you eat it."

Grandpa Sam dismissed Caleb's comment. "That was only a snack to hold us over."

"I'd like steak," Uncle Roy suggested. "And potatoes. Skip the green vegetables."

"We're sampling," Caleb said. At least that was what he assumed. He'd never actually tasted food options for a wedding reception before. "Not sitting down for a four-course dining experience."

"How will we know if we like all the courses if we don't try them?" Grandpa Sam countered.

"Can't have three good courses and a bad one," Uncle Roy said, his voice raised an octave. "It's the bad one everyone will be talking about the next day."

Caleb parked behind The Jamming Fig restaurant in Belleridge and cut the engine. "How about we head on inside and let the restaurant staff guide us?"

"Speaking of a guide." Grandpa Sam opened his truck door and peered back at Caleb. "Don't forget to grab Vivian's wedding notebook. If it's anything like Tess's and Maggie's, it'll tell you everything you need to know."

Caleb winced.

"You forgot it, didn't you?" Grandpa Sam accused.

"I left it at my apartment for safekeeping," Caleb hedged. He climbed out of his truck, pocketed his keys, and pretended all was exactly as he'd intended. "But I glanced over Vivian's catering notes."

"Great. Then there's nothing to worry about." Grandpa Sam followed Uncle Roy inside.

It was more like Caleb had flipped through the various pictures in the section marked Catering. Not that the stills of assorted fruit bowls, gardens, and candlesticks offered much direction for the menu. Still, Caleb refused to be concerned.

Surely, the caterer already had the couple's wishes. Vivian and Josh had booked The Jamming Fig months ago. It was their favorite date night restaurant. And according to Maggie, popular for local weddings. The caterer was the one with the culinary experience.

Sticking with that logic, Caleb stepped inside the trendy restaurant, took in the familiar face behind the reservation desk, and promptly forgot any worries. "KC Delvy."

"Caleb Sloan." KC reached out, gripped Caleb's hand in a firm shake, and pulled him in for a hearty pat on the back. KC's southern accent was unmistakable. "Haven't seen you since I tackled you in Amarillo at that rodeo roundup a few years back."

Caleb chuckled and introduced KC, short for Kurt Cash, to his grandpa and uncle. "KC is a saddle bronc rider. Few seasons ago, I went to assist KC off his bronc in the arena. Turned out that bronc had more bucking left to do after the buzzer. KC got sprung off, caught me around the neck and took us both to the dirt."

"Bruised my ribs something fierce that day. Could've been worse if Caleb and his first aid skills hadn't been there." KC rubbed his side. "I'm retired from the rodeo now. These days I'm slow cooking ribs on my smoker and taking risks with my spice blends."

"You're the chef here?" Caleb took in KC's white chef's jacket with The Jamming Fig logo embroidered on it. "Does Josh know?"

"I was promoted to head chef five days ago." KC tugged on his jacket as if the fit was suddenly uncomfortable. "I've been trying to reach Josh and Vivian. No luck."

"They're in the Alaskan backcountry," Grandpa Sam offered. "Josh's almost-in-laws had a bit of an accident."

"There's no cell reception where they're staying," Caleb explained. "But we're here to finalize the menu."

"That's good." Relief spread across KC's face. "I was worried about an anxious bride."

"Vivian will like you," Caleb assured his friend. "Vivian likes everyone."

"I'm more concerned about her liking my food." KC motioned them farther into the restaurant, which wouldn't open to the public for several more hours. "The former chef, who Vivian originally worked with, was offered an executive chef position at a five-star establishment in Dallas last weekend. He left immediately. He was talented in the kitchen but terrible at paperwork."

Worry pinched the back of Caleb's neck. "What does that mean?"

"I've got nothing about Josh and Vivian's wedding," KC explained. "Not even a theme."

"Right. The theme." The photo collection that was Vivian's wedding notebook came to mind. Caleb blurted, "Whimsical."

KC slipped his fingers beneath the collar of his jacket. "That's a start."

Caleb pictured his intended venue: a former rackhouse at the distillery. "Rustic too." He squeezed his neck. Swore he could see Lacey's gloating smile. She'd mentioned something about theme and romance last night right before he invited her to the wedding. The worry spread. "And romantic."

"It's more than what we had," KC said, yet he sounded less than positive.

Silence settled between the men.

Grandpa Sam hooked his thumbs around his large belt buckle. "When do we get to the tasting part?"

"That's what we really came for." Uncle Roy rocked forward in his boots. Certainty in his words. "Food doesn't need a theme if it tastes good."

There. Good common sense. What more did they need? Caleb stopped short of hugging his uncle and grinned wide. "I agree. Let's get to the sampling."

KC tipped his head back and laughed. "Can't tell you how glad I am that you're my first wedding."

"You've never cooked for a wedding reception before?" Grandpa Sam's mouth thinned inside his thick beard.

Caleb's enthusiasm dimmed.

"I've never been a head chef until now." KC headed for a swinging door marked Kitchen. Resolve was there in the stiff set of his wide shoulders. "But I do know how to cook, and I can prove it to you."

Caleb knew a thing or two about wanting to prove himself. He owed his friend that chance. After all, this was about the food.

Intent on maximizing his time, Caleb tugged his phone from his pocket and clicked on the first link for the contest that Maggie had texted him. Any interrogation of flavors and food combos, he knew he could leave to his partners here.

Grandpa Sam and Uncle Roy trailed after KC as if newly appointed sous-chefs.

"There are sample menus on the counter you're welcome to look over." KC tied an apron around his waist, and finally appeared more at ease. "If you have any other wedding details, feel free to share those."

Right. Details. About the whimsically rustic but romantic wedding Caleb hoped Vivian would like. Of course, there was no rustic without the rackhouse. He opened the email app on his phone, typed a message to the administrator at Three Springs's town hall inquiring about any health and business permits that might be required for the rackhouse to be deemed an event space, and hit Send. As for the romantic angle, he had time to figure that out later. He hoped KC was too busy cooking to notice Caleb wasn't exactly forthcoming with wedding details.

Uncle Roy picked up a menu and held it close to his face. "Don't see a gourmet fish veggie burger."

KC fired up a gas burner and tossed herbs and spices into a small sauté pan. "I prefer to keep the meat in my burgers and the fish and vegetables on their own plate."

"I knew I liked you." Uncle Roy beamed. "You can keep those fancy vegetables off my plate altogether."

"Yes, sir." KC laughed and moved around the commercial kitchen with the competence and professionalism one would expect from a well-seasoned chef.

Caleb grinned, propped his hip against the stainless steel counter, and scanned the Junior Royal Rodeo Contest guidelines. So much for simple. His unease jumped several levels. "Listen to this. A junior rodeo contestant must be knowledgeable about horse breeds. Skills in horsemanship to include but not limited to tack, saddling, and the completion of a set pattern in the arena. The contestant must give a two-minute speech on a Western topic and complete a one-on-one interview with a judge."

KC whistled and shook his head. "How old are these contestants?"

"Between the ages of seven and twelve." Caleb squeezed his forehead. That was a tall order for an adult, let alone a kid. The more he read, the more he realized Maggie had seriously downplayed the work involved.

"I'd rather ride a bucking bronc." KC tossed potato slices into a fryer basket. "And at that age, I wasn't speaking on a stage."

"Caleb was on the baseball field when he was eight," Grandpa Sam quipped. "Striking out more times than not. But he wasn't half bad as catcher."

"I liked the action behind home plate," Caleb said and mentally ran through his calendar.

Teaching Aspen was going to take more than one afternoon. He didn't even know her level of horsemanship. The last person he'd taught anything to had been Lacey. That had been roping and jumping back when they were kids and too fearless to pull themselves back.

Grandpa Sam wandered over to check the contents in the pan on the stove. Caleb heard his grandfather inquire about hot chilies and pimento but paid little attention to KC's response.

The risks of horseback riding were front of mind. Especially the potential injuries. He'd experienced plenty of them firsthand and had seen people he knew get hurt. How was he supposed to ensure Aspen's safety? He had to protect her; she was Lacey's daughter. Suddenly a wager placed in an empty bar looked much different in the daylight. Felt much different too.

Uncle Roy lowered the menu he'd been studying and asked offhand, "What types of glasses do you have for wine, Chef?"

Caleb paced around the kitchen, trying to walk off his growing nerves. He could teach Aspen just fine if he cleared away any distractions.

"Red or white wine?" KC took his knife skills to a piece of steak.

"Dandelion," Grandpa Sam replied.

Dandelion. Caleb froze near the double-door commercial freezer. This was what happened when he got distracted. His grandpa and uncle took advantage. He winced and took a step forward. Time to enter the fray. "We are not serving dandelion wine at the wedding reception."

"Why not?" Uncle Roy tugged on his salt-and-pepper curls. "The first batch is ready for sipping. The reception will be the perfect place."

Caleb set his hands on his hips. "For what?"

"For the introduction of our dandelion wine to the masses," Grandpa Sam stated, both his expression and words tinged with exasperation that it wasn't already obvious. "Where better to start building the buzz for our dandelion wine than the wedding?"

"Buzz," Caleb repeated.

"You know what buzz is, Caleb. It's what all the people want these days." Uncle Roy's thick eyebrows burrowed together. "To have a buzz. That builds a following, you know. And a following is what they say we need."

"You really should be up on all this already, Caleb, if you're going to be the big marketing executive at Misty Grove." Grandpa Sam's gaze narrowed on Caleb. "It's basic marketing for every great product."

But they had no product. Caleb smashed his lips together and glanced at KC. The chef's knife cuts gained speed as he shifted from the steak on the cooking island to dicing a tomato on the prep area in the corner. It seemed Caleb was on his own to deal with his grandpa and uncle. "How many bottles of dandelion wine do you have?"

"We've premeasured the servings," Uncle Roy said, a challenge in his voice. "We've got enough for at least one hundred people."

Caleb had finally caught a break. "Well, Josh mentioned the guest count was over one hundred and fifty before he left for Alaska." He spread his arms wide and tried to sound sympathetic. "Can't serve your wine if you can't serve everyone. Don't want to leave anybody out. That would build bad buzz. And that's the last thing you want."

Grandpa Sam pointed at Caleb. "This isn't over."

But it had to be. Offering their dandelion wine at the wedding, not to mention selling it later, would require following regulations, filing paperwork, and acquiring licenses. And the distillery wasn't licensed for dandelion wine.

Not to mention Caleb had a little girl to give horse-riding lessons to, as well as a long list of other commitments he'd made. He couldn't be introducing dandelion wine to the public. *No. Not happening.*

Caleb took in his grandpa and uncle, noted their earnest expressions and the determination in their gazes, and caved. He sighed, long and loud, more exasperated with himself than the duo. "What if I put together a separate tasting party specifically for your dandelion wine?"

Grandpa Sam's gaze switched to assessing. "What kind of tasting party?"

"An exclusive one that will build buzz," Caleb said, using their words to sway the wily pair. He appealed to his uncle. "It will be all about you and your product. What could be better than that to build buzz?"

Uncle Roy shared a looked with his brother, gave a barely-there nod, then said, "We want it booked on the calendar, Caleb, so it's official."

"And soon," Grandpa Sam said.

Crisis averted without disappointing his grandfather and uncle, Caleb agreed, "Fine." He motioned toward KC and asked, "Now can we please get back to the menu for the wedding reception?"

Uncle Roy wandered closer to the plates KC had set on the serving area. "Chef, there's something wrong with these French fries. They're stuck inside the meat."

Grandpa Sam joined his brother. "Nothing natural about that."

"Those are steak frites." KC chuckled, wiped his hands on a towel, and moved to stand next to the pair. "Just steak-wrapped French fries that you can pick up with your hands and eat in several bites. No utensils required." KC gestured with his arm out. "It's time, gentlemen, to sample."

Uncle Roy plucked a French fry bundle from a plate and took a large bite. He was reaching for a second fry bundle while still finishing off the first one.

Delight filled Grandpa Sam's face. "The wedding needs these. Add them to the menu."

"Glad you like them." KC pulled a tray from beneath a heat lamp. "But we need to start with the type of dinner I should prepare."

"Okay, Caleb, I reckon this is where you come in." Uncle Roy lifted a bacon-wrapped meatball from another platter. "We came for the tasting."

Dinner type sounded strangely close to theme. Caleb shifted from one booted foot to the other and stalled. "Maybe you should give us a rundown of our options."

"A plated, sit-down dinner," KC offered. "That's the most formal. I would need to know plate counts. Meal restrictions. Two course selections, single or double entrée, tableside dessert or not. Appetizers for the cocktail hour." KC set an empty frying pan in the industrial-looking sink. "I'm sure I'm missing something."

Caleb was missing the answers to everything KC had said after *formal*.

"Linen color." KC snapped his fingers and gave a satisfied nod. "For the tables and bar."

Grandpa Sam frowned. "Fancy silverware and all that is too fussy."

And confusing. Caleb stuffed a meatball in his mouth and sighed happily over the spicy flavor. When had this stopped being about good food?

"Buffet then." KC returned to the cooking island. "Table count and linen color is still needed."

What color was whimsical, rustic, and romantic? Caleb reached for another meatball.

"Never much liked standing in line for food," Uncle Roy mused.

"Stations are a new trend." KC set a plate of stuffed mushrooms on the counter. "They allow for the guests to move around throughout the evening. Each station has specific foods like small bites, pasta, carving roasts, fresh produce. Almost anything you can imagine."

Caleb was quickly warming to the idea. "So, it's like a pick-your-own-food adventure for the guests."

KC nodded.

"That's sounds fun." Caleb took out his buzzing phone and swiped on the screen. "Very on theme too. We want stations." A text from the fire chief about two feuding neighbors in Three Springs caught his attention. He opened it and frowned. "Okay, we need to wrap this up and get on the road."

"But we barely got to our sampling." Uncle Roy frowned.

Caleb glanced up. "Any chance we can take some of this to go?"

"Sure," KC said. "I can pack it up."

"Great," Caleb said. "I've got a call I need to get to."

"But we still have to decide on the foods at the stations." KC stacked steak frites into a to-go container.

Caleb did what came naturally. He improvised. "I like the stations you listed."

"But…" KC started.

"I trust you," Caleb said and threw out the culinary buzzwords he'd heard tossed around. "Locally sourced. Farm to table. We want that at the stations."

"How about I put together a full menu and email it to you?" KC asked.

"Yes." Caleb shoved his phone in his pocket.

"Don't forget the steak bites. We want these for our exclusive tasting party too." Grandpa Sam arched an eyebrow at Caleb. "We are having food to go with our wine, aren't we?"

"Isn't a proper party without good food," Uncle Roy chimed in.

Caleb looked at KC. "Can you fit in a dandelion wine tasting party?"

"I'll send you my available dates." KC grinned. "Don't forget I need the color for the linens."

"Right." *Color.* Caleb made a mental note, took the to-go containers from KC, and hustled his grandfather and uncle outside.

Once they were in his truck and heading to Three Springs, he realized it would be out of his way to drop off his uncle and grandfather back home.

The fire chief's instructions had been clear, yet also confusing. He evidently wanted Caleb at Wildflower Court before there was a problem between the Buckner family and the Engell family.

"Never been on an actual emergency call before," Uncle Roy said, his words upbeat. "What's the protocol when we get there?"

"The only protocol is for you two to stay in the truck," Caleb said. "And there isn't an actual emergency yet."

"There will be if we have to sit in the truck," Uncle Roy countered. "It's too hot this afternoon."

"I'll leave it running," Caleb argued.

"That's bad for the engine," Grandpa Sam said.

But it was worse for the crafty pair to get involved in a neighborly dispute. Caleb wasn't even certain what was going on with the feuding families. "I really need you to remain in the truck."

Grandpa Sam tapped on his phone screen. A satisfied grin on his face. "Breezy and Gayle are less than five minutes from Wildflower Court. Seems they're heading there on official business for the *Herald*."

"Tell 'em we're on our way," Uncle Roy ordered, suddenly cheerful again. "We'll be getting out of the truck now, Caleb. On account of needing to check on our friends."

"Fine." Caleb ground his teeth together and knew he wouldn't win this round. "You can wait with Breezy and Gayle but please try not to interfere."

"I stopped interfering in the feud between Harvey Engell and Jack Buckner years ago," Grandpa Sam declared. "More stubborn cowboys than those two, I never met."

Caleb refrained from correcting his grandfather, who happened to be the most stubborn cowboy in the entire Panhandle, aside from his brother, Roy.

"But, Caleb," Grandpa Sam said.

"Yeah?" Caleb glanced over.

Grandpa Sam looked up from his phone. "You're for sure going to be interfering."

"Why is that?" Caleb asked.

"Seems your deputy is smack in the middle of what's sure to become a skirmish between Harvey and Jack." Grandpa Sam frowned. "Don't you remember the last time those two old goats quarreled?"

Caleb shook his head.

Grandpa Sam's words were earnest. "They started a fire."

Caleb stepped on the gas.

CHAPTER TEN

A DUEL WITH water hoses.

What was the code for that? Lacey parked at the end of the cul-de-sac on Wildflower Court, climbed out of the SUV, and quickly assessed the situation.

Four large truck tires hung from an oak tree in the center of an immaculate lawn that looked like it belonged on a private golf course. Underneath the oak tree's thick branches sat a riding lawnmower also missing its wheels. And somewhere inside one of the houses, a dog barked. But it was the two older gentlemen in a standoff at the single-lane gravel drive dividing the two properties that had Lacey's attention.

One guy held a garden hose and garden shears and wore clogs with white socks that extended to mid-calf. The other gripped his own garden hose with a commercial-grade brass nozzle and adjusted his canvas tool belt stuffed with every piece of inventory from the garden section at Country Time Farm & Ranch Supply.

Lacey approached the pair, completed introductions, and asked, "What seems to be the problem?"

Mr. Engell reached down, unclipped a steering wheel from a carabiner on his tool belt, then waved it at Lacey. "He's holding my lawnmower for ransom."

"You have the lawnmower, Harvey." The morning sun highlighted the silver in Mr. Buckner's black hair and the glee in his grin. "Just not the wheels. No more mowing before the rooster crows now."

"Well, Jack, it sure seems like you have a similar dilemma," Mr. Engell retorted. His sand-colored beard was longer than the hair left on his partially bald head. He rushed on, "Now your namesake grandson can't speed around, run over my lawn, and bust my sprinkler heads."

"This is a shared driveway." Mr. Buckner aimed his nozzle toward the gravel. His words were terse. "Could be anyone in *your* house who keeps busting your precious sprinklers. Pay your family more mind than you do your precious grass, and I bet you don't have any more breaks."

Mr. Engell clenched the steering wheel. "The tread marks in the grass match Jack Jr.'s truck tires."

"Those tread marks match every truck on the street, even yours parked in your garage." Mr. Buckner started forward, his tone determined. "I'm getting those tires back right now."

"Not another step." Mr. Engell flipped his hose on and blasted Mr. Buckner's bare knees and socks. "Step on my lawn, and I'll have this nice deputy arrest you for trespassing."

"I'll have you arrested for vandalism." Mr. Buckner tossed his shears aside, adjusted his hold on his garden hose, and doused his adversary from his bald head to his army-green rubber gardening boots.

"And I'll have you both arrested for disorderly conduct," Lacey cut in. "Hoses off! Now." Lacey eyed both men and waited until the water slowed to a trickle from both nozzles. "Just so we are all clear. If I take you both in, and I will, I'll have you stay in the same cell for the entire weekend."

Mr. Engell's bald head glistened.

Mr. Buckner rolled forward in his squishy shoes but held his silence.

Satisfied that she had their full attention, Lacey said pleasantly, "And your stay might get extended into next week since Judge Rawlins is in New Mexico taking a hot-air balloon ride. And you do not want to ruin number eight on the honorable judge's bucket list. Do we all understand each other?"

Mr. Engell gave a curt nod and ran his palm over his damp head. "Jack can't prove nothing."

"The tires from my grandson's truck are dangling from your tree, Harvey." Mr. Buckner's face reddened. "In your front yard."

"I was asleep in my room all night. Ask my wife." Mr. Engell's sarcasm was hard to miss. "I woke up and found new lawn ornaments. Imagine my surprise." Mr. Engell pointed to the tree in question. "You know I'm growing fonder of the industrial art look the longer I'm out here."

Mr. Buckner proved his reflexes hadn't dulled

with age. Once again, his hose was back to full blast and soaking Mr. Engell from head to toe. But in a deft move, Mr. Engell dropped and rolled like a trained firefighter, sprang back up behind Lacey, and caught Mr. Buckner in the chest with the precision aim of his heavy-duty brass nozzle. Peels of delight filled the air, along with a cackling "gotcha!"

That was when the duel turned into an all-out water war.

Lacey lunged toward Mr. Buckner. He swung wide. Water doused her hair, splashed across her face. Mr. Buckner danced backward in his rubber clogs and wielded his hose, sweeping it in rapid arcs. He soaked everything in his path, including Lacey and Mr. Engell, all the while hurling taunts to his foe.

Lacey changed tactics and spun around, intent on Mr. Engell instead. He dodged to the right, soaked her entire front in his effort to keep Mr. Buckner in his spray line. At his adversary's shout about a low blow and his electronic hearing aids, Mr. Engell chuckled and slowed only to shimmy in celebration.

Lacey doubled down and leaped forward, reaching for the brass nozzle. Mr. Engell yelped and yanked back. Something hard knocked against her forehead. Water sprayed across her eyes. Lacey remained undaunted. Her fingers finally connected. She tightened her grip around the metal extension and wrenched the garden hose from Mr. Engell. Shoving the flow lever to the off position, she rounded on Mr. Buckner and ignored the water dripping down her face. "Turn it off! Now!"

Mr. Buckner's eyes flared, then his eyebrows zoomed up into his hairline.

"Not a word." Lacey held up her hand, palm out. Mr. Buckner opened his mouth, Lacey cut him off. "Do. Not. Talk."

"But…" Mr. Engell stepped toward her.

"Don't anyone move either." That order from a new male voice boomed across the gravel drive.

The two older gentlemen stilled instantly.

Lacey peered through the wet strands of hair stuck to her face.

Caleb.

He never bellowed. Never roared. Never lost his temper. Yet she knew from the impatience in his long, determined stride that carried him toward her and the firm set of his jaw that the command had come from him.

She noticed that witnesses had gathered—two older women were standing beside a bright green SUV with Sam and Roy Sloan. The taller of the white-haired women aimed a phone at them as if she was recording the scene. The other lady waved and kept her digital camera in front of her face.

Caleb reached Lacey and drew her full attention. He tipped her chin up and peeled her hair away, clearing the left side of her face in seconds. His touch was tender, efficient, and at complete odds with the irritation in his clenched jaw.

Lacey tried to swat his hands away. "Caleb. Stop."

"Hold on." He ignored her and tilted her head back farther. "I need to see how deep the cut is."

"Cut?" Lacey stopped fighting him. "What cut?"

"The one above your eyebrow." He blocked her arm when she reached up to touch her face. "The one bleeding down your cheek."

Lacey swiped her fingers across her damp cheek, then groaned at the blood staining her skin. "It can't be that bad. I hardly felt it."

His gaze narrowed. His mouth thinned. His words were stiff. "Just missed your eye. And you need stitches. I'd guess at least a dozen."

She heard the quick gasps of the two men behind her and frowned. "Don't exaggerate, Caleb."

"I'm not." Caleb reached into his pocket and pressed gauze against the cut. "It's deep and on the face."

"Can't you sew it up?" she asked.

"No. It's bleeding way too much." He lifted the bandage, cursed under his breath, and added more gauze. His gaze collided with hers. Frustration coated his words. "I'm too mad. And my hands are far from steady right now."

But his touch was gentle. Looking at him so closely, she could see there was no trace of the boy who would've encouraged her to laugh this off and teased her until she smiled. Examining her wound was a grown man, protective and concerned and undeniably appealing. This cowboy she wanted to know from the inside out.

"Stop," she sputtered. *Stop looking after me. Stop making me feel cared for. Protected. I do that for myself.* His gaze held hers. "Make it stop bleeding, please, so I can deal with this." *And you. I have to deal with you. Otherwise, my heart will start bargaining for more again. But those bargains never work in my favor.*

"You need to get this treated now," he insisted.

"I can do that after this situation is handled." She wanted to sound firm, decisive, despite the ache building in her temple.

"You can't drive and apply pressure to your wound." Caleb frowned and slipped more gauze underneath his palm. "You can't stop applying the pressure either."

"I'll take her," Mr. Buckner offered.

"I'll drive her," Mr. Engell said at the same time.

"I'll call the ambulance first." Caleb's expression darkened again. "Deputy Nash wouldn't need to go to the hospital if you gentlemen…"

Lacey pressed her hand flat against Caleb's chest, pulling his gaze back to her. "I got this. Let me handle it, and then I'll go to the hospital but not in an ambulance." That was the last thing she needed.

He inhaled and exhaled slowly. She felt him relax. Finally, he nodded but didn't move from her side or release his hand from her forehead.

Lacey reached for the radio clipped on her shoulder and gave Gertie a ten-thirty-three, requesting immediate assistance from Sheriff Hopson at Wildflower Court. Then she pulled Caleb's hand away and pressed her own palm to her wound.

At Gertie's acknowledgment over the two-way radio, Mr. Buckner said, "You don't need to be calling the sheriff to come out here."

"It was just a water fight." Mr. Engell's forehead wrinkled.

"I'm going to the hospital thanks to you two and just your water fight," Lacey said, displeased to her core. She'd always hated needles. "Now you get the sheriff. Congratulations, gentlemen."

"If you hadn't stepped between us, you would've been fine," Mr. Engell said.

Caleb stiffened beside her.

"Here's what's going to happen," Lacey jumped in. "It's called a truce, fellas."

Both men gaped at her.

Lacey might've laughed at their shared indignation, but the throb in her head was building with an insistence she couldn't quite quell. She spoke around the pain. "You're going to put the wheels back on the lawn mower and the truck together."

Both men started to argue.

Lacey's patience stretched thin. She pushed on, "Together, gentlemen. Or you will go to jail for the weekend. Same cell. Where you will stay until you've worked out your differences."

"I can't go to jail." Mr. Engell shifted from one rubber boot to the other. "I've got a Roots and Shoots garden club meeting tomorrow. I'm treasurer. They need me."

"My granddaughter has her first soccer game of

the season." Mr. Buckner set his hands on his hips. "I promised I'd be there."

Lacey worked her mouth into a stiff smile. "Uh-huh. So what's it going to be? Truce or jail."

"Temporary truce," Mr. Buckner stated, then extended his hand toward his adversary.

"Temporary," Mr. Engell agreed and shook his neighbor's hand.

Lacey started to correct the two men.

"Take the win, Lace," Caleb whispered. "They haven't shook on anything in years."

"He's not wrong, dear." That statement came from behind her.

Lacey turned to see that the amateur film crew stood within hearing distance. The taller of the pair tucked her phone into the zippered pocket on the bib of her ladybug-red overalls and introduced herself as Gayle Baker. "You can't end a feud that deep in one day, sweetie."

It turned out the other lady was Gayle's sister, Breezy, who nodded, then pointed to the quarrelsome neighbors. "All you can do is hope to fill it in. Cover it up layer by layer. Until one day it's no longer a tripping hazard and no one hardly gives it a second thought."

"Besides you're starting to leak again, dear." Gayle's thin brows lowered as if to hide beneath her moon-round eyeglass frames. She tapped a pale pink nail against her forehead.

Lacey scrunched her nose at the trickle she felt near the edge of her eye.

Breezy pressed a microfiber towel into Lacey's other hand. "This one's clean. Keep a package in our console for spills and such."

Lacey pressed the towel over the already soaked-through gauze and tried not to think about the stitches she needed.

"Come with us, Deputy Nash, we'll get you to the hospital right quick." Gayle slipped a thin arm around Lacey's waist.

"But I need to…" Lacey started.

"Get to the hospital," Caleb finished for her. "I can hear the sirens on the sheriff's car approaching now."

Sure enough, the sirens blared louder. Lacey watched the truck stop and her stepdad climb out. One sweep of the cul-de-sac, and his demeanor soured. "Someone needs to tell me why my deputy is bleeding."

Everyone started talking at once. The sheriff raised his hands and called for silence.

Gayle patted her zippered pocket. "I've got it all on recording, Sheriff Hopson. I'll send you the video on our way to the hospital."

Her stepdad's frown deepened.

"I just need a few stitches," Lacey offered. "I'm fine."

"You will be fine when you get a doctor to examine you," Caleb added, his words a mix of concern and exasperation.

"I have a job to do," Lacey countered.

"Deputy Nash, the Baker sisters will drive you

to the hospital," her stepdad stated, his words succinct. "Caleb will fill me in."

No sooner had her stepdad spoken than Lacey found herself bustled into the back seat of the Bakers' cheery green SUV. Breezy was behind the wheel, and Gayle buckled in beside Lacey in the back. For support, the petite woman claimed.

Lacey leaned back against the headrest and switched hands, giving her left arm a rest from applying pressure.

Breezy handed her camera to Gayle and started the car. "It's a good time to look through the pictures and see which ones are worth uploading."

"Uploading." Lacey met Breezy's clever gaze in the rearview mirror.

Breezy's eyebrows twitched upward before she slipped on a pair of teal-framed, blue-lensed sunglasses. "Gayle and I were at the scene today on official *Three Springs County Herald* business."

"Our great niece, Reyna Boland, is a reporter for the *Herald*." Breezy swiped through photographs on the digital camera. "The paper covers Three Springs, Belleridge, and Llyne and anything happening between our three towns."

"Reyna is up in Llyne today." Breezy lowered her voice to a confidential tone and turned onto the main highway. "She's investigating some cattle rustling claims up there."

"Not the first time cattle have gone missing up in those parts," Gayle mused, then grinned at Lacey. "When we called Reyna about the feud being re-

ignited, we assured her we'd get all the details."
She patted her zippered pocket. "And we certainly
did that. What with me filming and Breeze taking
pictures, we didn't miss a second."

"Now we need to get those photographs to Reyna,"
Breezy declared. "Can't keep the news waiting."

The spry pair was nothing if not efficient. Although it was not lost on Lacey that neither one
mentioned Reyna specifically requesting their assistance at the scene. Yet to be fair, the ladies hadn't
intervened and, for the most part, had done their
spectating from a safe distance. Still, Lacey should
deter them from sending anything to a news reporter. If only her head wasn't pounding.

It was as if Breezy scored extra points for every
pothole she hit. Every thump of the tires seemed to
throb double-time between Lacey's temples.

Gayle nudged her bony elbow into Lacey's ribs.
"Do you have a favorite side or angle, dear? What
with your rather stunning red hair and high cheek-
bones, it is hard to imagine you have a bad angle."

The compliment set Lacey back. She ran her
fingers through her damp hair, knowing the water
had drawn out the waviness and the humidity, the
inevitable frizz. Her hair had always been too red
to be truly auburn, yet not quite red enough for
her to be a classic redhead. Growing up, her height
had been a talking point, her indecisive hair a curiosity, and her impulsive nature a concern. But
stunning, well, that had never been attached to
her before.

"My sister is right," Breezy added. "Your hair is like a kaleidoscope of spectacular shades. It's sure to capture a cowboy's interest from the get-go."

A cowboy's interest. A cowboy like Caleb, perhaps? Lacey stopped smoothing out her hair. She'd let it frizz and watch those cowboys pass on by. After all, capturing a cowboy wasn't top of mind. Or even bottom of mind for that matter. As for Caleb, she only ever challenged him. Instead, his perfect cowgirl would do nothing less than captivate him.

"Speaking of angles," Breezy started and chuckled. "We once knew the most charming cowgirl, Darlene Berry. Everyone called her darlin' Darlene, and well, she believed all her angles were perfect."

"It wasn't true." Gayle shook her head forlornly. "But we didn't have the heart to tell the sweet woman. Darlene tried, but she always looked rather queasy in photographs." Satisfaction curved Gayle's smile up into her papery cheeks. "But you don't seem to have that problem."

"That's a relief," Breezy chimed and drove straight for another pothole. "We don't want the launch of your social life to start out poorly."

Launch of my social life. Lacey's stomach bounced. Her head pulsed.

"That means we've got to put your best face forward in the newspaper," Gayle explained.

"Although your wound could draw those caring cowboy types right to you." Breezy's words were thoughtful.

Her wound had certainly drawn out a side of Caleb that Lacey hadn't seen before. She couldn't remember the last time she'd been looked after like that. Lacey stopped her full-body sigh. She didn't need looking after or any such thing. She wiggled in her seat and pressed her own very capable shoulders into the soft leather.

Gayle's chin dipped. "Now, a compassionate cowboy is certainly worth catching."

Lacey straightened even more. "I think there's been a misunderstanding." A heart-size one.

Caleb was a well-trained EMT. Of course he was compassionate and skilled at looking after the injured. He'd done nothing more than his job with Lacey. It was so easy for her heart to read too much into it. But it was a quality that would certainly appeal to his perfect cowgirl—the one Lacey promised to find for him.

"You've a different cowboy type in mind, don't you, dear?" Breezy said, her expression understanding.

"Why don't you tell us about the cowboy partner you would like?" Gayle took Lacey's free hand. "We've got ideas, of course. But it would be good to hear from you."

Lacey jumped right to the point. "I don't want a cowboy." *Compassionate or otherwise.* Because she was home to mend the wounds she'd caused in her daughter's heart, not open her own to new ones. The only heart that really mattered was Aspen's.

"I fear it's the blood loss, Breeze." Gayle patted Lacey's hand and kept her voice low. "I think there's been more than we suspected."

Breezy gave a *hmm* sound of agreement.

"I didn't come back for a cowboy," Lacey said, adding resolve to her words, wanting these two sweetly misguided and oh-so-persistent retirees to understand. "I'm here for my daughter, Aspen."

"Right." Gayle squeezed Lacey's fingers with decided vigor. "We need to add a cowboy with an affinity for family to the deputy's ideal partner list."

The only list Lacey needed was a grocery shopping list. And perhaps Caleb's ideal cowgirl list if he even had one.

Lacey winced at Breezy's bull's-eye hit of another pothole and argued, "All of this is really unnecessary. My social life is fine as is." No jump start required.

"You should rest now," Gayle said gently. "Once we get your wound cleaned and fixed up, you'll see things much clearer."

Lacey closed her eyes and gave in. In truth, the throbbing had escalated to what felt like a viselike clamp around her head. All from one seemingly small cut. Fortunately, the conversation ceased. Not that it mattered.

Things were already perfectly clear for Lacey. Nowhere in her future did she see a cowboy. After all, falling for a cowboy would only mean giving her daughter less. And Lacey had vowed to give her daughter all she had.

If that meant keeping blinders on her heart to protect herself and Aspen, that was exactly what she would do.

CHAPTER ELEVEN

JUST HOW LONG did it take an almost nine-year-old to get settled? Lacey checked the time on the microwave clock the next morning. Aspen had arrived exactly twenty-eight minutes ago. Exactly three minutes after that, Lacey had shown her daughter to her bedroom and told her she'd let her get settled in. Now Lacey wondered what to do next.

Wait her daughter out? Another minute clicked by on the clock.

Check on her? Was that hovering too much? Ask her if she needed anything? Wanted anything? Was that too soon? It was well past breakfast time yet much too early for lunch.

Lacey paced around the small kitchen in her ranch house. Watched another minute tick by.

The debate in her head raged on.

Lacey started down the hallway, but the doorbell had her spinning around and heading for that instead. The cowboy standing on the other side of her screen door had her grinning. Seeing a familiar face grounded her. She picked up her pace. "Caleb. What are you doing here?" *Whatever the reason, I'm grateful.*

"I wanted to check on you." He smiled and held up the shopping bags he was holding. "And I brought you gifts. But if this is a bad time, I can go."

"No," Lacey blurted, then rushed on, "Please come on in." *And tell me what to do. Help me get this right.* She propped open the screen door and motioned him inside. "What is all this?"

He stopped in the foyer and faced her. "First, tell me how you are."

Scattered. Panicked. Fearful I'm gonna mess up being a mom. Take your pick. She reached up and glided her fingers lightly over the bandage above her eye. "Twelve stitches. You were right."

He hardly looked relieved by that news. He prodded, "Concussion? Headache? Tenderness?"

"No concussion. Mild headache and tenderness, yes." She lowered her arm. "And I'm sure there's going to be bruising." She smiled, hoping his frown would stop deepening. "But I was introduced to a lovely and extremely meticulous plastic surgeon. We bonded over the fact that we both don't like needles. She claims the scar will be minimal."

"You never much cared about scars." His frown finally softened. "But you always hated needles."

"And you always hated horror movies," she said.

"Still do," he admitted and adjusted the bags he held. A bright gleam took over the seriousness in his gaze. "And I still like gifts, giving and getting them. But these are for you."

There was the Caleb she wanted. The carefree, nothing-to-stress-about-here cowboy. Lacey took the purple paper shopping bag stuffed with glittery tissue that he handed to her.

"That is chocolate from Tess, my sister-in-law," he explained. "If you like it, you can find more at Silver Penny. Tess owns the general store, and her award-winning chocolate is known from the Panhandle to the Gulf."

Lacey started to peek inside the bag, but Caleb presented her with another larger shopping bag.

"Elsie, my other sister-in-law, sent chicken and dumplings with homemade biscuits and homemade honey butter," he said. "The honey is from her and Ryan's bee farm."

Her stomach rumbled, and she laughed. "Great, we know what we're having for dinner tonight."

"Maggie, my third sister-in-law, wanted you to know Aspen is cleared for the contest," Caleb continued. "Mags plans to find a way to help her that isn't a conflict of interest since she's the rodeo director." His grin shifted into mischievous.

This was what she needed. A light and easy distraction to allow her to get her parenting feet under her.

"Carter sent this from his private bourbon collection." He lifted a bottle from the last bag he clasped. "But considering you have a head injury at the moment, I'll be more than happy to hold on to it for you."

"You will not keep that." Lacey tipped her head toward the kitchen. "We can put everything on the table, including the bourbon."

Caleb swept up the bags and carried them into the kitchen.

Lacey put the casserole dish in the refrigerator, then sneaked a bite of Elsie's homemade biscuits—and discovered one bite wasn't enough. "These are delicious, and I'm afraid I won't be sharing." She took out the whole biscuit and proceeded to devour it without guilt. To Caleb's clear amusement. Savoring the last bit, she said, "This is all too much."

"It is the town's way of telling you that we look after our own," Caleb said and turned toward the door. "I'll get the rest."

"There's more?" Lacey trailed after him.

The rest included a vegetable basket with selections from Mr. Engell's backyard garden. A red velvet ice-cream cake from Mrs. Buckner and a handwritten apology. Cookie tins, homemade candies, and jars of nuts. A fruit basket from the neighbors next door to the Buckners and a note requesting that Deputy Nash please not judge the entire Wildflower Court by the stubborn ways of two cantankerous old men.

Lacey propped the note card on the table and took in the array of goodies. The house had been full of baskets and food when her mom was first diagnosed with cancer. It had seemed like the entire town had rallied around them. No questions, just support. Over a decade later, and that support was being extended to Lacey. It was more than she'd expected and made her especially determined to look after her hometown and the locals living there.

"Mom, the new shower is even better than the one at Dad's house." Aspen skipped into the kitchen, her twin braids swinging over her shoulders.

Score one for Lacey. She had to thank Wells again for his handiwork last night. Her daughter seemed comfortable. At home even. The tension in Lacey's shoulders released.

"Whoa." Aspen gaped at the kitchen table. "That's a lot of stuff. Is it for us?"

"Housewarming presents," Caleb said and introduced himself to Aspen. "You might want to hide the chocolate chip peanut butter cookies from your mom. Those are the best, and you won't want to share them."

Aspen pressed her hands over her mouth to muffle her giggle.

Genuine amusement. They were on the right track. "Hey," Lacey objected. "I'm right here."

"Fine." Caleb sighed and sorted through one of the baskets. He found a robin's-egg blue jar with the word *Sweets* on it, twisted off the top, and handed a cookie to Lacey. "You can have one." He pressed the jar into Aspen's hands. "But the rest are for Aspen. They'll be a good treat after her riding lesson."

"What riding lesson?" Aspen sobered and glanced from Caleb to Lacey.

Time to take a side: her daughter's or ex-husband's. Lacey lowered her cookie to a napkin on the table.

"Can't win a spot on the Junior Royal Rodeo Court if you can't complete the pattern in the arena properly," Caleb quipped.

"But I'm not competing." Aspen folded her arms around the cookie jar. Her bottom lip jutted out. "Dad said no."

"I don't recall giving my answer. I'm your parent too." Lacey brushed her hands together, wiping off the cookie crumbs and smiled at her daughter. She'd chosen her side the minute she began the paperwork to retire from the army. "And as it turns out, I'm here, and your dad is not."

Aspen's eyes widened. Hope filled her face. "Can I enter the Junior Royal Rodeo Contest?"

"Well, you can't enter twice." Lacey chuckled and stood up. "I submitted your application yesterday, which was accepted by the way."

Aspen's smile was pure joy. She lunged at Lacey and hugged her tight, despite not letting go of the cookie jar. "Thanks, Mom."

Lacey took in the moment, embraced her daughter, and told herself whatever the fallout, it would be worth it. Her gaze connected with Caleb's over her daughter's head. His expression was tender, affectionate, and unguarded. She could've hugged him. Instead, she mouthed a silent *thank you*.

He tipped his chin in acknowledgment, then seemed to distance himself.

Most likely her imagination. She was the one feeling emotional after all. Lacey concentrated on her daughter. "You're in the contest." She released Aspen and held her shoulders. "That means you need to work hard to get prepared, and Caleb is going to help us with that."

"I'll do whatever he tells me," Aspen promised and looked at Caleb. "I'm a real good listener. That's what Mama-Beth tells me. She also says I catch on real quick." She tossed one braid over her shoulder. "What do we do first?"

"That's for Caleb to tell us." Lacey broke her cookie in half and handed a section to Caleb.

He took a bite of the cookie and said, "First, you need a horse."

Aspen's face scrunched together. "I don't have one."

"Lucky for you, I know where to find one." Caleb pulled his car keys from his pocket. "Ready to go meet your new teammate?"

Aspen glanced at her mom.

Caleb smiled. "Don't worry. Your mom will be right there with us." His tone relayed understanding and patience. "Although, she will be watching from the sidelines and not riding with us today because of her head wound."

Lacey finished her cookie and pointed at her temple. "It's a small cut."

"Head wound," Caleb countered and started for the front door. Aspen chased after him as if afraid he might leave without her. His words were gratingly pleasant. "And it hasn't even been twenty-four hours since you suffered your injury, Lace. You need to take it easy."

"Caleb Sloan, you are not my doctor." Lacey grabbed her purse from the kitchen chair and two jars of snack mix from the Baker sisters' basket and rushed after the pair. "I will decide if I ride or not. Not you."

"Your mom doesn't like it when people tell her what to do," Caleb said to Aspen on the porch, his words secret-sharing low. "But I do it anyway. When she's riled, her cheeks turn a shade almost as pretty as her hair."

Caleb thought her hair was pretty. *He thinks I'm pretty.* Lacey fumbled with the key in the front door. It seemed cowboy compliments rattled her.

"Come on, Lace," Caleb called out. "We want to see what color your cheeks are."

Her daughter giggled.

Lacey's cheeks warmed, but she refused to call it a blush. Her cowboy might get her riled up. But he would not be the cause of her blush. After all, it was those blinders on her heart that made her resistant to cowboy compliments. Lacey inhaled and turned toward the pair.

Caleb's one-sided grin came slow, same as the spark of appreciation in his blue eyes. "Told you she was pretty."

The heat beneath Lacey's skin flared. She battened down her heart, sweeping aside her sigh.

Aspen nodded, her grin enthusiastic. "She sure is."

Caleb's grin stretched farther into his cheeks, compelling and captivating.

Again, she was tempted to get to know this cowboy. But his side wasn't the one she wanted to be on. And it wasn't her heart's turn this time around. It was about her daughter.

Lacey tipped her chin up and strode past the pair. "Stop trying to distract me, Caleb. I know my own mind, and you won't be telling me what to do."

"We will see about that," Caleb muttered behind her. "Especially if Aspen and I just want to keep you safe."

Lacey turned to see her daughter tucked up against Caleb. If he lifted his arm, Aspen would be sealed against his side. They'd bonded already. How easy he made it look. Lacey wanted to know Caleb's secret. She took in their earnest expressions and said, "Well, I appreciate you both wanting to look after me."

Pleasure washed over Aspen's face.

"You're welcome." Caleb stepped around Lacey and opened the passenger door for her. When she climbed into the front seat, he leaned in and whispered, "And I wasn't distracting you. I was serious. You've always been pretty to me, riled or not. That's just a fact."

Lacey's throat went dry. Her pulse picked up. And all because her cowboy just got to her and she had no idea what to do about it.

Caleb turned to open the door for Aspen and waited until they were both settled, then made his way to the driver's side. The truck started, and he pulled out of the long driveway.

Aspen buckled her seat belt and said, "I've been learning all about horses, Caleb. Mom sent me a book for Christmas. Remember that, Mom?"

"I do." Lacey shifted in the leather seat, avoided

looking at her cowboy, and smiled at her daughter, loving her excitement.

"Dad said I should be reading what he calls the classics instead of horse books," Aspen announced.

Lacey heard the frown in Aspen's voice and found herself frowning too. Perhaps she shouldn't have told Jeffrey all about her horse adventures growing up. Perhaps his dislike for the equestrian world was her fault somehow. Lacey had just wanted her ex to understand her passion. She'd wanted to share something about herself that had meant so much to her. If she had shared her joy for singing, things might have been different. Yet her self-assured ex would have most likely considered her stage fright an unfortunate weakness. Looking back, Jeffrey and she hadn't shared much in common, aside from a chemistry that had fizzled out too soon.

Lacey's gaze slanted toward Caleb. That hit of awareness sparked instantly. True, her cowboy captivated her. But she couldn't afford to bargain her heart away only to have it broken. She needed it whole for her daughter. "Aspen, I think you should read what makes you happy."

"That's what Mama-Beth says too. Horses make me happy." Aspen popped her head between the front seats. "What makes you happy, Caleb?"

Being with her daughter made Lacey happy. Her gaze returned to Caleb. *And you. You make me happy, cowboy.* And that was trouble. Good thing it would all be resolved with that perfect cowgirl match Lacey had promised him. His cowboy com-

pliments and blue-eyed charm would be for someone else. Just as Lacey wanted. No, she told herself,
that certainly wasn't a pinch of envy or even un-
happiness inside her. How could it be? Lacey had
given up trouble a long time ago.

"A lot of things make me happy." Caleb pulled up
to a stop sign. He tipped his head, skimmed those
daringly perceptive blue eyes over her face.

Lacey searched his gaze. Felt that awareness
flare through her again. Still, she held his stare for
a beat. Then another. *You feel it too, don't you? Stop
it. Shut me out.* She blinked. Retreated. *I can't...*

Finally, he slipped on a pair of tinted sunglasses,
blocking her out just as she wanted.

Lacey exhaled and faced forward in her seat. "I
can answer what makes Caleb happy."

"Is that so?" he asked, his words a challenge filled
with curiosity and amusement. And suggested affection between more than friends.

That way led to trouble. *Turn around. He's not
your happy.* Lacey blurted, "Super spicy food makes
Caleb happy." His eyebrows lifted, and Lacey rushed
on, "You were always daring me to eat peppers and
hot sauce and ordering everything extra spicy."

"I still prefer that extra spice on my food," he admitted.

Aspen wrinkled her nose. "Hot spices don't make
my stomach happy."

"I also like lima beans and spray cheese from a
can." Caleb grinned. "Those aren't spicy. Your stomach should like them, Aspen."

"But, Caleb, that's gross." Aspen giggled.

"Well, you don't eat them together." Caleb's laughter joined Aspen's and filled the truck cab.

Lacey added one more thing to her happy list: the sound of her daughter's joy. That was it. She would make her happy list so crowded that there would not be enough room for her cowboy on it.

"Aspen, there are two boxes next to you." Caleb turned onto the bypass. "One is for you. One's for your mom."

Lacey pressed her lips together, tried not to shout *no more gifts. You're not mine. I'm not yours.* Clearly, she had to find that cowgirl for him and fast.

"We got more gifts." Wonder spread through Aspen's features. She handed the box with Lacey's name on it to her, then asked, "Can we open them now?"

"Sure can." Caleb chuckled.

Lacey spread her fingers over the box resting in her lap and willed her pulse to slow.

There was a rustling sound from the back seat, followed by, "It's a real cowboy hat." Aspen sounded awestruck. "I never had one before. Thanks, Caleb."

"I already checked, and it's approved attire for the contest," Caleb explained and touched his own cowboy hat. "Figured you can't be a cowgirl without the hat."

"Awesome." Aspen stretched the word out with even more amazement. "I love it. Do you love yours, Mom?"

Lacey lifted the lid of the box and ran her fingertips over the classic felt cowboy hat inside. It was the color of desert sand with a simple silver buckle on the matching felt hatband. Simple. Understated. And exactly what she would've picked for herself. As if her cowboy already knew her so well. "I do like it a lot." *And you, cowboy. I like you too. But I can't let myself. You have to understand.* "Thank you, Caleb."

"Wait." Aspen shifted and leaned forward again to peer into Lacey's hat box. Aspen said, "Mom, our hats match."

Lacey glanced over the seat to take in her daughter. Her cowboy hat was propped expertly on her head as if she'd always been wearing one. Lacey asked, "Is that okay?"

"Yeah." Aspen adjusted her hat and grinned. "I think it's cool."

Now she was cool. Score another one for Lacey. All thanks to Caleb. She owed him. Lacey lifted her hat out of the box and set it on her head.

Caleb glanced over and said softly, "There's the cowgirl I remember. I knew she was still in there."

Cowgirl. No, she wasn't that. Hadn't been one in longer than she could remember. Couldn't be one now. Because then her heart just might get confused and make a bargain to become *his* cowgirl.

CHAPTER TWELVE

ARRIVING AT THE Sloan stables, Lacey remembered to take her cowboy hat off. She was returning it carefully to the box when Aspen caught her. "Mom, you gotta wear your hat too. Today, we're cowgirls."

"Right." Lacey propped the hat back on her head and climbed out of the truck. "Do we look like cowgirls?"

Aspen's mouth pinched toward the side. Her head shook. "We're gonna need real cowboy boots like Caleb's." She pointed at Caleb's weathered square-toed cowboy boots.

Lacey nodded and wiggled her toes in her old but reliable running shoes, concentrating on her daughter rather than the cowboy standing too close. "Anything else?"

"Jeans too," Aspen said decisively. "Like Caleb's."

Lacey patted the pockets of her olive green cargo pants, then tugged on her ivory tank top. "Let me guess, we need shirts like Caleb's too?" Making Lacey the cowgirl to his cowboy.

Aspen nodded solemnly, then brightened. "But purple plaid. That's my favorite color."

"Looks like we've got some shopping to do." Lacey held her hand out to Aspen. "How about today we just keep our hats on, be ourselves, and act like cowgirls?"

Aspen slipped her hand into Lacey's. "How do cowgirls act?"

"The cowgirls I know are brave, hardworking, and look after their families." Caleb walked with them toward the stables.

"Like we're looking after Mom by not letting her ride today, right, Caleb?" Aspen asked.

Caleb opened the door to the stable and grinned. "Now you're thinking like a cowgirl."

"Now I just need to be brave and work hard just like Mom." Aspen squeezed Lacey's hand, then released her and walked inside the stable barn.

Lacey's chest tightened. She hadn't known what her daughter thought about her until now. Aspen's words strengthened her in the best possible way. Sharpened her focus back onto her daughter where it belonged.

A cowboy with a pure white beard, white hair, and a sparkle in his gaze waited in the center aisle of the stable barn.

Caleb stopped inside the door, set his hands on his hips, and said, "Grandpa, what are you doing?"

"Lacey Nash." Sam Sloan ignored his grandson and opened his arms wide to Lacey. Sam was older but still the considerate, gentlemanly cowboy she'd known as a kid. Sam added, "Breezy and Gayle whisked you away yesterday before I could give you a proper welcome home. Hope your head's not paining you too much today."

"Hurts less now." Lacey smiled and stepped into Sam's embrace, then gently squeezed the older cowboy she'd always adored. "It's good to see you, Sam."

"Your mom sure would be proud of you. A decorated career in the army. Now a deputy sheriff." Approval was there in his words, fondness in his soft smile. "I sure know how proud Wells is of you. And I'm proud of you too."

"That's kind," Lacey said. And so very appreciated. His words settled deep inside her, filled her like her daughter's had. "It's good to be home."

Sam gave Lacey another quick hug, then released her and turned to Aspen. "And this must be Aspen, our Junior Royal Rodeo cowgirl."

Aspen beamed.

Sam extended his arm toward Aspen. "Pleasure to meet you."

Aspen slipped around his arm and hugged him instead. "Mom said I can be myself. And I usually get to hug Santa. And you look an awful lot like Santa except skinnier."

"Well, I'll take that as a compliment." Sam laughed, embraced Aspen cheerfully, then frowned at Caleb. "Did you see that, Caleb? That's a proper greeting for an old cowboy like me."

Lacey swallowed her laughter.

Caleb grinned wide and opened his arms. "Hello, Santa Sam."

Aspen giggled.

Caleb hugged his grandfather and hung on for an extra-long moment. His grandfather stepped back, and Caleb's grin stretched even farther.

"We don't have time for your foolery, Caleb Sloan," Sam admonished and set his hand on Aspen's shoulder. "We've got to get our young cowgirl ready."

Caleb nodded, his words dry. "I was trying to greet you properly like you requested."

"I already got the best hugs of the day from these two cowgirls," Sam retorted. "Now, I've saddled a horse for you, Caleb, in case you want to ride too. And I set everything out for Aspen. She'll need to do that herself in the contest. It's best to practice now."

Caleb scratched his cheek. "Let me guess, you read the rules, didn't you?"

"This morning in fact." Sam wrapped his fingers around his large belt buckle and smiled. "Can't help her win if we don't know what it takes. Of course, you could've told me yesterday about helping Aspen, so I had more time to prepare." Sam frowned. "Instead, I had to hear it from Maggie at breakfast, which you skipped."

Lacey peered at Caleb to see how he was taking Sam's scolding.

"I had gifts to deliver, but I'm glad you missed me, Grandpa." Caleb chuckled.

"We made some decisions this morning I reckon you'll be wanting to know about," Sam said. He spoke with a casual attitude, but his gaze was shrewd.

"What were those?" There was a reserve to Caleb's words and expression.

"Glad you asked." Sam's grin disappeared inside his thick beard. "We've booked our private dandelion wine tasting event. It's on the calendar for next weekend."

"That sounds fun." Lacey smiled.

Caleb frowned. "And soon."

"Your uncle and I told you we weren't waiting," Sam warned. Then he adjusted the silver clasp on his bolo tie, cleared his throat, and said, "Lacey, I'll make sure you receive a formal invite, of course." His lips twitched, and his eyebrows waggled, returning him to his good-natured ways. "Caleb is organizing our private affair. It'll be an evening you won't want to miss. I can promise you that, right, Caleb?"

Caleb looked like he wanted to miss it. He scrubbed a hand over his face. "Grandpa, we can talk about this later."

"The date is set," Sam insisted. "There's no bowling league or garden club that night. Everyone has already marked their calendars for the tasting. That means it's officially booked." Sam preened at Lacey. "Around here, we prefer full calendars. Being social keeps us young."

"Or it keeps them merrily mixed up in everyone's business," Caleb whispered to Lacey.

Lacey tried not to laugh, but it was hard work.

"What about me?" Aspen thrust both her arms out.

"Don't you worry, we'll do something just as fun." Sam smoothed his fingers through his beard, his words reassuring. "What if we set a date for ice cream?"

"Can we have root beer floats?" Hope seemed to rise behind Aspen's eyes. "I like those so much."

"Now you sound like your mom. If she wasn't riding, I'd catch her down at Frosty Dreamer's Parlor, sipping on a root beer float." Sam chuckled, then turned to Caleb, his words firm. "Mark your calendar, Caleb. We need to take Aspen for root beers floats and soon."

"I'll get right on that." Caleb rubbed his hands together. "But right now, we need to get back to the horses."

"Sam, I see the stunning Arabian I rode the other day at the lake." Lacey pointed toward the far end of the barn. The sleek Arabian had his head extended over the stall as if he wanted to be included.

"You won't be riding Denny today." Sam shook his head and crossed his arms over his chest. "What with your head all banged up like that."

Not Sam too. Lacey adjusted the brim of her hat to hide the bandage. "It's just a slow ride around the arena with Aspen."

"Sure it is," Caleb mumbled, then coughed, covering the rest of his words.

Lacey began to confront Caleb and defend herself, but Sam stopped her.

"Don't think I'm gonna fall for that one, my dear."

Sam tapped his forehead and rattled on, "Age has only made me wiser. I haven't forgotten what you used to tell me way back when." Sam's eyebrows hitched up underneath his cowboy hat. "You'd look me right in the eye and say: *we're just going to take it easy today, Mr. Sloan. Enjoy the grounds with the horses.*"

Lacey tried not to wince. Those had been her exact words to Sam every time she and Caleb had been caught leading horses from the Sloan stables. Lacey glanced at Caleb.

He smoothed his hand over his mouth, but his smile remained. He shrugged. "He's not wrong. We used to say that all the time."

Aspen flicked her attention from one to the other as if not wanting to miss a word.

"Now don't go denying it. It's much too late for that." Sam swished his finger between Lacey and Caleb. "In truth, it was too late when you two were kids. Don't think we didn't know what you were up to."

Lacey clasped her hands behind her back as if she'd been caught sneaking in after curfew.

"We?" Caleb pressed.

His grandfather chuckled. "We as in me and your gran Claire. Lacey's darling mama." Sam ticked the names off on his fingers. "Wells too."

Sam made it sound like Lacey and Caleb were up to more than riding. Back then they'd been friends only. But now. Now, she wanted…

One side of Caleb's mouth lifted. That private

grin hooked her, hinted at shared secrets and heated her cheeks. Lacey slapped her palms over her face and willed her sudden blush to subside.

"What did they do?" Aspen asked.

"Jumping," Sam replied. "The kind on horseback."

"No way." Aspen rounded on Lacey. "You actually did jumps and stuff?"

"Oh, yeah. Couldn't hardly get your mom out of the saddle once your grandpa Wells plopped her in it," Sam explained all too cheerfully. "She was jumping everything from hay bales to fences to streams on her horse."

"Whoa." Aspen looked Lacey up and down like she was trying to imagine it but couldn't.

"Your mom was a highflier." Sam raised his arm. "Graceful like an angel as she and her horse soared over whatever was in her path. A real natural."

"I wouldn't go that far," Lacey said, although Sam's praise wasn't entirely unwelcome. Her two passions had been singing and horseback riding. Her horses had been her most loyal listeners.

"You were that good, Lacey," Sam countered. "Otherwise, I wouldn't have let you go and ride on our property. Especially after your gentle-hearted mama would call and blister my ears something good." Sam touched his ear. "My ears are still ringing from her phone calls."

Aspen giggled softly, her shoulders shaking.

Her mom had known what Lacey had been up to? Here Lacey had thought they'd been so clever all those times. She looked at Caleb. He seemed as surprised by Sam's admission as Lacey.

"It's true," Sam insisted and eyed Aspen. "Your late grandma was a force to be reckoned with. She'd call and tell me: *Sam Sloan, those kids are at it again. You'd best make sure my girl gets nothing more than a scratch. You hear me?*"

Aspen pressed her hands against her mouth. "What did you do?"

"Listened, of course," Sam said, wisdom crinkling the skin around his clever eyes. "You don't interrupt moms when they are giving you a piece of their mind. Remember that."

Aspen nodded. "Yes, sir."

"No sooner had Dana blistered my ears than my own sweet Claire would come out to tell me those two were are it again. And I'd best watch over 'em," Sam lamented, then pointed his finger at Caleb and Lacey again. "If one was jumping, the other was jumping higher."

Aspen spun toward them. Hands on her hips, eyebrows arched. Accusation was written all over her face. "You *both* jumped."

Caleb rubbed the back of his neck.

Lacey started to deflect, then glanced at Sam. "Sam helped us. More than once too."

"That he did." Caleb chuckled and edged closer to Lacey as if to make a united front. "Grandpa stacked more than a few hay bales for us to jump."

"I had to look after you somehow, didn't I?" Sam

turned but not fast enough to hide the twinkle in his eyes. For all his bluff, he'd enjoyed himself.

"When do I get to jump?" Aspen hopped up and down and clasped her hands together. "Who's going to teach me? Mom. Caleb. Santa Sam."

The stables quieted as if even the horses were anxious to find out.

"Best to leave these sorts of decisions to the grown-ups." Sam cleared his throat. "Think I'll just head on over to the arena and get it opened up for you all." With that, he scooted silently and rather spryly out a side door.

Lacey's first instinct was to put her foot down and declare no jumping. Not ever. She'd lose a point for sure with that decision. But Aspen was a child. *My child.* Jumping was dangerous. The idea of Aspen getting injured was like a full-blown nightmare. Lacey managed a calm, "We can talk about jumping when you get older."

"Now you sound like Dad." Aspen crossed her arms over her chest.

Lacey understood Jeffrey's point of view a bit better. Kids didn't always have to get what they wanted. It was just that looking at her defeated daughter made all the guilt for the years Lacey had missed well up inside her. Disappointing Aspen was the last thing Lacey wanted. Talk about a parenting rock and a hard place. She touched her forehead.

Caleb moved to her side, set his hand on Lacey's lower back. His words and touch were gentle. "My gran Claire was a real deal cowgirl, and she loved her horses more than anything."

Lacey managed not to lean into Caleb, yet she stayed still and right beside him, grateful for his steady touch and quick assist.

Aspen's frown softened. "I bet your gran did lots and lots of jumping."

"She sure did," Caleb said, a smile in his words. "But she also did lots and lots of learning first."

"I already learned lots of stuff in my horse books," Aspen said, her frown returning. "Every night in my bed I read and read."

"But I'm talking about a different type of learning," Caleb continued, unruffled. "This is learning about your horse. What she likes to eat. Her favorite treats. If she likes a blanket at night or not. Where she likes to ride. What scares her."

That was the type of learning Lacey wanted to do with her cowboy. Or would want to do if she wasn't finding Caleb his one true cowgirl. Lacey eased away from his side.

"Spiders scare me." Aspen slipped her hand into Caleb's and walked with him past the stalls. "And mean snakes. Are your horses afraid of snakes?"

"That depends on the horse." Caleb slowed by a stall and stroked his hand between the ears of a brown quarter horse. "Denny over there is too curious for his own good. While Winston here is too lazy to be bothered by much of anything. And the farm cats sleep with Catnip down in the first stall, so she hasn't had to worry about critters of any variety bothering her."

"Catnip is lucky. I want to sleep with a cat," Aspen admitted and reached up to touch Winston's face. "Or a dog. Then I wouldn't ever get scared at night. Do you get scared, Caleb?"

"Sometimes," he confessed. "But I think you're right. I should get a pet too."

Lacey was scared she was already learning so much about her cowboy the longer she watched him with her daughter. She was even more scared that when he moved on with his cowgirl match, not even a pet of her own would be enough to fill the loneliness. But that was impossible. This was Caleb. And she was Lacey. And they were not... They were just *not*.

Aspen grinned and swung their joined hands between them. "When I learn about my horse, can I jump then?"

"So you start with having to learn all about your horse," Caleb explained. "Then you become friends. After that, partners. And that's when you trust each other."

"And then we jump," Aspen announced.

No. Lacey shook her head. There would be no jumping on horses for Aspen. And certainly no other kind for Lacey that included leaping from friends to something more.

"Gran Claire always told me you can't move straight to jumping. That's just poor planning. And nothing good ever comes from that," Caleb said.

"And I'm going to add, you can't jump without trust."

Right. Lacey couldn't trust. Not her cowboy. Not herself. She'd keep her feet planted right where she was, and friends was how they would stay.

Caleb stopped at the stall with a striking tan-and-white Paint inside. "Ready to meet your teammate and get to know her?" He handed an apple to Aspen. "Her name is Biscuit. She's calm, friendly, and one of my favorite horses."

Aspen gripped the apple and leaned toward Caleb. Her whisper was heavy with worry. "What if Biscuit doesn't like me?"

Caleb lowered to a knee in front of Aspen. "Biscuit will like you because you have what my gran Claire would call heart."

"How do I know if I have heart?" Aspen's gaze never left Caleb's.

"You're here, aren't you?" Caleb countered. "Can't get where you want to be without taking that first step, right?"

But if Lacey didn't let her heart take any step, then she would stay where she wanted to be. Here, with her heart intact and all for her daughter.

Aspen pursed her lips, then finally nodded.

"Come on." Caleb opened the door to Biscuit's stall and led Aspen inside. "Biscuit is waiting."

The pair moved from treats to grooming to finally braiding Biscuit's mane together. The conversation never paused, switching from horse breed facts to horse care to horse tack and its specific uses as they saddled the patient mare. Aspen listened, followed directions, and kept up her own steady stream of praise for Biscuit.

All the while, Lacey watched the pair and feared her own heart was showing. Yet she couldn't move away and wanted to be closer. To join in. Fortunately, the closed stall door reminded her to keep to her side.

Finally, Aspen ran her hand down the length of Biscuit's neck, complimented the mare's light blue eyes, and declared, "Biscuit likes her mane braided. Now we match." Aspen leaned in, whispered to the mare, then grinned at Caleb. "We're ready to ride now."

Caleb put the brushes away and led Biscuit out of the stall. Outside, he handed the reins to Aspen and let her guide Biscuit into the covered arena. Caleb, Aspen, and Biscuit moved into the soft, sandy arena.

Lacey paced in front of the metal gates, trying to walk off her sudden apprehension. She caught sight of Sam strolling toward her and joined him at the curve of the arena. "I'm a little more anxious than I thought I would be. She's ridden before but not much. I just want her to…" *Love it as much I did. Not fall. Have fun. Not get hurt. Enjoy herself. Not get defeated. Get back up.*

Sam set his hand on Lacey's arm, drawing her gaze to him. "Worry is what comes with loving someone the way you love your daughter. There's no getting around it."

Lacey considered Sam. "What do you do about it?"

"You make sure when it can't be you watching over her that the right people are doing it for you." Sam tipped his chin, and Lacey followed his gaze toward the center of the arena. Caleb was now seated behind Aspen on the mare.

Their heads were bent together as Caleb talked to her daughter and guided Aspen's hands around the reins. Lacey's shoulders loosened. "Wells taught me to ride the same way."

"Your mom knew Wells was one of the good ones." Sam propped his arms on the metal gate. "My Claire would've called Wells a cowboy worth keeping."

Wells was certainly that. Her stepdad had always looked out for Lacey and her mom.

Lacey watched Caleb and Aspen circle the arena. Aspen waved as they passed, pure delight on her face. Joy was in her gaze. Lacey had felt all that when she'd first learned to ride all those years ago. And those feelings had only grown the more time she spent with her horses.

Her gaze landed on her cowboy and stuck. She needed to find his cowgirl match soon, before she decided he might be her cowboy worth keeping.

CHAPTER THIRTEEN

CONGRATULATIONS WERE DEFINITELY in order.

It was after lunch, and Caleb was driving Lacey and Aspen home. That Aspen's practice had gone better than he'd imagined wasn't his cause for celebration.

Rather it was the fact that he could finally look at the bandage on Lacey's forehead and not get irritated all over again. Finally, he was not thinking about what could've happened if the nozzle had struck an inch lower or an inch to the right. True, her cowboy hat covered part of the bandage, and she was staring straight ahead, but Caleb meant to take small successes where he could.

"Can we stop at Cider Mill Orchard?" Lacey asked. "Breezy and Gayle told me about the farmers market there. And I wanted to pick up some fruit and vegetables. Breezy said the owner has a selection of homemade baked goods featuring her fruit that are not to be missed."

Caleb glanced at Lacey and got distracted by that bandage again.

"I promise I'll be fast," Lacey said, misreading his frown.

"Have you ever been to Cider Mill Orchard?" Caleb switched on his blinker and pulled into the left turn lane.

"No," Lacey said.

"Well, I can promise you it won't be a quick stop," Caleb said.

"Wanna bet?" She leaned on the console, her grin teasing.

"I'm not going to accept." Because a new wager would mean higher stakes. And for things that changed friendships. Things he should not be considering. Caleb concentrated on the road. "You're going to thank me later." Meanwhile, he would be grateful he'd stayed inside those long-standing friendship boundaries.

Lacey laughed. "We shall see about that."

And he would see that he friend-zoned Lacey. Caleb pulled into the parking lot and glanced into the rearview mirror. "Ready to get lost sampling apple cotton candy and apple cider in the biggest farmers market you've ever been to?"

"Yes!" Aspen cheered and climbed out of the truck.

Caleb guided the pair through the entrance to the outdoor market.

Aspen came to a halt. "Whoa. This place is huge."

Lacey nodded.

Caleb leaned in and whispered, "You can thank me now."

Lacey shook her head, but her shoulders quivered. Her amusement was obvious. "We never really defined quick, did we?"

"Nice try." Caleb lifted his hand and waved to a woman carrying a bushel of apples. "Come on and meet Whitney Carson. She owns the place. And then you can shop."

"I can come back another time if you're in a hurry," Lacey said.

He wasn't in a hurry to leave her. That thought should have him running back to his truck. Caleb was never one for lingering. But that was exactly what he did. "Take your time. Aspen and I have sample tables to find." He grinned at Aspen. "It's like a treasure hunt."

"Uncle Caleb," a familiar voice shouted. "Uncle Caleb!"

Caleb turned and caught the two young girls careening into his arms. Autumn and Gemma Parks were energetic and animated and his sister-in-law Elsie's nieces. Caleb wasn't quite sure how the family tree worked regarding Elsie's nieces. Elsie and Ryan had officially married in a small private ceremony in June. And Caleb had suddenly earned the uncle title. He'd been too thrilled and honored to make a correction or worry about the bloodline details.

He lifted them both and spun around in several circles to their collective delight. Then he asked the adorable pair, "Who are you here with?"

"Auntie Elsie and Uncle Ryan are picking out onions." Gemma Parks pointed to the vegetable sign, then grabbed his hand and twirled around underneath his arm.

Autumn said, "Dad needed to work today and

Uncle Ryan said we could help with exercising Midnight Rose and Sundancer when we get back."

"Can you come over and ride horses with us too, Uncle Caleb?" Gemma asked. "We get to go visit the dandelion fields."

"I can't think of anything better that I have planned. I'm sure I can find a horse in our stables who would enjoy some exercise." Caleb accepted their excited hugs and introduced the lively pair to Lacey and Aspen.

"Can we show Aspen the apple sweets section, Uncle Caleb?" Autumn asked.

"With the candy apples and fudge and apple ice cream." Gemma sang the words and wiggled her hips.

"Can I go with them, Mom?" Aspen asked.

Elsie and Ryan joined them. The girls barely lasted through another round of introductions; their collective excitement was ready to burst free.

"I'll take these three to the candy cottage." Ryan kissed Elsie and added, "And you can shop at your leisure."

"I'm going to show Lacey the scented soap and candles Whitney just started selling." Elsie linked her arm around Lacey's. "We'll catch up with you guys later."

Caleb shook his head at his sister-in-law. "It's not what you think, Elsie."

"You have no idea what I think, Caleb Sloan," Elsie countered. "And if you're worried about what I might ask Lacey, then it is exactly what I think."

Caleb frowned.

"Come on, little brother." Ryan's hand landed on Caleb's shoulder. "My wife is not going to let up until she talks to Lacey alone."

"But it's not what she thinks," Caleb called out, ensuring his words reached Elsie and Lacey.

Elsie laughed and tugged Lacey down an aisle of potted plants until they were out of sight.

"So what is it?" Ryan bumped his elbow into Caleb's side, then clarified, "Between you and Lacey."

"Why does it have to be something?" Caleb nudged his brother away.

"It doesn't," Ryan said. "It just feels like there's something. You know?"

No. He didn't know. Or rather didn't want to know. That would only blur things between him and Lacey. And he wanted to be clear where they stood for his heart's sake and hers. "Look, I'm really happy for you and Elsie and what you've found together." Caleb nodded vigorously at his older brother. "Love looks good on you."

Ryan pressed his hands over his chest and gave an exaggerated sigh. "That's the sweetest compliment you've ever given me."

Caleb chuckled. "Just because you like love and wear it well that doesn't mean everyone around you wants to try it on too."

"You've never tried on love, little brother." Ryan lifted his arm and flashed his wedding ring at Caleb. "How do you know it won't fit you?"

Because that meant opening his heart fully. Without restraint. Without restrictions. That was opening himself to things that hurt. And nothing about that fit him well. "Trust me, I know."

"That's the thing about love," Ryan said, his words wise, his expression sincere. "It's like those new trend-setting boots in the store window. The ones that look impractical and stiff and entirely unsuitable. But then one day those same boots show up in your favorite color, and you finally try them on. And you discover they're a perfect fit, and you never want to take them off."

"Do you hear yourself? You're talking about love and boots as if they are the same." Talking to his love-sunk brother was testing his patience. Caleb picked up his pace to catch up with the kids. "I already have enough pairs of boots that fit perfectly fine. So how about we agree to disagree on this thing you call love?"

"Only if you agree to admit I'm right," Ryan said. "When the time comes, of course."

Caleb crossed his arms over his chest. "You're serious?"

"I like to be right," Ryan said, with too much satisfaction. "I like it even more when my brothers publicly admit I was right and they were wrong."

"Fine," Caleb said. "Now can we talk about the dandelion wine tasting party?"

"You mean event," Ryan corrected. "Grandpa Sam and Uncle Roy were very specific about the name this morning. It's not a private wine tasting party.

It's an *event*. Apparently, that sounds more exclusive. And exclusivity builds buzz."

Caleb's head was starting to buzz. He yanked off his cowboy hat as if that was the cause of his tension and ran his hand through his hair. "Why did you and Elsie agree to let them use the greenhouses for their *event*?"

"Why did you agree to put together the *event* in the first place?" Ryan countered and set his hands on his hips.

"To keep them from interfering with the wedding reception," Caleb admitted. "And I didn't want to disappoint them."

"We didn't either." Ryan nodded and sighed in solidarity. "I'll get the wine bottles moved from the barn to the greenhouse."

"I'll take care of the rest," Caleb said. "Shouldn't be that complicated."

"Don't look at me for more help." Ryan lifted his hands. "I'd tell you to plead with Elsie to lend a hand, but I'm taking her to Arkansas this coming week to pick up two more retired bucking broncs. We're making an extended road trip out of it and leaving tomorrow."

"You're not going to be here?" Caleb asked.

"We'll be back in time for the tasting event," Ryan said, sounding far from reassuring. "But I'm sure you're right—it can't be all that complicated to organize. Send out invites. Get some good food, and you're done."

"Except Grandpa and Uncle Roy expect an exclusive event." Caleb smashed his hat back on his head, wondering when it'd gotten so complicated.

"Yeah, I don't even know what that means." Ryan chuckled and tapped his fist lightly on Caleb's shoulder. "Good luck with that one, little brother."

The girls raced up, grabbed their hands, and started pulling them across the farmers market.

Caleb laughed and asked, "What's the rush?"

"Dogs." The reply came simultaneously from the spirited trio.

Elsie and Lacey suddenly appeared in the aisle. Elsie lifted her arm, blocked their path like a crossing guard at the elementary school, and said, "We are leaving now. Ryan cannot go see any dog."

There were grumbles of discontent from the trio.

Elsie continued, "Ryan cannot get attached to another dog. Smarty Marty and Butter-Belle won't like it."

"Are those your dogs?" Lacey asked.

"Those are the goats," Gemma announced.

Elsie chuckled. "Goats who think they are dogs. If they aren't following me around the farm, they are attached to Ryan. Of course, he gives them treats and picks them up as if they are baby kittens."

"So you're a rancher too?" Lacey asked.

"I'm a transplanted event planner," Elsie said. "Learning my way around a farm with a few more mishaps than grace."

"Don't let her fool you." Ryan swept Elsie into his arms. "My wife is amazing and can do anything she sets her mind to."

Elsie wrapped her arms around his neck and kissed him. "And my husband is one of the good ones."

Gemma groaned and lamented, "They are always doing this."

Autumn nudged herself between them. "You both promised, not here."

"Fine. I'll kiss my wife later." Ryan laughed and bent down near Autumn. "Climb on. It's a free ride back to the truck."

"No fair. It was my turn." Gemma set her hands on her hips.

Ryan swept the little girl up into his arms before her pout could fully form. "Hang on tight, Autumn. I've got to shake Princess Gemma's smile free."

"Hold on." Caleb motioned for Ryan to prop Gemma on his back, then he glanced at Lacey. "I'll meet you and Aspen over at the dog adoption tent." He grinned at his brother. "Race you to the truck. Last ones buy ice cream at Frosty Dreamer's after our ride later."

Gemma cheered on Caleb, and the race was on with Elsie following close behind. Minutes later, Caleb found Lacey at the edge of the dog adoption tent. She was biting her lower lip and watching Aspen peer into one kennel after another.

He moved to stand beside Lacey and said, "Looks like maybe it wasn't Ryan we needed to worry about getting attached."

"Caleb, tell Mom she needs a dog," Aspen pleaded

and rushed on, "'Cause then she won't be alone when I'm with Dad and Mama-Beth."

"I'm not sure it's a good time," Lacey hedged.

"But, Mom, it's a dog," Aspen argued. "She can sleep in your bed. Protect you. Give you kisses when you're sad." An excited brown terrier licked Aspen's face through his cage. Aspen's laughter peeled out around her.

"She makes a good case," Caleb said. He could make a similar case as a cowboy. One who could kiss Lacey when she was sad or happy or simply standing beside him. *Lacey and kisses.* That was dangerous territory. Caleb moved closer to Aspen and the dog kennels, but those unwise thoughts nipped at his boot heels.

Aspen spun around and pointed at a blond Labrador retriever curled up at the back of a kennel. "We need to adopt her, Mom."

Lacey joined them. "Why this one?"

"All her puppies got adopted." Aspen tapped the laminated card attached to the dog's kennel. "And now she's a mom with no family. We need to be her family."

Caleb had no argument. No counter for Aspen. Family was everything to him. Always had been. He noted Lacey opened her mouth, tucked her hair behind her ear, then closed her lips together softly. As if she too struggled for a sound rebuttal. Family meant something to her. It was good common ground for friends—like they were. Even more important for that "something more" that he was starting to think about more than he should.

"Her name is Butterscotch, Mom." Aspen clasped her hands together in front of her and heightened the imploring plea in her words. "She's so sad. And alone. Look at her. We gotta help her. Give her a family."

The struggle was there in Lacey's unblinking brown eyes. The indecision in the seal of her lips, not firmly set, yet still holding back. Caleb searched for a way to help. But Aspen had already swayed him. He wanted to adopt Butterscotch, gather up Aspen and Lacey, and call them his own. What he needed to do was turn around and walk away. Fast and far. What he actually did was stay put.

"Please, Mom." Aspen stretched her words out, clearly not ready to concede.

Lacey collected herself. "I suppose it doesn't hurt to meet her."

Caleb supposed it wouldn't hurt for him to greet the dog either. It wasn't like he was adopting her. Or claiming a family. He already had one.

The dog rose and slowly inched toward the front of the kennel. Her tail barely twitched, but she sniffed Aspen's fingers wrapped around the wire door. "Can she come out?" Aspen asked.

One of the adoption workers was there in an instant, clipping a leash onto Butterscotch's collar, and leading them all into a portable pen. Aspen sat on the grass and patted her legs. The sweet dog dropped into Aspen's lap without hesitation. Aspen's arms wound around the dog's body.

"She likes me," Aspen said, her grin stretching from cheek to cheek. "Come meet her, Mom."

Lacey had no sooner sat down than Butterscotch was wiggling to get to her, her tail whipping back and forth in excitement. Lacey laughed and moved, allowing Butterscotch to press right up against her.

"Look, Caleb," Aspen called out. "Butterscotch likes Mom the most."

"I think you're right." He knew someone else who was starting to like Lacey more and more. Maybe even the most.

Aspen hugged her mom and Butterscotch. "I told you she needed us."

He was starting to think he might need them too. Caleb bent down in front of them and greeted the dog.

"I think I'm getting a dog," Lacey whispered and touched his arm. "Tell me this is a bad idea."

Caleb considered her hand on his arm for a beat. It was a bad idea of colossal proportions. Caleb only needed a career pivot, not a relationship upgrade. Yet when he looked into Lacey's enchanting brown eyes, he tended to lose himself and forget. "I want to, but I can't." *I'm not good with people's hearts, even my own.* He leaned in and said, "I think Butterscotch is smiling right now."

Lacey shifted, and her fingers flexed around his arm. "It's hard to tell who's smiling more, Butterscotch or Aspen."

"Or you." He reached up and tucked her hair behind her ear. Just the smallest shift, and he could brush his lips against hers. Just a light caress. But those heart-strings tugged. And he guessed one brief kiss wouldn't be nearly enough. He pulled his hand away.

"I think I'm getting a dog." Lacey's eyes sparkled at him, then she waved to the volunteer. Her grin was sunshine bright and everything he could want aimed his way. She spoke to the volunteer. "What paperwork do I need to sign? We choose her."

I could choose you. But that means choosing my heart first. And that was not something Caleb had ever done. He wiped his hands on his jeans and stood up. "Guess we better get some dog supplies as well."

It wasn't long before the paperwork was completed and submitted. And the dog supplies, conveniently available for purchase at the adoption event, were stashed in the truck. Butterscotch leaned against Aspen on the back bench, the pair already content and looking inseparable.

Caleb turned onto the street that led to Lacey's ranch.

"I almost forgot the best news in all the excitement of meeting Butterscotch." Lacey lowered the volume on the radio and grinned at him. "You have a date tonight."

"I have a date," Caleb said carefully. *Please let it be with a deputy, her daughter, and their new dog.*

"Yes. Her name is Eryn. She is Whitney Carson's cousin, and she's free tonight." Lacey fumbled with her phone. "I told her you would text her about meeting up for movie night tonight downtown."

Caleb flexed his fingers around the steering wheel and hoped his expression was neutral.

"Elsie mentioned that movie night is really popular." Lacey tapped on her phone screen. "I thought it would be good to have a first date in a crowded place. Elsie and I both really liked Eryn, and Whitney vouched for her."

"You've thought of everything." *Except asking me what date I really want.* Caleb was pleased his words sounded almost indifferent.

"You can't back out," Lacey warned. "I heard you tell Ryan and Elsie's nieces that you had no plans tonight."

"I'm not backing out," he assured her and pulled to a stop in Lacey's driveway.

In fact, he was leaning into a date. All the way in. Just to prove that there was nothing between him and Lacey. That Ryan was completely wrong about there being something between them. And that Caleb had just gotten caught up in the moment earlier. His boots had taken a bit of a detour at the farmers market, but he was back on the right path now.

"Look, I'll text her right now." He put the truck in Park and picked up his phone from the console. "Happy?"

"Very," she said, albeit a little too quickly and a bit too briskly.

Caleb eyed her, then decided that was only his ears deceiving him. After all, she'd orchestrated the whole date thing. The wager was entirely her idea. And she'd vowed to win. Of course, she was happy about finding him a date. Same as he would be. He would be thrilled in fact. As soon as he got over that annoying bit of disappointment that his date wasn't with his deputy. Surely that would happen any minute now.

He typed his text and hit Send. Eryn's response came immediately. Caleb worked his best smile into place. "We're meeting at six in the square. Looks like I have a movie night date."

"Great." Lacey gathered her purse. "It's a triple feature. Should be good weather too."

"What more could I ask for?" Other than more time with a certain trio.

Lacey glanced into the back seat. "Come on, Aspen. We've already taken up enough of Caleb's time. He's got a date to get ready for."

"Can we go to movie night too, Mom?" Aspen opened her door. "Autumn told me that Riley would be there. She says I gotta meet Riley 'cause she's in the Junior Royal Rodeo Contest too."

"Riley Bishop is the daughter of Evan Bishop, the cattle rancher you met at the lake the other morning with Walter," Caleb explained to Lacey. At her nod, Caleb added, "Evan is married to Paige, who happens to be Tess's sister."

Lacey chuckled. "I think I got it straight."

"And Ms. Paige is a veterinarian. That's what I want to be when I grow up," Aspen announced. "I gotta meet her too. So does Butterscotch. In case she needs a doctor."

"Can't argue with a proper vet meet and greet," Caleb said cheerfully.

"Okay, looks like we'll be heading to movie night as well." Lacey climbed out of the truck and waited for Aspen and Butterscotch to jump out.

Aspen led the dog around the front yard, then straight into the house.

Lacey smiled at him. "Thanks again for today. Maybe we'll see you tonight."

He wanted to tell her she could count on that. But he had a date. Although not with her. He started the truck and touched the brim of his cowboy hat. "Hope you enjoy your evening, Deputy."

And he hoped that the notion of being friends with his deputy would start to fit right again. And soon. Because it was the only thing between them.

CHAPTER FOURTEEN

THE OUTDOOR MOVIE night was as popular as Elsie claimed. Lacey took in the bustling crowd filling the square, sitting in chairs, stretched out on blankets. Friends and neighbors mingled. The kids played. The laughter swirled with its own melody. All while a popular children's movie about a collection of animated toys played on the jumbo movie screen at one end of the square.

Lacey watched Aspen with her new friend, Riley Bishop, as the pair chatted nonstop and walked Butterscotch around a small group of trees. Riley's stepmom, Paige, had set up a collection of chairs and blankets for friends and family nearby. Lacey had promised to come back after she returned her ex-husband's call about an urgent situation.

Wanting to make sure Sarah-Beth and the baby were well, Lacey walked across the street, seeking a quieter location. She moved under the dim awning of Rivers Family Hardware and dialed Jeffrey.

Her ex-husband answered on the second ring, gave a curt greeting, followed by, "This is not what we agreed, Lacey."

"Jeffrey, what are you talking about?" Lacey wandered down the sidewalk.

Her ex-husband's sigh rolled across the speaker. "I overheard Aspen and Sarah-Beth talking earlier. I know Aspen went riding today."

Lacey stopped abruptly. "First, is everything okay with Sarah-Beth and the baby? They are fine, aren't they?"

"Couldn't be better," Jeffrey quipped. "But could we please stay on topic?"

Lacey was trying to. "You texted me about an urgent situation." She gripped her phone tighter. "I thought something was seriously wrong."

"Something is wrong," Jeffrey stated flatly. "You entered Aspen in that contest, and we agreed not to."

That was his urgent situation? Lacey inhaled and worked to keep control of her growing frustration. "No, we didn't agree." She turned back toward the crowded downtown square. "You told me. Same as you told Aspen."

"We discussed this, Lacey," Jeffrey retorted. "This isn't how we coparent correctly or effectively."

"We didn't discuss anything," Lacey countered. Discussions and the right conversations had never been their specialty. Perhaps if they had, Jeffrey and she might've worked out differently. But debating the past was hardly productive. It was over. Her gaze skimmed the sea of happy smiling faces. "But I did talk to Aspen like I told you I would. She wants to do this, and I'm going to help her."

"This is not a good idea," Jeffrey stressed. "You're making me look like the bad parent."

"Jeffrey, this isn't about you," Lacey said. Her gaze landed on a familiar cowboy who wasn't so far away that she couldn't get to him. Or see that he was completely alone. But that wasn't right. "Look, this is about Aspen. She needs to be our focus."

"Well, make sure this is not about you either, Lacey," he challenged. "Aspen is not you."

He said it as if being like her was a bad thing somehow. Lacey fought the urge to apologize. Her gaze returned to her cowboy and stuck. She kept her cool. "What does that mean exactly?"

"Look, this conversation is better in person," Jeffrey said, his words yielding slightly. "I've been trying to do what's best for Aspen since you deployed. It's not too much to ask that you follow my lead now, is it?"

There it was. That guilt surged again. Along with the urge to apologize. It took a minute, but she managed to unclench her jaw and loosen her grip on the phone. "You're right, Jeffrey. This is a conversation best had face-to-face."

"We'll meet as soon as Sarah-Beth and I get back to Three Springs," he stated.

With that, he ended the call. No good night. No sleep well. Just silence, doubt, and second-guessing herself.

But Lacey had watched Aspen with Caleb in the Sloan stables and the arena. She knew in her gut that horses were more than a phase for her daughter. Aspen had a passion and a natural affinity for them. And that elusive *heart* that Sam and Caleb referenced.

Aspen is not you.

Surely, she wasn't just wanting to see herself in her daughter, was she? Grasping for common ground that wasn't there. Misreading everything. She caught sight of her cowboy, still alone on that blanket.

Lacey tucked her phone into the pocket of her denim shorts and started across the street. She should head back to Paige and sit with the veterinarian's family. Keep the evening entirely about Aspen.

But her gaze was fixed elsewhere, and her feet followed, leading Lacey toward her cowboy. As if he'd called her. It was more that she felt drawn to him, wanting him to help her feel something other than uncertain.

Lacey navigated around several blankets and finally reached her cowboy. "Where did your date go?"

Caleb grabbed her hand and tugged her onto the blanket. "If you keep standing there, the people behind you are going to start hollering because you're blocking the screen."

Lacey waved an apology to the family behind them and settled beside Caleb. "Well, where is Eryn?"

"She left halfway through the first movie to find mosquito spray," he said, his words bland and unbothered.

Lacey looked around. "But the second movie just started playing."

"Yeah, well, it seems Eryn ran into Matt Molina, the mayor's son, inside Goodstart Pharmacy," Caleb explained. "Eryn and Matt got to talking. And they decided to grab banana splits and watch the movie from inside the ice-cream parlor."

Lacey gaped at him. "Eryn bailed on you for the mayor's son."

"Don't underestimate the power of a banana split," he said, laughter coming from his lips.

"It's not a root beer float with homemade ice cream," she countered.

"No, it sure isn't." He dropped his hat on the blanket, tousled his hair, and grinned at her.

She studied him. "You're not mad."

"Not really." He stretched out on the blanket and stacked his hands behind his head. "It wouldn't have worked out between us anyway."

"You don't know that," she argued. She needed to argue. Otherwise, she would give in to her pleasure that his date had sputtered and failed. And that was entirely the wrong kind of thinking.

"Eryn wanted a banana split." He tipped his head toward her. His expression was serious, yet there was an undercurrent of his usual good humor in his words. "And I don't like to mix my fruit or my ice-cream flavors. I like to keep things simple and uncomplicated."

He'd always been straightforward, never pretending to be anything he wasn't. Never apologizing either. She'd always admired that about him. She stretched her legs out and leaned back on her arms. "What now?"

"We watch the next movie." He motioned to the screen. "Enjoy the evening. Let Aspen have fun with her new friends. The same way we used to have fun while the adults sat around."

"I never much thought about my mom and Wells having fun together when I was a kid," she confessed.

"I think most kids are too busy thinking about their own entertainment." Caleb stared up at the night sky, his words wistful. "I know I was."

Lacey drew her legs up and rested her arms on her knees.

"What's on your mind, Lace?" He shifted beside her and sat up. "Something tells me it's not about the fun we had as kids."

"We did, didn't we?" she said. "Have fun."

"Why do you sound surprised?" he asked and propped his arms on his raised legs, mimicking her position. "You were there for our adventures. Heck, you came up with most of them."

"Not after my mom was diagnosed with cancer." She set her cheek on her knees and looked at him. "And everything stopped being fun."

He scooted toward her as if he wanted to block out everyone around them. As if he wanted to be certain she heard his next words. His gaze drifted over her face, part stunned and part alarmed. His eyebrows lifted slightly. "That's why you broke up with Grady Welton and stopped coming around?"

Did you miss me? She nodded. *I missed you.* "I had to be there for my mom. I had to be responsible, do whatever I could to help her and Wells."

"I would've helped you," he said softly. "If you'd asked."

She believed him. "Your gran Claire dropped off meals. The Baker sisters and neighbors did too. I'm not sure Swells and Mom knew what to do. There was so much food."

His gaze searched hers. "I would've…"

She reached out and set her hand on his arm, stopping him. "I know."

But she hadn't wanted his pity. Caleb had been the one she turned to for excitement and adventure. An escape. A good time. He'd always made her laugh. She hadn't wanted him to see her cry. She'd never wanted to be the one to ruin his fun.

He covered her fingers with his hand as if wanting to stay connected. "You gave up fun in high school." She opened her mouth to object, he rushed on, "For good reason. When did you start having fun again?"

"That's just it." Her fingers tightened around his arm. She felt his strength and his warmth underneath her palm. Felt it inside her chest. She exhaled and admitted, "I never really did."

He didn't pull back. Didn't let go. Simply studied her, questions in his intensely appealing eyes. "You even went into the army. Wells and your mom would fill me in when they got your letters. They were always so proud, they'd tell everyone who'd listen to them about you."

She smiled. "I enlisted because the army paid for my college degree. There were so many medical bills, I couldn't burden Wells and Mom with paying for college."

He pressed his lips together.

"I don't regret a minute of the time I served," she said, wanting him to understand. "The military made me a better person. Don't get me wrong, I liked serving. I would do it again."

"But," he pressed.

"But it was lonely most of the time." Her fingers flexed around his arm again as if he was her anchor while she spilled her unspoken truths. "Then I married Jeffrey." Her words swept around her sigh. "And I was still lonely."

Caleb edged even closer until their knees and shoulders touched and kept his hand covering hers.

"You asked what was on my mind before, and it was just that." She bumped her shoulder against his, but it didn't lighten the mood. Instead, she leaned right into him as if she needed another connection with him. Or perhaps she just wanted to feel steady. "I realized Jeffrey and I never had fun together."

"You dated and got married." His fingers caressed her wrist. A back-and-forth slide. His gaze searched hers. "There had to be good in there."

"We had a baby and responsibilities and more important things to always think about," she said. His fingers continued that slow slide, his touch so light against her skin, yet so very soothing. "It all happened too fast. In the wrong order."

"Why did you get married?" he asked.

"It was the responsible thing to do," she admitted. A surprise pregnancy had fast-tracked them past dating and straight into parenthood. And she'd been so certain what they felt for each other would be enough. "We needed to come together as parents for our child."

"But you weren't truly happy," he guessed.

"That shouldn't have mattered," she countered. "It was the right thing to do for us."

"You made the best decision in the moment, and according to Gran Claire, that's all any of us can hope to do," he said, his expression pensive.

Would Gran Claire think it wise or foolish if Lacey twisted her wrist and linked her fingers with Caleb's? Was the best decision moving her hand out from underneath his or holding on tighter? Lacey kept her arm in place, afraid to make a choice. And perhaps that was for the best. In this moment.

"What now?" he asked.

"What do you mean?"

"You are home," he said. "Isn't it past time to find that fun again?"

With you? That idea was entirely too tempting. "I'm home to prove I can be the parent Jeffrey needs me to be." Although, on that front, she was falling short already. Her ex had made that clear during their phone call.

"I'm not going to offer parenting advice. That

wouldn't be right." Caleb squeezed her hand. "But I don't think it's wrong to want to be happy too, Lace. You shouldn't have to apologize for that."

I could be happy with you. But would you keep my heart safe? Not just in this moment, but always? Because she vowed not to bargain for temporary ever again. Her heart wasn't up for a trial run. Not this time around.

She slid her hand from beneath his, eased away from his side and back into that easygoing banter shared between friends. "Hey, I owe you an apology for Eryn. I wouldn't have suggested this date if I knew mosquitoes would chase her away and straight to Matt Molina."

Caleb chuckled. "That's okay." He reached into a picnic basket nearby and handed her several frosted animal cookies. "Now there's more snacks for us."

"You brought animal cookies." Lacey plopped a bite-size unicorn cookie into her mouth and savored the crunch of the colorful sprinkles and sweet frosting. "I never did like sharing the good snacks anyway." She swallowed and examined the cookies in her hand. "Wait. These aren't store-bought. Did you make these?"

"Of course. I made them earlier with Gemma and Autumn for their princess tea party." He grinned. "Gran Claire taught all her grandsons the basics. How to cook, how to dance. Some of us are better than others."

She laughed and shook her head. "Smug is not a good look on you."

His grin tipped farther into one cheek. "But it's true. Ask my brothers."

"I just might," she challenged, then finished off her other animal cookies. "Now tell me, why is it Gran Claire taught you to crochet and none of your brothers?"

He stuck his animal cookie into his mouth and grinned. "Weren't you listening? I'm the best. Gran Claire knew it."

Lacey shoved him playfully. "What's the real reason?"

He brushed his hands together and eyed her. "I never sat still. Gran Claire used to say: *if that child doesn't learn to sit still once in a blue moon, his run is going to run out before he turns eighteen.*"

Lacey chuckled.

"It's true," Caleb said, not looking the least bit put out. "She'd say it to anyone who came to the house. I was apparently an ongoing topic in her weekly crochet group."

Lacey smothered her laughter, trying not to be too loud.

"Someone—and I'm fairly certain it was Breezy Baker—suggested Gran Claire give me something to do while I was sitting." Caleb opened a bottle of root beer and held it out to her. "Turns out I can sit still if my hands are occupied."

If I held your hand, would that be enough to keep you beside me? Just for a moment? Just for right now? Because I'm happy. And I know it won't last. She sipped her root beer and gathered her words.

Now wasn't the time to go chasing after her heart. "I'm quite certain the rodeo's auction will be more than pleased with your handiwork. Word around the station is that they are short on donations this year."

Before he could respond, Aspen came and plopped down on the blanket. Butterscotch stretched out beside her. "We came to watch the movie with you. Our feet and paws are tired." Aspen rolled over onto her stomach and eyed the picnic basket. "And we sure could use a snack."

"Help yourself." Caleb chuckled and slid the basket closer to Aspen. "I'm sure there is something in there that Butterscotch will like too. But keep the grapes to yourself."

"Those are bad for dogs." Aspen sorted through the basket. "Onions and chocolate too. I read about it."

"Is there an animal you haven't read about?" Caleb teased.

Aspen opened a bag of peanut-butter-filled pretzels. Her expression was thoughtful. "I like all animals. Farm animals especially."

"Why is that?" Caleb reached into the basket, took out a bag of popcorn, and tossed Butterscotch several pieces.

"I want to be a veterinarian like Riley's bonus mom, Ms. Paige, so I gotta know all about farm animals." Aspen sighed like it should have been obvious.

"Are you sure you want to be a veterinarian?"

Lacey reached into the popcorn bag and scooped out a handful.

Suspicion crossed Aspen's face. "Dad told you, didn't he? Then he also told you it was just a phase."

Seemed everything with their daughter was a phase. When did it stop being a phase? Lacey feared it might be when Aspen chose something Jeffrey approved of. Lacey frowned. "Why would your dad say that?"

"'Cause we aren't farmers." Aspen tossed another pretzel into her mouth and crunched down on it.

"Doesn't mean you can't become a veterinarian and treat animals, even ones on farms," Lacey said, unless Jeffrey already had a vision for his daughter's future.

"That's what Mama-Beth told me." Aspen smiled and rolled back over to watch the movie. "I love this part of the movie. It's so funny. You gotta watch."

Lacey was too busy looking at her contented daughter and trying not to look at the cowboy beside her. The one who made her feel pretty content herself. She warned herself not to read too much into it.

Yet the movie ended all too soon for Lacey. She stood and took in her daughter who was trying to cover up yet another yawn.

Aspen frowned. "But there's another movie."

"It's getting late, and we have lots to do tomorrow," Lacey said. "And I see Grandpa Swells headed this way. He's our ride home."

"Can't we stay a little longer?" Aspen pleaded and fought off another yawn.

Lacey saw her stepdad wave and waved back. Lacey noticed his other hand was clasped around that of a tall, elegant woman.

"Who's that with Grandpa?" Aspen jumped up and waved both arms at Wells.

Caleb stiffened beside Lacey. His words were bleak. "That's my mother."

Caleb's mother. She was there and with Wells. Not just walking beside Lacey's stepdad but appearing to be very much *with* her stepdad. But this was the woman Caleb never talked about—not even in passing when they were growing up.

Lacey turned to Caleb. "Wells mentioned he was going out to dinner when he dropped us off here. He never told me who he was going with."

Caleb nodded, plucked his hat off his head, and finger combed his hair.

"This is awkward." Lacey knocked the loose grass from her shorts.

"Awkward doesn't even begin to cover it." Caleb tapped his cowboy hat against his thigh and slanted his gaze toward Lacey. "Guess it's time to meet the parents."

CHAPTER FIFTEEN

HER FIRST DATE in more decades than she wanted to count, and Lilian Sloan felt as if she was a teenager already breaking the rules. She took in the guarded expression on her youngest son's face and slowed her steps. She'd wanted more than a cool indifference from Caleb. Well, she had Caleb's attention now. For good or ill was still to be seen.

Perhaps Caleb's obvious reservations were valid. She had no business holding hands with the handsome sheriff and strolling through the park like they did this every evening. The heavens knew Lilian had gotten relationships and love wrong before. She was supposed to be older and wiser.

"Too late for second thoughts, Doc." Wells squeezed her fingers and drew her gaze to his. "We're all but caught." He looked rather delighted, sounded rather pleased with the outcome. "If our kids hadn't seen us, well, I reckon most of Three Springs has, and word would've reached 'em soon enough."

"You don't mind?" She searched his gray eyes. The ones she had decided over dinner were steel-colored and wonderfully expressive. "You don't think we're moving a little fast?"

"At our age, we don't have the luxury of taking it slow." His gaze gleamed. "And I'm feeling things I thought I left behind long ago."

She'd always preferred a straight talker. "You're not alone in those feelings." Lilian tightened her grip around his hand. "And this is nice. Quite nice."

"I'll take that," he said, his smile tender. "But just so you know, I'd like to see this become something special and quite lasting, if you're of a mind to agree." He raised their joined hands and pressed a soft kiss against her fingers. "But for now let's enjoy nice."

Lilian's smile sank deep inside her. "I'd like that."

"Since that's settled, it's time to quit stalling." Amusement curved across his face. "Can't leave the kids waiting."

Lilian laughed and walked with him to meet his stepdaughter and granddaughter. Her son was civil yet cautious.

Introductions concluded, Wells grinned and said, "We've decided to switch cars and take Lilian's instead. We put the top down and let the night right in beside us." Wells dropped his arm around Aspen's shoulders. "We figured Aspen would enjoy a ride in the convertible."

Aspen grinned. "Can we ride with Ms. Lilian, Mom? Please?"

"Sure." Lacey tucked her hair behind her ear.

Her gaze slanted toward Caleb as if she was wait-ing on him for something.

But Lilian's son remained quiet and seemed far from enthusiastic about a top-down drive home.

Lilian took in a stoic Caleb, then Lacey and de-cided there was a definite undercurrent there. Her gaze shifted to the bandage on Lacey's forehead. Her inner doctor might be retired, but she was still alive and active. "Lacey, how is your head? No pain? Lingering side effects?"

That question snapped her son from his com-placence. His focus shifted to Lacey and locked on the deputy as if she was his only concern. And that undercurrent stirred.

"It's fine. I'm fine." Lacey barely touched her bandage. "It hardly bothered me at all today."

Lilian nodded and smiled.

"Never did thank you properly for looking after Lacey yesterday." Wells turned to Caleb and ex-tended his arm. "Sure do appreciate it."

Caleb and Lacey's stepdad shook hands. Then Lacey stepped toward Caleb and thrust her arm out too. She said, "I never thanked you either."

Caleb considered her hand, then wrapped his fingers around hers.

Lilian was convinced she'd never seen a simple handshake look more like a promise of something more. Perhaps it was how her son held on to Lacey's hand for a beat longer than necessary. Or perhaps it was the catch of their fingertips on the release. Whatever it was, that undercurrent swelled.

Her son was back to looking guarded. And poor Lacey looked plain perplexed. Lilian supposed it didn't matter if one was young, old, or in-between, love was simply hard to get right.

Lilian smiled wide and held her arm out to Aspen. "Ready to feel the night wind in your hair?"

Aspen chewed on her bottom lip. "What about Butterscotch?"

"Butterscotch will fit perfectly between you and your mom in the back seat." Lilian reached down and rubbed the friendly dog's ears.

Wells stepped up beside Aspen and the dog. "I think Butterscotch just might love the car ride more than any of us."

Aspen took Lilian's hand and kept her grip on Butterscotch's leash. "Hear that, Butterscotch? You won't have to put your head out the window. Just put your nose in the air."

They waited for Lacey and Caleb to settle on a practice time at the Sloan stables for the next morning, then they were off. Their pace slowed to allow Butterscotch the appropriate sniffing of the fire hydrant and stop signs and whatever else caught the dog's interest. As for Lacey, with every pause, she glanced back toward the downtown square.

Stopping at a tall pine tree, Aspen asked, "Mom, can Ms. Lilian and Grandpa Swells come shopping with us tomorrow? Grandpa knows cowboys, and Lilian dresses pretty. We gotta be cowgirls, Mom."

Lacey pulled herself back to the conversation. "If they are free, they're welcome to join us." She set her hand on Aspen's shoulder. "Aspen is in the Junior Royal Rodeo Contest and wants to look her best."

"And we gotta be cowgirls," Aspen stressed, then added more emphatically, "'Cause cowboys and cowgirls go together, right?"

Lacey nodded absently and again glanced back to where a certain cowboy was standing.

Lilian considered her own hand clasped securely in the sheriff's and smiled. "I could use a pair of cowboy boots myself. I've been thinking it's time to expand my wardrobe."

Wells grinned. "I was going to stop in at the station tomorrow, but I'd be willing to meet you three for a bite to eat between stores."

"Then it's settled," Lacey stated, although still looking distracted.

"It's a shopping day for us," Lilian said. And if the topic of Caleb and Lacey as a couple came up, well, she'd take that conversation one store at a time. Surely that was good listening, not meddling. After all, she'd vowed not to interfere in her sons' lives when she moved back, and she intended on keeping her word. Still, she couldn't help but ask, "Is something wrong, dear?"

Lacey wrung her hands together, then pointed toward the square. "I forgot something."

More like someone, Lilian was willing to bet.

"I can run back and get it," Wells offered. "What'd you leave behind?"

Lacey tapped her mouth and looked away.

Lilian chuckled softly. "I think Lacey needs to find it herself."

Lacey's cheeks warmed.

"Wells and I can take Aspen and Butterscotch home." Lilian touched Wells's arm, drawing his attention to her. "And we're happy to stay until you get home, Lacey, aren't we?"

Wells scratched his cheek, considered Lilian. Then his eyebrows lifted, and his eyes widened as if reading into Lilian's unspoken words. "Absolutely. Aspen and I can show Lilian how to make our special yogurt smoothies."

"Yes!" Aspen cheered. "Those are the best."

"No need to rush, dear." Lilian squeezed Lacey's shoulder lightly and said, "Often things like these can't be found in one night. But the more time you spend together looking, you realize it was always right there in front of you."

Lilian hustled Aspen and Wells away before Lacey could disagree.

Wells leaned in and whispered, "I've got my eye on you, Doc. I know what you're up to."

"I haven't the faintest idea what you're referring to." Lilian kept her tone bland.

"And after all that talk at dinner about not messing in our kids' lives." Wells chuckled and squeezed her hand. "My doc...the matchmaker."

"I always fancied myself more of a big-city career-minded girl," Lilian replied lightly.

"I always fancied a woman who knows her mind

and exactly who she is," Wells said, appreciation clear in his expression.

Lilian used to know who she was. Now, she wasn't so sure. She tucked herself closer into the sheriff's side.

But for the first time, in a long while, she thought maybe she was starting to find herself again.

CHAPTER SIXTEEN

ALONE. JUST LIKE he preferred.

Caleb watched the opening credits scroll across the giant movie screen. He pulled out his cell phone but kept the screen on lock. All that waited there was the email from the county detailing his permitting problems for the rackhouse. Nothing that could be solved until Monday when the town hall was open.

The night stretched out before him. Though the solitude that had once appealed was now oddly off-putting and slightly uncomfortable.

Of course, all he had to do was pack it up, ditch the musical rom-com movie about to play, and skip into The Feisty Owl. Then he would be far from alone among the Saturday night singles and the weekend merrymakers. They would welcome him. They always did.

He looked across the street at the brightly lit Feisty Owl sign. All he needed was a few hours inside. Then the night wouldn't seem quite so endless. And surely a line dance or two would cure him of whatever strange melancholy seized him now.

Caleb packed up the picnic basket and fastened the lid.

A pair of sandals, revealing bare toes and a thin silver ankle bracelet, stepped into his line of sight. Caleb lifted his head, skimmed his gaze over white jean shorts and a flowy light purple shirt to a pair of deep brown eyes. His grin came as easy as the anticipation inside him.

Caleb suddenly reevaluated his evening plans. "Thought you were headed home, Deputy."

"You seemed a little taken aback about your mom and Wells," she explained. "I came to check on you."

Check on you. Not to be confused with *I wanted to be with you.* Caleb's smile dimmed. He folded up the blanket. "I don't want to talk about whatever that was between Wells and my mother."

"We don't need to talk." Lacey grabbed the other end of the blanket and walked the ends to him. "But we are getting out of here."

Caleb took her ends of the blanket, being careful not to touch her. Otherwise, he might be tempted to hold her hand, same as Wells had clasped his mother's. Like a cowboy who'd found his partner and had no intention of letting go. But Caleb was more of a go-it-alone cowboy. He buried his hands in the blanket. "Where are we going?"

"I know a place." She extended her arm and flexed her fingers. "Give me your keys. I'll drive."

There was a playfulness to her soft smile. A challenge in her brown eyes. A confidence in her stance.

And it was all so very appealing. *She* was so very appealing. He doubted she even knew how much.

She was asking for more time with him. He wanted the same with her. What was the harm? It wasn't any sort of permanent detour. Just a way to spend the rest of the evening. Besides, she'd piqued his curiosity. And his curiosity always got the better of him. He reached into his pocket and set his truck keys against her palm.

Lacey accepted the keys, then pressed the picnic basket into his arms. "Come on. Let's go."

Twenty minutes later, Lacey steered his truck onto a barely visible side road covered in brush and cut the engine.

Caleb glanced out the window and rubbed his chin. "This is Clearwind Lake. And the front gate is closed and locked."

"That never stopped us before." Lacey opened the truck door. "You coming or waiting here so you can hear all about it later?"

That had been their taunt to each other years ago. *You can sit back and hear about it later. Or you can join in and experience it. The choice is yours, but get a move on.*

Caleb grinned. "Do you remember where the back trail is, or do I need to show you?"

"Grab a flashlight, cowboy, and follow me." With that, Lacey hopped out.

Caleb took two flashlights from the toolbox underneath his back seat and joined Lacey on the dirt road that narrowed to a single-file trail. Soon enough they wound their way down to the shore of Clear-wind Lake and then onto the dock.

At the end of the dock, Lacey slipped off her sandals, sat, and dipped her feet into the cool water. "I used to come out here a lot and wait for a shooting star to fall into the lake on the horizon."

"Gran Claire used to tell me that those shooting stars were the ones that granted wishes." Caleb sat, leaned against the last post on the dock, and propped his arm on his raised knee.

"The wish granters, she called them." Lacey swirled her bare feet in the water. "And to cover all my bases, I wished on all the stars in the sky, just in case one fell while I wasn't here."

"That was very thorough," he said.

"I was a desperate teenager."

"What were you wishing for?"

"For my mom to get better," she confessed, then lifted one shoulder. "For more time with her."

He felt himself tense and tossed a small pebble into the lake. "I didn't ever wish to be with my mom. Not once." Strange how his body relaxed at the admission. The words somehow freed him. "That's bad, isn't it?"

Lacey reached over and set her hand on his leg, just above his knee.

He considered her touch, gentle yet solid enough to tether him to the moment while the past swept around him. He set his head back against the post and stared at the stars. "I should've wished for her. Kids should want to be with their moms."

"But you had your gran Claire, your grandfather, and your four brothers," she said, a sincerity to her words that suggested he let himself off the hook.

"All my memories start and end with them," he said. "They've always been there for me. Whenever I needed them." For so long, his brothers and grandparents had been all he ever needed. Yet now, when he looked at Lacey, he needed…

He lifted his gaze out over the dark lake waters. But he couldn't quite ignore the feel of her hand on his leg. A simple show of support. A connection he shouldn't want to encourage. "Now my mother is back in my life, and I don't know what I'm supposed to feel."

"Maybe it's not about deciding how you're supposed to feel." She shifted to face him, drawing one leg out of the water so her thigh touched his. One more link between them. Her hand never moved. "Maybe instead it's just honoring how you feel."

Like accepting that he felt more at ease right now with her than he had in years. Here, completely surrounded by the stillness of the night, which he usually avoided, but wanting nothing more than for this moment to last. "I'm starting to think my mom isn't the person I made her out to be."

"I would be surprised if she was," Lacey said, her smile brief. Her expression was all compassion and tenderness. "We all have sides we show and others we hide."

I'm hiding now. From you. Because I can't—won't—show you my heart. He searched those stars, then shifted his gaze back to hers, not surprised to find her watching him. "I need to get to know my mom and the person she is now, don't I?"

"That's a good place to start." She nodded. The motion made her hair sweep across her cheek. "Then you can decide how you really feel as the person you are, not the boy you once were."

The boy he once was had liked the girl who challenged him to keep up. But the cowboy he was felt something more than simple affection for the cowgirl sitting beside him. Yeah, he knew full well what he felt; he just wasn't certain he liked it. "What do we do about your stepdad and my mom?"

She blinked and brushed her hair off her cheek. "Nothing."

Could he do that with Lacey? Nothing?

"If they are happy, then we should let it play out," she said, sounding certain. "Not interfere."

Happy. He was perfectly happy with the way things were between him and his deputy, wasn't he? He shouldn't let something like his heart interfere with that. He pressed, "Then it doesn't bother you? Them dating."

The corners of her mouth dipped down. "It bothers me more to think of Wells unhappy and alone."

But Caleb was alone. And not unhappy. Although, he supposed, he hadn't really given his happiness much thought...until recently. He nodded. "We will let it play out then." Same as he would with his deputy.

"I don't know what's worse, how skeptical you

sound or how bleak you look," Lacey said, her words teasing. She dipped her fingers in the lake and splashed him. "They're grown-ups. They can date."

He liked the sound of her laugh. The playful tilt of her head. Her candid smile. "What about you?"

"What about me?" She trailed her fingers in the water.

"You're grown up," he said. "You could date too." *Would you say yes if I asked?*

She dried her fingers on her shorts and shook her head. "I've got to concentrate on Aspen. She is my priority. I don't want anything to interfere with that."

He understood her position yet wanted to disagree.

"In fact, I should probably get home to my daughter." She picked up her sandals and put them on. "It's her first night at the ranch. Wells and your mom will want to be getting home too."

Caleb pushed away from the post and stood. Lacey was on her feet before he could offer her any assistance. He switched the flashlights on and handed her one, then they made their way back to the fence and the trail.

Inside the truck, Lacey asked, "Mind if we roll the windows down?"

Caleb obliged, lowered all the windows, and reversed out of the dirt road.

"Usually if I'm not asleep at this hour, I'm working." She buckled her seat belt and rested her elbow on the doorframe. "But now I can enjoy the night a little while longer."

And Caleb could enjoy the picture she made.

Her arm out the window, her fingers floating on the night breeze. Her head rested against the seat back. Her eyes were closed. Her face was peaceful, her barely there smile blissful. Sitting next to her inside his truck, catching glimpses of her, he realized how much he wanted to make her happy. For more than this one moment.

But he feared she wouldn't be happy with what he offered—a heart more locked down than open. Caleb concentrated on the road and left Lacey free to appreciate the night on her own terms.

Too soon, he was pulling into her driveway. Walking her to the front door. Preparing to end the moment.

Only two steps onto her front porch, she turned and thrust her arm out to him. "Good night, Caleb."

He stared at her hand for a beat, then slipped his fingers around hers. If he'd been a different cowboy, he might've eased her arm up and pressed the softest kiss against her knuckles.

Or perhaps he might've tugged gently until he could gather her up into his arms and simply hold her close.

Instead, he skimmed his thumb across her palm, watched her eyes flare slightly and her breath catch. And he wondered again what it would take to be her cowboy. But he already knew. It would cost him more than he could give.

One more caress against her skin, as if he needed the memory, and he released her. He touched his hat and retreated. Back behind those friendship barriers where hearts were safe and happiness guaranteed. "Night, Deputy."

She slipped inside without a backward glance. And then he was alone again. Just like he wanted.

He kept the truck windows down on his drive home, willing the midnight breeze to carry away his foolish thoughts. Then he turned up the radio to crowd out his sudden discontent.

He drove up the driveway, noted the dim light over the back porch of the farmhouse and the two figures waving to him. And his discontent doubled. So much for being alone.

What was it with coming home late and running into his family? Didn't his family sleep anymore? Caleb walked around his truck and up onto the back porch where his older brothers, Carter and Grant, were sipping bourbon and talking.

"Glad you're here." Grant transferred baby Sadie into Caleb's arms and shook out his own arms from his shoulders to his wrists. "Your niece missed you."

Caleb adjusted the blanket with stars and moons and unicorns around his niece. "What are you two doing exactly?"

"Maggie fell asleep, and I didn't want to wake her," Grant explained and stretched his arms over his head as if he was warming up for a midnight jog. "So we're having a sleepover." Grant tapped Sadie softly on her nose. "Only this little one refuses to sleep."

"She's been rather insistent about being held

however," Carter added, trying to sound vexed. But his doting-dad smile gave him away. "We came out here so she wouldn't wake the rest of the house."

"How long have you been out here?" Caleb asked. Sadie gave a full body yawn.

"Long enough for a glass of bourbon." Carter lifted his tumbler.

"And two servings of Tess's Black Forest cake," Grant added, not looking the least bit regretful about overindulging. "If you want any, you better get in there quick. It'll be gone by morning."

Carter touched his stomach. "We were just discussing another slice when you pulled in."

"Don't let me stop you." Caleb tipped his chin toward the back door.

"We've moved on," Grant said and considered him. "We decided we'd much rather hear about your evening. Tell us about all the fun you've been having."

What could he tell them? The venue was questionable, the reception in jeopardy unless he secured the necessary permits. Not going there. He could tell them that he hated handshakes. Or more specifically, handshakes with a certain deputy. That would ignite too many questions.

Caleb paced around the porch, then turned back to them. "Did either of you know Mom was seeing Sheriff Hopson?"

"Mom is dating…" Grant dropped into a chair beside Carter and stared into his tumbler as if searching for his response. Finally, he nodded. "I always liked Wells Hopson."

"I don't think Mom is looking for your approval." Caleb frowned.

"She has my support." Carter sipped his bourbon. "I always liked Wells too."

"This is not about liking Wells Hopson," Caleb charged, then lowered his voice at the baby's wrinkled brow.

"What is it about then?" Grant asked and exchanged a look with Carter. Grant set his elbows on his knees and studied Caleb as if he was one of his brother's patients withholding information. His grin finally came. "You don't like the idea of Mom with Wells because of Lacey."

Carter nodded and murmured his agreement. "That makes sense."

"What does Lacey have to do with this?" Caleb asked and rocked Sadie.

Grant and Carter exchanged another silent look. Grant shrugged, his words simple and direct to better emphasize the obvious. "You like her. That's what Lacey has to do with this."

"And I suppose it's weird to have your mother dating your girlfriend's stepdad," Carter mused and swirled the single ice cube in his tumbler.

Girlfriend. Caleb looked at the baby in his arms as if she could rescue him. She gurgled and kicked her legs and fisted her tiny fingers. *Good advice, little one. I need to fight.* "Lacey and I aren't dating. The only label we have is friends."

His brothers completely ignored him. Grant tapped his tumbler against Carter's glass and said, "I suppose it could be weird, but it is not a deal-breaker."

"Definitely not a deal-breaker," Carter agreed.

The deal-breaker was his two older brothers and their misconceptions. Caleb thrust his hand through his hair and kept swaying for Sadie's benefit. "I'm not dating. But thinking about Mom dating doesn't feel right."

"Why not?" Carter shook his head. "It's not like we're kids and wanting Mom and Dad to reconcile."

"Yeah, that ship sailed decades ago," Grant said flatly.

"More like sank," Carter quipped. "When they divorced."

"It's not that," Caleb argued. "I don't know how to explain it." Other than he thought of his mother as perpetually single, like himself. Determined to prove they could face the world on their own—no partner required. Because a closed heart was better than a broken one.

Grant made one of those annoying *hmm* sounds as if that summed up everything.

Caleb narrowed his gaze on his brother yet tried to relax his body for Sadie's sake. "What does that mean?"

"It's simple." Grant waved his hand toward Caleb, a satisfied gleam in his gaze. "If Mom finds someone, you really will be the last single Sloan."

"But he has Lacey," Carter offered as if suddenly eager to help.

"I don't have Lacey," Caleb countered. "And I don't mind being single. The last one *or* the only one." Was that a crack he heard in his voice? Like he lacked conviction? Impossible.

Grant steepled his fingers under his chin and looked thoughtful. "Little brother, who exactly are you trying to fool?"

"I'm serious," Caleb said. He had Lacey's friendship, and if he wanted more, well, that was only a momentary lapse, wasn't it? In the morning, the moment would have passed, and he'd be on to the next thing. Without his deputy. "If I was with Lacey, why would I let her set me up with someone else?"

"Wait." Carter held up his hand and blinked at Caleb as if clearing his head. "Lacey is setting you up?"

"She claims she can find me the perfect cowgirl." As if she existed. Okay, she might. And she could very well be his deputy. But that wasn't the point. Caleb winced. "It was all part of a wager we made."

"And you agreed to be matched up?" Grant smoothed his fingers over his mouth, but the dismay was there on his face.

"It's not like she's going to succeed." Tonight's movie date fiasco was a prime example. Caleb had been more than a little relieved when Eryn had texted him about running into Matt. So relieved he'd encouraged her to go enjoy her evening. Caleb asked, "Why do you think I took the bet in the first place?"

Grant's words bordered on grim. "You never bet against love, little brother."

"Love," Caleb sputtered. "This has nothing to do with love."

"It's always about love, even when it's not." Carter stretched out his legs and yawned.

Now the two of them sounded like Ryan. Caleb should *not* be surprised.

"He's right." Grant was solemn.

"This from two cowboys who are so blinded by love all you see are rainbows and unicorns," Caleb said. Same as Ryan. And his twin, Josh.

"I'm not complaining." Grant shrugged a second time. "I always liked rainbows."

Caleb swallowed his groan.

"I like my view. It suits me." Carter propped his boots on the coffee table as if he wanted to get even more comfortable and eyed Caleb. "But you, little brother, seem to be the only one all riled up tonight. Maybe you should try on our love-tinted lenses."

"It's impossible to have a conversation with you two," Caleb muttered.

"You just don't like what you're hearing." Grant sipped his bourbon and considered Caleb over the rim of his glass. "But being the very supportive older brothers that we are, we feel it's our duty to say it anyway."

"You've made your point." Caleb frowned and sped up his rocking for his niece.

Carter and Grant chuckled, then toasted each other again as if pleased with their results.

"Speaking of things I don't like hearing," Carter started. "What is this about a dandelion wine tasting party?"

"You mean the dandelion wine event," Caleb said, glad for the change in topic. "It's nothing. It's for Grandpa and Uncle. I've spoken to Ryan. We're hosting it out at the greenhouses on Elsie and Ryan's farm."

Carter paused. "You really think you have time for that with everything else?"

"It's a simple party," Caleb said, working that missing conviction back into his words. "Nothing to it. Besides, if I don't do it, Grandpa Sam and Uncle Roy plan to serve dandelion wine at Josh and Vivian's reception."

Carter frowned.

Grant laughed. "Nice save, little brother."

"That's what I do well—improvise and think on my feet." Caleb grinned. "Now that my niece is back to sleep, my work here is done too." Caleb handed a snoozing Sadie back to her dad and said, "Believe it or not, Carter, I've got this."

Carter nodded and said, "And I still have a tent ready as the wedding reception backup plan. Let me know when you need it."

"I won't," Caleb assured him. "Like I keep telling you, I have everything in hand."

With that, Caleb walked into the farmhouse, picked up the last of the Black Forest cake from the counter, and strolled back outside. He was off the porch, cake container in hand, before Grant and Carter caught on. Wishing his brothers sweet dreams, after assuring them he was only looking after their health, he headed to his apartment.

He was confident he had the wedding reception and rehearsal in hand. Or he would as soon as he solved the permit problem. The very one he'd discovered when he checked his email after Eryn ditched him during the first movie. Turned out the rackhouse needed to meet fire codes and other building restrictions to be fully permitted as a multi-use venue space. Caleb needed that mutiuse venue space at the distillery to prove to his brother he had both vision and the ability to handle the marketing director position. He'd been working through possible solutions for the rackhouse when his deputy showed up and he chose to be distracted.

Now all he knew for sure was that if his deputy offered him one more handshake, he just might kiss her instead. But he feared there would be no walking away after that.

CHAPTER SEVENTEEN

LACEY LIFTED HER face toward the summer sun beaming down on her inside Lilian Sloan's stylish convertible. She let the wind tangle her hair and soaked in Aspen's enthusiastic back-seat radio sing-along. She even joined in for a verse or two, earning Aspen and Lilian's approval.

If only Caleb could see her now—having fun, finding her happy. Like he'd suggested she do last night.

Well, it was a new day. Aspen had ridden alone with Caleb beside her on his horse during their morning practice. Lacey had watched her daughter's confidence grow with every turn around the indoor arena. That feeling of contentment from the night before filled Lacey all over again.

"Everyone ready to shop until they drop?" Lilian parked her car in the public parking lot in downtown Belleridge and pressed a button on the dashboard to lift the convertible top back in place. "What does a cowgirl wear for the Junior Royal Rodeo Contest?"

"I gotta have a white shirt, jeans, and boots."

Aspen unbuckled her seat belt. "Caleb already got Mom and me hats."

"She also needs to dress up her jeans for the speech and group interview portion of the contest," Lacey explained.

Aspen wrinkled her nose at the mention of the speech.

"I scouted the boutiques and boot store online last night." Lilian dropped her key fob into her purse and climbed out. "Several should have Aspen's size."

Aspen scooted along the back seat. "Mom needs stuff too."

"I'm good." Lacey helped Aspen out of the two-door car and smiled at her daughter. "Today is about you."

"But you told Caleb you were gonna ride next time. No matter what he said." Aspen set her hands on her hips. "And you told Grandpa Swells you could use new boots. I heard you."

Lacey met Lilian on the sidewalk. "Steel-toe boots seem to be all I own." Along with a pair of old sandals and worn running shoes. Khaki uniforms and monotone colors rounded out her closet. Nothing overly fun there.

"I understand." Lilian pointed at her feet and wiggled her toes inside her strappy sandals. "I've been discovering the joy of a flirty sundress and sassy sandals now that I've traded in the scrubs and white coat."

"I've been in neutrals so long I can't remember what my style is," Lacey admitted.

"I suggest a little of everything," Lilian said. "Then you put on whatever fits your mood and makes you feel your best."

Feel my best. She wanted that. More, she wanted her mood to stay right where it was now. She linked one arm around Lilian's and the other around her daughter's. "Ladies, it's time to let our inner cowgirls shine."

Aspen cheered, and the shopping spree was on.

Successfully finding all the required clothing and a few extra outfits was relatively easy, thankfully, and eventually, they made their way to the final store of the afternoon, Horseshoes and Boots. Just inside the entrance, Aspen promised to find Lacey the prettiest boots and sprinted down an aisle to begin her quest.

Lacey watched Lilian act demurely again when another local stopped to greet her and mentioned that she had seen Lilian with the sheriff the other night. It had happened in practically every store. Someone commenting on what a charming couple Lilian and the sheriff made. Or how nice it was to see the sheriff out with Lilian. And Lilian, for her part, was gracious if slightly flustered. But Lilian Sloan didn't strike Lacey as a woman who flustered easily.

"I could use your advice on boots," Lacey said and earned a grateful glance from Lilian, who wished the woman a good day and walked beside Lacey down the wide aisle. The shelves were filled with boots from top to bottom.

"Wells tells me that you and he are an item," Lacey said casually.

"We haven't labeled things between us." Lilian held up a pair of pink cowboy boots. "Too much?"

Lacey nodded yet refused to be diverted. "Does Wells know you aren't at the labeling stage?"

"We're taking it slow," Lilian hedged, then showed off a pair of vivid teal boots.

Lacey shook her head. "It's funny because just this morning, Wells told me you've been texting and doing that video call thing every day." Lacey picked up a plain brown boot. "Rather late into the night, in fact."

A blush colored Lilian's cheeks. She took the boot from Lacey and set it back on the shelf. "One would think he and I were teenagers all over again."

"I can tell you that he's really happy." Lacey stopped and met Lilian's gaze. "And Wells hasn't been happy for a long time. I think that happiness is thanks to you."

"I'm sure it's having you home again," Lilian countered, yet her small smile hinted that Lacey's words pleased her. "Now you and Wells are work-ing together."

"It's perhaps partly from my return," Lacey con-ceded. "But you've put a certain twinkle into his gaze."

Lilian touched her cheek and laughed. "I'm not sure I've been accused of that before."

"Does it bother you?" Lacey asked, searching Lilian's face. She could see why Dr. Sloan had captured her stepdad's attention. Lilian was not only attractive, she had poise and confidence too. Not to mention a warmth that Lacey herself seemed to be getting accustomed to.

"This is nothing I expected to find when I moved back," Lilian confessed.

"What did you come back for?" Lacey asked.

"I suspect the very same thing as you." Lilian dipped her head toward Aspen down at the end of the aisle. "Family called me home. It was past time to make amends."

Lacey nodded. She knew all about making amends. She accepted two boot boxes from Aspen with instructions to try them on. She waited until Aspen was out of earshot before asking, "How is that going? You being home and making amends."

"There have been speed bumps," Lilian said. "That's to be expected. My sons aren't the boys I walked away from."

"Aspen isn't that same little girl anymore either." Lacey watched her daughter run her fingertips over one pair of sample boots after another. "I'm worried I'm giving in too much. Giving her everything she wants to make those amends. Worried it's too easy. Worried I'm getting it wrong, that I'm going to mess it up all over again."

Lilian chuckled. "I can guarantee you'll mess it up again."

"That's not very reassuring." Lacey hugged the boot boxes.

"I prefer to deal in facts." Lilian tugged a boot

box from the shelf and placed it on top of Lacey's. "None of us are perfect. At best, we get perfect moments that add up to something special."

Lacey had spent perfect moments with Caleb and Aspen recently. In the arena together. In the truck, laughing and teasing. Then alone at the lake with Caleb. She sat down on a chair. "What if I can't trust in those moments?"

"Then I'd say we have even more in common than I first thought." Lilian dropped into the chair beside Lacey and kicked off her sandals. She leaned her shoulder against Lacey's and said, "Perhaps we can figure it out together."

"I'd like that," Lacey said and picked up the first boot box from Aspen.

Lacey missed her mom. It had been more than a minute since she had opened up to anyone. Now she had shared with not one but two Sloans in a matter of days. Still, she appreciated Lilian for her candor and support. Same as she appreciated Caleb for his friendship.

And that was what she wanted—his friendship. Despite feeling like those handshakes she'd shared with him recently had been somehow "less than." They had left her wanting more. Like a kiss. Unrushed and under the stars. *Foolish thought, that.*

Lacey lifted the lid on the box and quickly swallowed her laughter. "But first we need to figure out how to tell my daughter that sparkles and rhinestones are not quite the style upgrade I had in mind."

"It glitters brighter than a disco ball." Lilian lifted

one of the red rhinestone high-heeled boots from the box. "*You* may want less sparkle, but I do believe I just might need more. May I?"

Lacey smiled and handed the box to Lilian. "Aspen will be thrilled."

As it turned out, Lacey kept to a traditional cowboy boot but chose a rich indigo color. The intricate stitching covering the deep blue suede shaft that reached mid-calf added extra flair according to the salesperson. And Aspen and Lilian convinced her the denim color would go with her new dresses.

As for Lilian and Aspen, they both opted for more flare in their step. Lilian kept her pearl bedecked and rose gold metallic trimmed boots in the box. Aspen wore her new boots right out of the store. After she excitedly declared the glittery gold starbursts on the boot shafts were good luck and the deep pink on the stitching her favorite color ever.

Outside on the sidewalk, Lilian checked the time on her phone. "We can do one more stop before we have to meet Wells at the All-Day Corner Diner for an early dinner."

"I don't think my hands can carry any more shopping bags." Aspen kept her arms down at her sides.

"We're done shopping," Lilian announced and started down the sidewalk. "It's time for some pampering. I can't think of a better way to celebrate our success than manicures and pedicures."

Lacey checked her fingernails. "I can't remember the last time I put nail polish on."

"Put clear on if you'd prefer." Lilian held open the

CARI LYNN WEBB 223

door to the nail salon. "But this is my treat for letting me tag along today."

"Mama-Beth goes to a place like this." Aspen walked inside, her eyes wide. "Mama-Beth says it puts a spring back in her toes."

"We could all use more spring in our step." Lilian checked in with the receptionist who led Aspen and Lilian to the nail booth together.

Lacey followed a friendly nail technician to the only vacant spot in the row of pedicure chairs. Within minutes, Lacey's feet were soaking in the warm whirlpool bath and her entire body was relaxing. She was starting to see the appeal.

Lacey was about to doze off when the doors to the salon opened and a pair of lively and familiar retirees swept in. The Baker sisters exchanged hugs with the staff and complimented the customers on their fashionable looks.

Gayle Baker caught sight of Lacey and bustled over. "Nice to see you sprucing yourself up, Deputy."

"We have the perfect event to supercharge your social life." Breezy handed Lacey a colorful flyer. "Mark your calendar, dear, for this Wednesday. We've already tapped several cowboys for you."

"Simple meet and greets." Gayle's eyebrow lifted over her glasses, revealing her light purple eye shadow. "Nothing formal. Bring your new dog, and everything will feel even more natural."

Lacey glanced at the flyer for the Last Dog Day of Summer. An annual event for dogs to show off their agility and style, make new four-legged friends, and win prizes. In the corner, she noted that the special emcee was none other than Caleb Sloan.

The woman beside Lacey lifted the flyer Breezy gave her and whispered, "They remind me of my own grandmother." The flyer flickered as the woman peeked around it to track the Baker sisters in action. "I wonder if they are in cahoots with my grandmother."

Lacey laughed. The Baker sisters did a circuit around the haircutting stations, passing out flyers like free candy before sashaying back to Lacey's chair.

Gayle tapped a metallic yellow fingernail against her lips and grinned. "I do like your color choice for nail polish, dear." The woman beside Lacey chuckled and wiggled her fingers polished with a similar sunflower yellow. Gayle continued, "I'm quite sure there will be a cowboy at the dog festival to catch your fancy too."

"Do you have a dog, dear?" Breezy plucked at her short, bold white hair.

"It's not a requirement." Gayle rocked back and forth in her rubber clogs. "You could simply tell 'em you're just shopping."

"For a cowboy and a canine companion." Breezy nudged Gayle and burst into laughter. "Best kind of two-for-one around if you ask me."

Lacey laughed too. She couldn't help it.

The woman beside Lacey chuckled and said, "I do have a dog that I was planning on bringing."

"Then you'll be there." Gayle beamed and squeezed in between the two chairs. "What's your name, dear?"

The woman shook the Baker sisters' hands and said, "I'm Georgia Moure."

Lacey lowered the flyer and shifted to take in the woman beside her. "Georgia Moure from Three Springs High School, home of the Prairie Dogs?"

The woman tipped her head and studied Lacey. "Oh my. Lacey Nash." Georgia gasped, then laughed. "I can't believe we've been sitting here for this long and didn't recognize each other."

"It's all that foil in Georgia's hair." Breezy peered at Georgia and shook her head. "Can't even tell what color her hair really is."

"Still, we should've recognized each other," Lacey said. "We spent our junior and senior years working together at Double Dutch Donut Shop, glazing and topping dozens and dozens of donuts."

"I haven't eaten a donut since high school." Georgia chuckled. "I think my clothes and my hair just stopped smelling like burnt donuts last year."

"I thought the same." Lacey laughed. "What have you been doing?"

Lacey and Georgia spent the next hour getting caught up. Georgia was a local general contractor with a list of adventures under her belt longer than Caleb's. She dabbled in breakaway roping when time allowed. And from the hilarious stories she shared, she didn't take herself too seriously.

The more they talked, the more Lacey realized Georgia was Caleb's ideal cowgirl. Georgia could help him with the building permitting issues he'd told Lacey about earlier. Even more, Georgia practically *was* Caleb, from their shared nature to their carefree outlook to their mutual love of the rodeo. Georgia was *the* cowgirl to his cowboy.

Excited, Lacey pulled out her phone and texted Caleb to see if he was still in town. He'd mentioned needing to meet with the caterer and run a few errands for his grandfather's event.

His reply came quickly. He was around the corner, just finishing with the caterer. Luck was on her side.

Lacey paid, checked on Aspen and Lilian who were still drying their toenails, and stepped outside to meet Caleb to give him her news.

When he rounded the corner and caught sight of her, that slow half grin lifting into his cheek— the one she thought of as for her only—she wanted nothing more than to launch herself into his arms. And claim him as her cowboy. Lacey blanched.

Her cowboy kept coming toward her. His gaze fixed on her.

Her heart raced. *He's mine.* No, that was wrong. All wrong.

He closed the distance. Almost in launching range. Two quick steps and one leap. He would catch her. She knew it. But catching a cowboy had never been her goal.

He finally reached her.

Lacey tempered herself, tucked her arms at her sides, and kept a friendly space between them. "I have good news. I found a solution to your permit issues for the rackhouse reception space and located your perfect cowgirl." *It's not me.* Her heart pounded. *But we already knew that.*

"Wow." He crossed his arms over his chest. "That's quite the productive day."

"It was," she said.

Something like disappointment flashed in his gaze.

Lacey shut down her imagination and adjusted those blinders back over her heart. Then rolled on, "Anyway, I ran into a friend from high school. Georgia Moure is a contractor with experience at getting town hall officials to permit old buildings."

"That is good news." Caleb nodded, his expression guarded.

The salon door opened, and Georgia stepped outside. Her blond hair floated around her shoulders before she propped a cowboy hat on her head, shadowing her pretty face.

No turning back now. Lacey smiled wider. "And here she is now." Lacey drew Georgia over for introductions.

"If you are free now, I'd be happy to discuss converting your rackhouse into an event venue and see if I can help." Georgia oozed authenticity and genuine kindness that only made her more attractive.

Lacey tried not to fidget and fix her own hair.

Before Caleb could respond, Lilian and Aspen were there. Aspen rushed to hug Caleb and show off her nails.

Lilian flashed her phone. "Wells just texted that our table is ready at the diner."

"Perfect timing," Lacey said, making sure her smile was perfect. Her words perfect. Because it was all so very perfect. Caleb and his perfect cowgirl. Just like she'd imagined. "We'll just be going and leave you two to get to know each other."

Caleb held Lacey's gaze for a beat, rubbed his hand over his cheek, then he grinned at Georgia. "I happen to have some time now. The Four Fiddlers shouldn't be too loud this early."

"Great." Georgia hugged Lacey with a promise to see her at the Dog Day event on Wednesday.

And like that, the perfect cowboy pair walked away.

Lacey tried to stay upbeat. "Ladies, I am starving, and I'm suddenly in the mood for a triple chocolate fudge brownie milkshake."

Aspen glanced over her shoulder. Her frown puckered her eyebrows. "Why didn't you invite Caleb to come with us? He likes milkshakes. He told me so."

"Caleb has work he needs to do." Lacey took a step in the direction of the diner, hoping the others would do the same. "And my friend Georgia is going to help him."

Aspen cast one more glance over her shoulder. "You shoulda worn your cowboy hat and boots, Mom."

"Why is that?" Lacey asked.

"'Cause cowboys and cowgirls go together," Aspen said.

Yes, they certainly did. Cowboys like Caleb belonged with perfect cowgirls like Georgia. And if her own heart hurt just a little at that thought, well, that was nothing for a onetime cowgirl like Lacey to simply dust off.

CHAPTER EIGHTEEN

CALEB'S MOOD WAS SOUR. It had started to turn three days ago when his deputy thrust his perfect cowgirl at him on the sidewalk in Belleridge and strolled away without a backward glance—or, it seemed, even a second thought. And his mood had been on a steady decline ever since.

The wine tasting event was proving more labor-intensive than he'd assumed. He still couldn't reach his twin, and the caterer, KC, needed a color theme to ensure he could get the linens on time. That meant a check of Vivian's notebook, but it was back at his place. One more thing for his rapidly expanding to-do-later list. Same as finalizing the menus for all events. But he wasn't about to reverse course now.

So here he was inside the rackhouse, waiting on Georgia Moure and her electrician to give him an update about the needed repairs. *Let it be good news.* Noting the pair was still in deep discussion on the other side of the vast space, he leaned against an empty bourbon barrel, pulled out his cell phone, and checked his text messages.

His mood flatlined.

The first text was a picture of Aspen, Lacey, his grandfather, and uncle sipping root beer floats at the ice cream parlor and looking more than joyful.

Caleb had had to cancel on Aspen the last two days. Fortunately, his uncle and grandpa had stepped in to help Lacey work with Aspen in the arena. But Caleb wanted to be the one to teach Aspen. To be there with Lacey. Spending time with the mother-daughter duo was the only place he'd wanted to be since Lacey left him on that sidewalk.

If ever there was a warning sign he was in way too deep, it was flashing at him now. He shoved his phone into his pocket, then joined Georgia and the electrician. He shook the electrician's hand, thanked him for his time, and watched him leave. He turned to Georgia. "Tell me this can be fixed."

"Your current electrical can be updated to satisfy the permitting requirements," Georgia said.

Caleb had liked the general contractor instantly from her straight talk to her quick action. He grinned. Finally, good news.

"But it's going to cost you." Georgia tore a paper off her clipboard, folded it, and handed it to him. "Maybe have a glass of bourbon in your hand when you read the estimate."

Caleb stuck the paper in his shirt pocket and walked outside with her to her truck. "My only concern is whether you can have the work completed and inspected in time for the wedding."

"If you've got the funds—" Georgia opened her truck door and turned back to him "—then your brother will have his reception in the rackhouse, not the tent."

"That's all I needed to know." Caleb shook her hand quickly and headed for his truck.

His phone buzzed again. More pictures filled the screen. This time it was Lacey on his Arabian Denny, riding bareback, her smile pure joy.

Caleb's mood dipped again. He knew full well that Lacey didn't need looking after, not even on a horse. But that didn't stop him from wanting to be with her all the same, watching out for his deputy. As if she was his to look out for. But that wasn't what Lacey wanted.

As for what he wanted… Those warning signals flared again. *Take the contractor out. Move on like you always do. It's what Lacey said to do.* He called out to Georgia. Her truck door was still open, and her boots rested on the truck frame.

Georgia glanced up from her phone and smiled.

She was pretty, he noticed. A true cowgirl from her scuffed cowboy boots to her well-worn hat. *Ask her out.* He rolled the words around in his mouth. Tested them out. "Anything else I should be worried about?" *Aside from my heart. Which I might be losing to my deputy.*

Georgia laughed. "Other than some minor repairs on the structure, I think we're going to be good."

Caleb nodded. If only he could claim the same for his heart. He hopped into his truck and called out, "See you tonight at Dog Days."

Georgia waved him off with a "see you there."

EMCEEING THE LAST DOG DAY event proved the distraction Caleb needed to keep his thoughts off his deputy. If only it had been more than a temporary reprieve. As it was, he'd gotten a brief hug from Aspen and a slobbery greeting from Butterscotch during a break between the agility competition and the contest for the dog face that only a mother could love. He'd caught glimpses of his deputy, still in her uniform, talking and mingling with the locals. It wasn't nearly enough.

Finally, dusk gave way to night, the last award was given out, and his emcee duties concluded. The dogs were let off leash to enjoy the temporarily fenced-in park, and the crowd lingered. Now was his chance to get to his deputy.

Caleb had Lacey in his sights but found himself waylaid by the fire chief and his family. Then by Kellie Pratt and her son, who wanted Caleb to sign his cast. Followed by friends he knew from working the rodeo.

With every delay, he watched Lacey slip farther away. And finally, Georgia stopped him. Her crew was ready to begin work at the rackhouse on Friday, which allowed for one week to finish the space. All Georgia needed was for Caleb to meet her and her crew there to let them inside Friday morning.

It was then that he saw a familiar dog bolt for the open gate on the far side of the park, followed quickly by a familiar red-haired woman in uniform. Caleb told Georgia to text him a time for Friday and took off after his deputy.

He found Lacey on her hands and knees in front of a section of tall bushes and trees.

"Need some help, Deputy?"

Lacey glanced over her shoulder. Relief passed across her face before she turned back to peer between the branches. "Butterscotch got spooked. I think it was all the chaos with the other dogs." Lacey set the dog leash beside her and sweetly called out Butterscotch's name.

The bushes didn't move.

Lacey frowned. "She's not budging. What should we do?"

"We sit with her." Caleb sat down and patted the grass beside him. "And we wait until Butterscotch is ready to come to us."

Lacey wiped her hands on her pants. "You don't have to wait with me."

"I must admit Butterscotch found a good spot." Caleb stretched his legs out. "The Last Dog Day is a bit more energetic than I recalled. I don't mind taking a moment." *With you.*

"You looked like you were in your element judging and emceeing, then leading the dog parade." She bumped her shoulder against his but didn't lean against him like he would've preferred. "You worked the crowd well and encouraged even more adoptions."

"I enjoyed it." He tipped his hat lower on his head. "In fact, I'm starting to appreciate these sorts of moments a lot." *But only the ones spent with you.* He cleared his throat. "Where is Aspen?"

"Wells took her to the diner. They wanted grilled cheese sandwiches." Lacey glanced at the bushes. "You could still catch up with them if you want to."

Oh no. His deputy wasn't chasing him off that easily. He was finally alone with her. He propped his arms behind him and leaned back. "I hear some rustling in the branches behind us. I can't leave now and risk startling Butterscotch again."

Lacey nodded silently, and her shoulders lowered. Whether she was relieved he was staying or that the dog might be coming out was up for debate.

He decided to press and find out. After all, if he opted to dive deep into the quicksand of his so-called *feels*, he sure as certain wasn't going to go it alone. Not that he had fully committed to that kind of dive quite yet. Still, it was time to find out if he'd possibly sidetracked her too. "You were right about Georgia."

Lacey yanked a weed from the grass. "That's good to hear."

Is it? She sounded far from pleased with his admission. "Georgia is quite possibly the perfect cowgirl."

There went another weed and a handful of grass. "That's why I introduced you." Her words were clipped as if stuck between her clenched teeth. "That's who I promised to find you, and I did."

But was it still only about the wager for her? Sure, the wager had given him an excuse to spend more time with Lacey. But now it wasn't the wager that kept him beside her. "Did you know Georgia just came back from a camping trip where the whole group took their horses? They rode into a remote area, camped, and went white water rafting." Caleb kept his words easy and light. "I've always wanted to do something like that."

She smashed the weed in her fingers. "I'm sure you two will have a lot of fun times together."

Except the fun I want to have is with you. The rustling started up again behind them. Caleb set his hand on Lacey's leg.

Her gaze jumped to his, but the night sky cast too many shadows across her face to read her usually expressive eyes. Still, he heard her soft inhale. Felt her relax beneath his steady touch. He whispered, "Don't move. Butterscotch is coming closer."

His words were no sooner out than a wet nose pressed against his skin, and a blond furry head burrowed underneath his arm.

Lacey grinned. Her shoulders shook. "Looks like someone else wants your attention."

Caleb straightened and showered Butterscotch with pats while Lacey clipped her leash back on. One problem solved. But what to do about his deputy?

"Butterscotch!" That cheerful shout came from Aspen.

Lacey let the dog run to Aspen. The young girl dropped to her knees to greet the dog with a whole-body hug. Lacey and Caleb walked to join Wells.

"Lacey, we need to get back on duty." Wells looked grim. "Two cars collided with an electric pole in

Llyne. Knocked out the power to most of the town. Multiple accidents have been reported."

In a blink, Lacey went from relaxed and easy-going to alert and ready. Until her gaze landed on her daughter, who was rolling in the grass with Butterscotch.

Caleb touched Lacey's arm. "I can take Aspen home and wait with her."

"You don't have to." But Lacey shook her head as if realizing she had no other options. Her father was headed to Llyne too. Her ex-husband and his wife were out of town.

"I want to," Caleb urged. *Please rely on me. Let me show you I can be who you need.* That put him precariously close to the edge of those so-called *feels*. He met her gaze and said softly, "You have to get to work, Deputy. There are people who need you."

She opened her arms as if she wanted to hug him, then dropped them just as quickly. "Text me if anything comes up."

"Aspen and I are good," he assured her. "We've got a speech to write and shows to binge-watch."

"The binge-watching will be easy." Worry crossed her face, and she added, "But I'm not so sure about that speech part. She's been resistant whenever I bring it up."

"I'll see what I can do." Caleb walked with Lacey over to Aspen and Butterscotch.

"Thanks for this," Lacey said. "You're a really good…"

Do not say friend. Caleb held her gaze, willing her to find another word. Any other word.

She rolled her lips together, sighed, and said, "Just...thanks for this." Then she spun around, hugged Aspen, and explained the situation.

Caleb smiled. He would take that. And hope the night ended on an even more positive note than a handshake. Because then he just might start to believe he wasn't about to take that deep dive all alone.

CHAPTER NINETEEN

CALEB WAS AT the front door, propping it open before Lacey's boots touched the porch. He was holding a steaming mug and looked rested. Lacey held on to the image, memorized it for the days when she might need it.

But her cowboy wasn't supposed to be a part of her daily life. Not like this. Not as the person she always leaned on. The one she always looked to. She slowed her steps.

"Evening, Deputy." He pressed the mug into her hands, guided her inside, and whispered, "Aspen is asleep on the couch. Can I make you something to eat?"

Lacey shook her head. It was too much. Too homey. Her daughter curled up under a blanket on the sofa. Her cowboy beside her to help her decompress. It was everything she could want. Everything she could pretend was hers. It was like coming home to her own family—the one she always envisioned.

But she'd messed all that up before. How could she trust she'd get it right now? Lacey wrapped her hands around the hot mug and took a deep sip of the honey-sweetened tea.

Aspen sat up and rubbed her eyes. "Mom? Caleb?"

"I'm here." Lacey set her mug on the coffee table and sat on the edge of the couch. "I'm home. How about we get you to bed?"

Aspen yawned, wrapped the blanket around her shoulders, and stood up. She shuffled over to Caleb and hugged him tight. Her whispered words were too hushed for Lacey to hear. She watched Caleb's grin, heard his "you got it," then watched the pair share a pinky promise.

Once more she felt that pull inside her. The one that wanted to step into his arms and share a group hug with the pair.

Suddenly Aspen pulled away, handed Caleb the blanket, and hurried back to the family room. She slipped on a pair of purple-tinted clear-framed eyeglasses that Lacey hadn't seen before and snatched up a different pair from the coffee table. Her words were sleepy. "Don't forget these, Caleb. Your eyes need them."

"Thanks." Caleb slipped the black frames into his front shirt pocket and wound the blanket back around Aspen.

It wasn't the eyeglasses on her daughter's face that set Lacey back.

Her daughter had fallen for Caleb. She was certain of it now.

Lacey had been so concerned about protecting

her own heart, she hadn't been paying attention to Aspen's. She had to pull back for both their sakes.

"Come on, Mom," Aspen said through her yawn. "You gotta tuck me in."

Lacey blinked and followed her daughter to her bedroom. With her eyeglasses tucked into a case in the nightstand drawer, Aspen burrowed underneath the blankets and cuddled Dash, her favorite horse stuffed animal. Lacey gave her daughter one more kiss on the forehead, then slipped out.

She found Caleb in the kitchen, leaning against the counter. "All good?"

"She was asleep before I got out of her room." Lacey retrieved her tea and carried it into the kitchen. "How did you know? About Aspen's eyeglasses. I didn't."

"I had a hunch after she wouldn't look over the contest rules with me." He shrugged one shoulder. "I never liked wearing my glasses when I got them in high school. I did all my reading in my room where no one saw me wearing them."

"I should've known." About her daughter's glasses. About her daughter getting attached. Lacey rubbed her hand over the small scar on her forehead. Suddenly exhausted.

"Jeffrey probably thought Aspen told you," Caleb said. "And Aspen probably figured you knew."

"I should've guessed about the glasses." Seen the bond her daughter was forming with him. Lacey sighed. "Or noticed her case. Something." Anything that would've warned her to step in before it was too late.

"You know now." Caleb lifted the kettle from the stove and refilled her mug. "And it's not a big deal. You would've found out eventually."

He was right, and yet Lacey struggled to let it go. But that was the problem, wasn't it? She was struggling to let her cowboy go. But this was Caleb Sloan. Her all-play, no-commitment cowboy. Losing her heart to him would be a misstep she might not recover from.

Panic sent her pulse into a fast beat. Her words rushed out, bumping into each other. "You should go. I've kept you long enough. Asked too much of you already."

He set the kettle on the stove and turned to look at her. "You haven't asked anything of me yet. I offered to help."

"Still, it's late." *And you look like someone I could lean on right now. For just a minute until I get my feet back under me.* He would hold her too. She knew that deep inside her. Also knew it might be impossible to remember that it was only temporary. But she was responsible for two hearts now.

He closed the distance between them, reached up, and tucked her hair back behind her ear. His fingers barely skimmed the small bandage on her forehead. His words were gentle, his tender gaze almost her undoing. "You're right. You need to get some sleep. I can let myself out."

Or you could let me hold you. We could hold

each other. But what would happen when he let her go and took her heart with him? And he would. Caleb Sloan had always claimed he was too restless to stay put long, while Lacey meant to put down roots and stick around for good. She crossed her arms over her chest. "What about you? Don't cowboys sleep?"

"Not this one." He pulled out his truck keys and grinned. "I've still got some run left in me before I call it a night."

But her cowboy had slowed down with her. Never seemed to mind either. Lacey shut down that thought. That was only her heart fooling her into believing she could change a cowboy. She picked up her tea rather than reach for him. "Night, Caleb."

He touched the brim of his hat. "Tell me you're still coming to the dandelion wine tasting event on Saturday. Grandpa Sam and Uncle Roy will be upset if you cancel."

"I'll be there," she said. "Early too. I promised Sam and Roy I'd keep an eye on you."

That drew his full smile. "Is that so?"

"Apparently they are concerned about your decorating aesthetic," she replied dryly. "It's an exclusive event, you know. They want it to feel special."

"I won't let them down," he promised and headed for the door. "Hey, Deputy, don't forget to lock up behind me." With that, he was gone.

Lacey turned the dead bolt on the door, switched off the lights, and headed to her bedroom. A quick check on Aspen, then she showered, climbed into bed, and finally secured her heart.

After all, if she gave her heart away again, she meant to do it for longer than a whim. Something more like a lifetime. And that just might be a moment too long for her cowboy.

CHAPTER TWENTY

IT WAS TIME to set his deputy straight.

It had been three days since the Last Dog Day event and their late-night rendezvous in her kitchen. Lacey hadn't ended that night with a handshake. For that, Caleb was grateful. But he had been dismissed all the same. When all he had really wanted was to be there for her. For whatever she needed.

Worse, that was the last time Caleb had been alone with his deputy. They had crossed paths at Aspen's practices. But if Lacey wasn't leaving for work, Caleb was late for a meeting. Their schedules never quite overlapped for more than a few quick conversations in passing.

He would've settled for a passing-by kiss. If it had meant they would've made time for each other soon. But that implied they were something more than friends. Something more like partners. There were those heart-tugging feelings winding through him again. Making him reconsider the appeal of having something more than a friendship with Lacey.

But Lacey had called in Caleb's mother, not him,

for an assist picking up Aspen from day camp when her shift ran long.

Caleb didn't begrudge the friendship between Lacey and his mother. In truth, he appreciated that Lilian Sloan was finally showing up for her family and friends. Still, Caleb wanted Lacey to call him. Lean on him. Let him show up for her like a partner would.

Even more, Caleb was bone-tired of his deputy asking him if he had been out with Georgia. Tired of her filling him in on another one of Georgia's thrilling trips. As if Caleb couldn't get enough of Georgia.

The truth was Caleb wasn't interested in talking about his contractor. He wanted to talk about his deputy and his feelings—the ones he was holding Lacey solely responsible for. The ones that had him twisted up tighter than the braids on a steer rope.

Oh yes, it was past time to set his deputy straight. Tonight, in fact.

Caleb just needed to find the perfect moment. When it was just him, her, and no interference.

However, that was not right now. Now, Caleb was guiding KC's catering van into the parking space behind the commercial greenhouses at Elsie and Ryan's farm. The dandelion wine tasting extravaganza was scheduled to begin in less than two hours.

Tonight was a dry run of sorts for Caleb to prove he was responsible and capable of managing projects. The rehearsal dinner and wedding reception next weekend would be the showstopper. And proof that Caleb could add value beyond tour guide while also bringing in an additional revenue stream to Misty Grove Distillery.

After ensuring KC was situated in the greenhouse reserved for food service and dandelion wine sampling, Caleb passed through the connecting hallway into the greenhouse dubbed the dance hall.

His deputy was on a ladder, adjusting long vines of live ivy around a tall trellis in the corner where the DJ would set up. She smiled down at him. "I like those tall vases with the floating gold pearls and candles inside. The ones you put on the tables in the dining area. Very elegant."

"You don't have to sound so surprised." Caleb reached up to help her down. "The atmosphere can be elevated, even though it's only dandelion wine."

"You had a vision, didn't you?" She stepped off the ladder and studied him.

He had a vision about dancing with her under the glass ceiling of the greenhouse. The moon and stars shining through. "Again, you sound so amazed. I had an idea of what my grandpa and uncle would appreciate. I went with it."

"I like it." She set her hands on her hips and shifted her gaze around the space. "A lot."

I like you. It's those feelings. I don't typically deal in those much. But with you... Caleb cleared his throat. "Ready to go?"

"Where are we going?" She aimed her smile at him.

"Out to the dandelion pasture," he said. "I want

to pick fresh dandelions for the sampling tables."
And dig into those feelings.

"Did I hear you're heading out to the pasture?"
Grandpa Sam strolled across the cement floor. "Count
us in."

Another roadblock. Caleb wanted to count his
family out, so he would have his deputy alone.

"Lacey will be wantin' a tour of the barn." Uncle
Roy followed Sam. In his hand was what looked suspiciously like a steak French fry bundle. He stuck
a bite in his mouth and grinned. "As the winemak-
ers, we should be the ones to show Lacey around.
It's more personal that way."

"I don't want to take you away from anything
you're doing here," Lacey said.

"They've been snacking on the appetizers with
Chef KC," Caleb said under his breath.

Lacey coughed to cover her laugh.

"Of course we were tasting with Chef KC." Uncle
Roy wiped his hands on his plaid shirt. "That's
called good quality control."

Except his grandfather and uncle had refused to
let Caleb or anyone else in the family, for that matter, sample their dandelion wine. According to the
stubborn cowboys, that was part of the evening's
allure. No one could taint someone else's opinion if
everyone was sampling the wine at the same time.

"Besides, Caleb has got all this well in hand."
Something suspiciously close to surprise lifted his
grandfather's eyebrows. Grandpa Sam nodded,

more of that surprise in his murmur. "Very well, indeed."

Caleb frowned. Not his grandfather too. Did no one genuinely believe he could make tonight a success?

"There's a working waterwheel at the barn where we make our wine and a stream that divides Sloan land from Elsie's." Uncle Roy took Lacey's arm in his and walked her toward the door. "Ryan built a bridge to connect the Sloan property with this one. You can see it from the barn window."

"It's like our very own piece of paradise for our winemaking." Grandpa Sam came up to Lacey's other side. "Private and soon to be profitable."

Caleb wasn't letting his grandfather and uncle out of his sight. He hurried after the departing trio and called out, "There are no wine sales tonight. Only tastings."

"But once they've had their first sip of our elixir, they're certain to be back for more." Grandpa Sam chuckled and held the door open for them.

"Tonight starts the buzz," Uncle Roy declared. "It will only build from there like a frenzy. Everyone wants a frenzy."

No one wanted that. Caleb chuckled and immediately lost his irritation. The gang climbed into the four-seater UTV, Caleb in the driver's seat. He handed Lacey a basket he had set in the UTV bed earlier. "For the dandelions."

"We'll be sure to fill that right up," Grandpa Sam offered. "After the tour, of course."

Caleb took the fastest route out to the old barn that sat on the far corner of Sloan land. After visiting the barn and checking out the inner workings of the waterwheel, his grandfather and uncle showed Lacey around the rest of the property and took her to the bridge. The one where Ryan had proposed to Elsie after he built the bridge to join Sloan land with Elsie's family farm. Lacey was seemingly touched by the story and wanted to walk across the bridge herself.

The view of the stream and bridge was quite striking. But what captivated him most was his deputy.

As she stood in the center of the bridge, the afternoon sun highlighted her radiant smile and the stunning shades of red in her hair. His grandfather handed her a dandelion stem, its head a white puffball. They exchanged a few words. Her smile grew, and her laughter floated through the breeze. Then she closed her eyes and blew, scattering the dandelion fluff every which way.

He guessed she'd made a wish. Would've liked to have known what it was…to see if he could grant it. Maybe then his deputy would discover he had more to offer than wagers and good times.

Or he could simply tell her. Set her straight, as it were.

Caleb grabbed the basket and headed to the dandelion fields. The sooner the task was finished, the quicker he could get his deputy alone for that straight talk.

Later, back at the greenhouses, Lacey and Caleb arranged the last of Caleb's dandelions at each of the tasting tables and stepped back. Caleb turned a slow circle and nodded. "I think we're done decorating."

Lacey checked the time on her watch. "And sooner than we thought. I have plenty of time to shower, change, and check in with Wells and Aspen."

This is it. Caleb rubbed his hands together. "Since we are early, do you want to take a walk with me? Elsie and Ryan worked all summer to finish the garden maze. There's a fountain in the middle I think you'd like."

"You had me at garden maze. I've always wanted to walk through one." She grinned and motioned toward the door. "Let's go. I can't wait."

Their pace was unrushed through the maze. Partly because Lacey stopped to smell the roses and every other flowering plant along the way, declaring each one her favorite scent until she reached the next. Caleb spent the time willing his heartbeat to slow and the right words to come.

But the deeper they walked into the maze, the more tangled his tongue felt. He finally gave in and started joining Lacey, smelling one flower after the next right alongside her.

With a cornucopia of scents swirling in his head and the right words no clearer than when they'd entered, Caleb led Lacey into the center of the maze. There, water spilled over multiple tiers of a tall vintage fountain and real pink and red rose petals floated in the wide circular basin.

Lacey gasped. "This is more stunning than I imagined." She hurried over to the fountain. "It's like our own secret garden."

Caleb followed her. Felt the sweat bead on the back of his neck. "Lace, there's something I wanted to tell you."

Lacey set her finger on a pink rose petal and glided the flower over the water. The smile she aimed at him was open and gentle.

Were his palms sweaty now too? Caleb smoothed his hands over his jeans. *Get it together.* This was Lacey. An old friend. A good friend at that. Nothing to be nervous about. He cleared his throat. "I wanted to tell you…"

"I know. You need to be hosting tonight's event and won't be able to leave. I won't ask to come back out here later." Lacey swirled her fingertips through the water. "Even though this place must be even more magical at night."

"I've never been good with these sorts of things," he muttered. Heck, he had never given his heart a voice before. He had always preferred action to explanations. And fearing he was blundering this beyond repair, Caleb leaned into what he always did. Jump in first and explain later. With more conviction, he said, "But this should sum things up."

He took Lacey's hand, twirled her away from the fountain, and straight into his embrace.

Her hands landed on his shoulders. Her breath rushed out, along with a startled, "Caleb."

He wanted her breathless. Wanted her to understand what he couldn't seem to put into words. He framed her face, tipped her head up. "There are things I need to say."

Her wide gaze searched his face. "You have my attention."

Her brown eyes were enchanting. His words scattered like that dandelion fluff she'd blown into the wind earlier. But the time for wishing had passed. Finally, he managed to say, "I can't take another handshake, Lacey."

She blinked. One achingly slow sweep of her eyelashes against her cheeks.

And he was transfixed all over again. He could get lost in her. Willingly. Gladly. Every day if she let him. "And I can't take one more night thinking about what it would be like to kiss you."

"Kiss me..." One more sweep of those eyelashes. A catch of her breath. A quiver of her mouth. Her words were more a puff of air than substance. "You want to kiss me."

Her pulse raced under his fingertips. His kept pace. "More than you could possibly know."

"But..."

"There's only one but that matters." Suddenly, he was second-guessing not making that wish. *Please, tell me I'm not wrong. That you feel this too.* "If you haven't thought about kissing me, then tell me now." *Or don't say anything. Just turn around. Walk away.*

254   A PROPOSAL FOR HER COWBOY

Her eyes flared. Her breath hitched.

"Tell me, Lace," he said without pulling her closer like he wanted to. "Tell me, and we walk away now."

Her teeth nipped into her bottom lip. "What if it's a bad idea?"

"I'm quite sure it is." He smoothed his thumbs over her cheeks. "But I'm tired of running from this."

"One kiss." Her arms curved up and around his neck. Her gaze held his, bold. Direct. Fearless. "Right here. Right now."

He didn't move. Didn't speak. Knowing she was setting the parameters as if this was one of their dares. But it was so much more than a game.

"If it doesn't sit right for one of us, no hard feelings." She closed the distance between them. "We leave as friends."

There was that word again. But she was in his arms. Her fingers tangled in his hair. He leaned in, then paused when their breath collided. "Fine. Friends."

His mouth brushed hers. Just the briefest catch of their lips. More of a tease. A skim. Nothing lasting. Everything they could walk away from. Dismiss, even. Yet there was nothing friendly about the sensation spreading through him. It was more of a jolt. A permanent imprint.

His eyes snapped open. Met hers, which were large pools of wonder fixed on him. He heard her inhale. She felt it too. That rush of awareness. Still, he held back. Gave her time to retreat. To push him away. Claim she felt nothing.

She shifted, her hand suddenly cradled his cheek. Her thumb smoothed over his bottom lip. Her gaze followed as if entranced. Oh, there would be another kiss. It was building between them. Pushing their pulses past rapid.

There would be no dismissing this kiss. No walking away and forgetting about it. It would be perfect and haunting. Friendship shattering. He should release her. Step back. His curiosity was satisfied. That was what had started this. But there was still so much left unsaid.

He gathered her close.

And she pressed more fully against him. Tightened her embrace as if anchoring them inside that garden maze in that moment with its rose-petal-strewn fountain. "Caleb Sloan, we made a deal." Her thumb paused mid-caress on his bottom lip. Her gaze lifted to his. "For a kiss."

One side of his mouth lifted. "I've never been one to back away."

"Neither have I." Her smile flashed bright.

They moved at the same time. Their lips only just connected, and shouts shattered the silence.

The first one was for Lacey. That halted them in place.

The second one was for Caleb. That forced them apart.

Another round of shouts. They spun away from each other. The thump of footsteps approached. And the moment was gone before it ever really started. Suddenly, what had been building was now nothing more than a could-have-been.

"There you guys are." Ryan jogged toward the fountain, waving a cell phone. "Lacey. There's an emergency."

"That's my phone." Lacey lunged toward Ryan. His brother tossed her phone to her, and Lacey snatched it midair.

"It's Aspen," Ryan finished and came to a stop. Worry splashed across his face. "Wells is taking Aspen to the ER right now."

Lacey swayed.

Caleb wrapped his arm around her waist, held her steady. "What happened?"

"Lacey's phone was ringing," Ryan said, his words rushed. "You left it in the greenhouse. It wouldn't stop. Elsie answered it finally. Aspen was stung by several bees on her walk with Butterscotch."

They were suddenly on the move, weaving swiftly through the maze. Ryan was on one side of Lacey, Caleb on the other. Confusion covered her words. "I don't understand. She's never been stung before?"

"She's had a reaction this time," Ryan said.

Lacey gasped.

Caleb picked up the pace and dug in his pocket for his truck key. "Ryan."

"Go. I got this," Ryan replied.

That was all that needed to be said. What had always been said between the Sloan brothers whenever one of them needed backup. His brothers would rally and take care of the evening. So Caleb could take care of Lacey and Aspen.

They were out of the maze and across the driveway in minutes. He helped a stunned Lacey into the passenger seat of his truck and shut the door. Giving a quick nod to his brother when Ryan told him to check in, Caleb climbed into the driver's seat and headed for Belleridge Regional Hospital.

He reached over and covered Lacey's clasped hands, already too cold to the touch.

She adjusted her hold, as if seeking his warmth, and looked at him. Her expression was bleak. Her face pale. Her eyes filled with alarm. "Caleb. Please hurry."

CHAPTER TWENTY-ONE

SEVERAL HOURS AFTER her frantic arrival at Belleridge Regional Hospital's emergency room, Lacey was curled around her daughter in a bed on the third-floor children's unit. She watched the slow drip of the IV attached to Aspen's arm and listened to her daughter's steady breaths.

There was nothing slow about the if-only's surging through Lacey. If only she'd called home sooner. If only she'd been at the ranch. If only she hadn't been indulging in a moment—a selfish one at that. If only she'd stayed focused on her daughter and not gotten sidetracked by wagers, crooked grins, and a no-good-for-her-heart cowboy.

The door opened, and Lacey's stepdad eased inside. He clutched a paper to-go coffee cup and looked as worn-out as Lacey felt. He settled into the chair beside the bed and took hold of Aspen's good hand. "How's our patient?"

Aspen's cheek was swollen from a beesting, as were her left palm and forearm from the other stings. Aspen whispered, her voice hoarse with worry. "What about Butterscotch, Grandpa?"

"Dr. Paige says Butterscotch will be perfectly fine soon. Same as you." Wells cleared his throat and tucked the blankets around Aspen. "Seems her face is swollen like yours, and she's getting medicine too."

"Dr. Paige will take good care of Butterscotch." Lacey smoothed the hair from Aspen's forehead even though her fingers still trembled with concern for her daughter. "Same as the doctors are doing for you here." *Same as I promise to do from here on out. You have my word.*

"I want to see her." Aspen frowned. "What if she's scared?"

"Dr. Paige took her home to her house," Lacey said, grateful for the kind veterinarian's quick response and continuous text updates. "Riley already made a bed for Butterscotch in her bedroom."

Aspen nodded, seemingly satisfied that her new friend would know how to comfort the dog.

"Lacey, you've got a cowboy pacing the shine off the tile floor out there in the waiting room," her stepdad said, his gaze compassionate. "Might be time to put his worries to rest."

"Caleb." Aspen shifted and looked at Lacey. "He's here?"

Lacey nodded.

"Can I see him?" Aspen whispered.

"Are you sure?" Lacey asked. *Because I'm not.* "You aren't too tired, are you?" *Maybe we could rest here awhile longer. You. Me. And none of those hard, uncomfortable truths.*

Aspen shook her head. "I gotta tell Caleb about the bees' nest. And how Butterscotch found it. And how I protected her." Aspen's brow wrinkled. "Well, how I tried to."

"You were very brave," Lacey assured her and rubbed the frown from her daughter's brow. "Those bees just got startled and a little scared." *I'm scared now. Scared I don't know how to get this right.*

"'Cause the bees weren't trying to be mean," Aspen finished and wiped her hand under her nose. "They didn't know we wouldn't hurt them. I gotta tell Caleb."

There were things Lacey had to tell Caleb. The time for stalling was over. Lacey pressed a kiss against Aspen's forehead and unfolded herself from the bed. "I'll go get him."

Lacey stepped into the hall and headed for the waiting area. She found her cowboy standing at the tall windows overlooking downtown Belleridge. His back was to her. He clutched a caramel-colored stuffed pony in one hand and ran his other hand over his face, then around to massage the back of his neck. Then he stilled.

She saw her reflection in the darkened window. Knew he saw it too. He turned slowly, his gaze took her in with one long sweep from her head to her toes and back, as if assuring himself she was there and that she was fine.

Lacey ran her hands over her T-shirt. Smoothing out the wrinkles was ridiculous. She was in the same clothes she'd worn to help set up the dandelion wine tasting event. The same clothes she'd worn when he held her near the fountain. That felt like a lifetime ago. Or perhaps it was another lifetime. She pressed her palm against her stomach. "Aspen wants to see you."

He nodded and lifted the stuffed animal, gripping it with both hands while he seemed to search for his words. All the while his gaze searched hers. Finally, he said, "If she needs to rest, I can come back in the morning."

But the morning would be too late. Lacey was letting him go. Tonight. "She knows you're here. She'll be upset if you don't see her before you leave." *I'll be upset too. Even though it's for the best. But that's for later.* She motioned to the hall. "Her room is this way."

Inside the room, Caleb shook hands with Wells as Lacey's stepdad vacated his chair and gestured for Caleb to sit. Wells stepped to Lacey's side and whispered, "I'm going to get a refill. I'll be back shortly."

Lacey nodded yet never took her gaze off her cowboy and her daughter.

Aspen's face lit up at Caleb's arrival. "Caleb."

"There's my favorite cowgirl." Caleb's words were quiet, sincere, and tinged with fondness.

For her daughter. For Lacey too. But in his arms earlier, there had been more than simple affection. Lacey had wanted to be swept up in those feelings. In him. But her feet were back on the ground. Her focus back on her daughter. Where it belonged. That first knot cinched inside her chest.

"Caleb, I swatted at all the bees," Aspen said, her words urgent. "To save Butterscotch. And then we ran real fast."

Caleb scooted the chair closer to the bed. "Courageous, just like your mom."

"You think I'm like my mom?" Wonder filled Aspen's words.

"I do," Caleb said softly.

Courageous. No, she wasn't that. That knot tightened, cutting into Lacey's breath.

Delight danced in Aspen's gaze, making her eyes sparkle in the dim room.

No. Couldn't her cowboy see? Her daughter's heart was on her sleeve. Too exposed. Too open. Too easy to break. Lacey had to protect Aspen. Caleb couldn't have her daughter's heart. Not when Lacey couldn't trust her cowboy with her own. She wanted to step between the pair. Chase her cowboy out of the room. Surely that wasn't wrong. Surely that was the responsible thing to do. After all, hearts were at stake. She widened her stance as if preparing to defend her position.

Aspen was hugging her new stuffed pony, ecstatic that Dash, her favorite horse stuffie at home, now had a partner. "Now they can always be together. And make each other super happy."

Partners…but for how long? And when it all fell just a little bit short, that was when partners drifted. And the loneliness sneaked in. And the hurt. Then

CARI LYNN WEBB 263

not even fondness and affection could hold it together. And it all crumbled. Lacey had picked up the
pieces once. Vowed not to have to do that ever again.

"That's what a good partner does." Confidence
tinged Caleb's words. "Makes sure his partner is
always happy."

"If they aren't happy, then you gotta squeeze them
real hard." Aspen hugged her pony tight against her
chest with her good arm and kissed its head. "And
you hang on until love makes them smile so much
they glow."

*Or you let them go. Certain you will smile again.
And so will they, one day.* Bargaining with pieces
of her heart, or worse, her cowboy's was not going
to make either one of them happy. And Lacey had
to have her whole heart for her daughter. How else
would she prove she loved her?

Caleb and Aspen discussed names for her new
pony. He drew out her muted giggles more than once.
Wells returned and gave Lacey a hot cup of tea.

At Aspen's first yawn, Caleb took her hand and
said, "You need to sleep now."

"But I'm not tired." Aspen ruined that declara-
tion with another yawn. "And we didn't decide on
a name yet."

"I bet you'll find the perfect name in your dreams."
Caleb rose and squeezed her fingers. "Night, Aspen.
Dream all things happy."

"Night, Caleb," Aspen said around another yawn.
"You dream happy too."

Caleb returned the chair to Wells. He set his hand

on her stepdad's shoulder. The two men spoke quietly before they shared another handshake. Then Lacey set her tea on the counter and stepped out into the hall with her cowboy.

"Do you need anything?" he asked, his words hushed.

I need you to tell me how to say goodbye to you. Then remind me that this is the smart thing to do. Because when she looked at him, she wanted only to step into his embrace and find her strength again. Discover those misplaced dreams. She shook her head. "You've done enough."

"Hardly," he said. "Anyone can buy a stuffed animal."

But not just anyone gets to my heart. At least they were not supposed to. And she could not risk losing it again, only to realize too late that she was not the one he truly wanted. That all this was just another whim. She couldn't be a whim. She thrust her arm between them. "Thanks for everything, Caleb."

His chin dropped to his chest. His eyes slammed closed. Not before she saw a flash of hurt there.

Lacey held herself still. A chill seeped into her.

He lifted his gaze to her. Hurt flared and was just as swiftly banked behind a stiff composure. "Lacey Nash, we are way past handshakes."

Lacey kept her arm in place.

"Listen well, Deputy." He stepped closer until her fingertips barely touched his plaid shirt. His gaze remained fixed on her, distant and guarded.

"If I take your hand now, I'm going to pull you into my arms." His words lowered below a hush. "And I'm going to kiss you to remind you who we are to each other."

Her breath hitched. Her throat went dry. Her heart raced. If she kissed him, she would be his, possibly forever. If that were possible. She curled her fingers into her cold palm and dropped her arm to her side.

"What is this, Lacey?" he asked.

"Goodbye," she blurted.

He crossed his arms over his chest. "Why?"

I'm not the one you belong with. You'll realize it soon enough. I'll ruin your fun. I have to be responsible. Always. She stressed, "So you can live the life you want, with someone like Georgia."

That distance between them fractured into a divide. "And what life is that exactly?"

"The carefree, no-commitment one you prefer. The one you've always claimed to prefer." The accusation was unfair perhaps, but she couldn't stop herself. "The very one you've been living since high school." The one that made them no good for each other. He'd resent her for reining him in. They'd become strangers. And no good could come from that.

Caleb ran his fingers over his closed mouth and started to shake his head.

"Don't deny it," she charged on. Her words were sharp inside her low tone. "In fact, tell me this. Tell me that you seriously intend to accept that full-time position at the distillery."

His lips parted. But only a thick silence settled between them.

She grimaced. "You can't tell me that. Because you can't accept that job."

"Why not?" His words were clipped.

"Because you can't commit to anything long-term," she said. "Tell me I'm wrong." *Please. I'm calling your bluff. Call mine.*

His lips pressed together.

Her short laugh was more anguished than triumphant. No use for it now. He always preferred straight talk, and he was getting it. "I can't have temporary, Caleb. Or a fling. Or take whatever this is while I wait for you to move on."

His eyes flared. He set his hands on his hips. "Is that what you think this is?"

"When has it ever been more than that with you?" she countered.

"Maybe it's more right now." His words and expression softened. "Maybe this is everything. Maybe I have no intention of moving on."

But she couldn't bet her heart—or Aspen's—on maybes. Not again. Lacey willed her tears to stand down. Still, she felt those cracks inside her heart.

"It doesn't really matter, does it?" His expression went back to stubborn and sour. "You've already decided for us both."

"I'm looking out for myself and my daughter," she said, her words sounding more like a pain-filled hiss. "That's my job as a mother."

"Right," he said. "You mean the job you think you're failing at."

She sucked in a breath.

"That's what you've convinced yourself anyway." He waved his arm between them. "That all the wrongs and mistakes in the past and the ones now are entirely your fault. Your doing." He shook his head slowly. "I'm surprised you can stand straight with all the blame you're shouldering."

"That's not fair," she charged.

"But I'm not wrong." He lifted one eyebrow. "If you're not perfect, then your love is somehow less than, isn't it?"

"Don't talk to me about love."

"Right." Impatience gave an edge to what would be his normally light tone. "Because what would a frivolous, reckless cowboy like me know about something as consequential and enduring as love?"

She was only saying what needed to be said. What they both already knew. Couldn't he see that? She whispered, "I can't be who you need."

"Funny." The corners of his mouth lifted. There was nothing easy or indifferent about his half grin. "I only ever wanted you to be you."

"This is me." She speared her arm at the closed hospital door. "I'm a mother. A deputy. I live to serve and protect. That's who I am."

"You really don't see yourself, do you?" he asked.

She thrust her fingers through her hair. "You want a happy-go-lucky cowgirl, Caleb. And that's not me anymore."

"I want the woman whose heart is bigger than this state." He stepped into her space. "I want the woman who embraces life with joy and passion and showers those she loves with the same. The one who is fearless."

I want a cowboy who will stick. She lifted her chin. "You've got the wrong person."

"Do I?" he countered.

"I have to get back to my daughter." Beside her daughter, she would surely be steady again. Not quite so numb. Surely in time this would all feel right and not so very wrong. "I'll make arrangements for Aspen to practice for the contest someplace else."

He nodded. "If that's what you think is best."

"That's exactly what I'm doing." She flattened her palm against her chest. "Making the best decision for myself and my daughter." *For our hearts.*

"Then it looks like you win, Deputy." He took a step back. "Congratulations."

The cowboy she knew faded away before her eyes. *Don't go. Tell me you can stay. Tell me I'm wrong.* Lacey curled her fingers into her palms. *Don't quit on me. On us.* The words clogged her throat. *Fight, cowboy. Don't flee.*

One more step back, and he added, "You're getting exactly what you want."

But she didn't feel like celebrating. She felt like crying. Hard and long. And soul deep. She reached blindly for the door behind her.

"Hey, Deputy," he called out, so much emptiness in his expression. "I lied earlier at the fountain."

Lacey willed the cold metal door handle to freeze out his next words. She clutched the metal harder and waited. Knew her cowboy's final words would buckle her knees. But her cowboy would not see her break. Not a crack. Not a single tear.

"It's not fine. Not even close," he said, "and if it's all the same to you, you can keep the friendship too."

Just like that, it was over.

She'd lost her cowboy, but she'd won. She'd been right all along. The fun stopped, and he had given her up. Certainly, the rush of satisfaction would fill her soon. Any minute now, really.

Instead, tears surged all at once. Unstoppable.

Lacey sagged against the door and slid to the ground. Easier to pick up those pieces of her heart there, when she finally got around to celebrating.

CHAPTER TWENTY-TWO

LILIAN SLOAN WAS a coward.

True, she was a skilled heart surgeon known for her compassion, patience, and good judgment. She took detail-oriented to extremes. And she possessed exceptional hand-eye coordination. It was the heart-mind connection—her own—where she faltered.

After all, if she was brave, she would not have spent the last few hours lingering inside the first-floor waiting area of Belleridge Regional Hospital.

If she was brave, she would not have lied.

But she was lingering. She had lied. And she sure as certain was a coward.

The elevator doors opened in the lobby, and her youngest son stepped off. Or rather, a version of her son. This one was a far cry from the fun-loving, never-takes-himself-or-life-too-seriously son she knew Caleb to be.

Now, he looked defeated and defiant. Never a good combination, that. Lilian had felt the very same after her divorce. And then she had gone on to blaze a path that burned bridges she was now trying diligently to repair. Lilian wound her way through the empty waiting room chairs and called out, "Caleb."

"Mom." He blinked as if she had flashed a penlight directly into his eyes. Then he rubbed his forehead and seemed to finally focus on her. His frown deepened. "Where were you, dressed like that?"

Lilian passed her hand over her crisp, cream-colored blazer, sweeping down to the waist of her matching tailored, pleated trousers. The formfitting power suit was a remnant of her city life. Her armor of sorts. "I was out with a colleague from the university. An adjunct professor at the medical college there."

Caleb eyed her and remained silent.

Tell the truth, Lilian. It was a date. Lilian touched her pearl earrings. The ones she hadn't worn since she moved back to Texas and discovered the appeal of more casual jewelry. She tipped her chin up and added, "I had my phone turned off at dinner." That was true. Guilt was a powerful motivator. She finished with, "I got here as soon as I could."

Caleb finally nodded, but the motion seemed automatic as if he'd stopped listening to her.

Lilian added *distracted* to her description of her son. "But enough about me. What happened?"

"Aspen was in the backyard at their ranch with Butterscotch and decided to pick flowers." Caleb tugged off his cowboy hat and scrubbed his hand through his hair. His gaze shifted to the elevators and caught. "Butterscotch was sniffing around and stuck her nose into a beehive in the ground. Aspen was stung swatting the bees away from the dog. And now we know she's highly allergic to bee-stings."

Lilian let Caleb fill her in despite already having those particular details thanks to the voicemail updates that Wells had left on her phone. The one Lilian had turned off during her dinner date.

Caleb exhaled, the sound long and weary. "Aspen is fine, she's recovering now. You can go up." He cast one more dark glance at the elevators. That defiance hardened across his face before he smashed his hat back on his head. "I'm sure Wells and Lacey would like to see you."

She was quite sure that was not true. Wells had told Lilian about his feelings for her. And Lilian had gone on a date with another man. Not exactly the most appropriate response to a good guy who wanted to love her and confessed he was willing to wait for her heart to catch up.

Lilian wrapped her arm around Caleb's and said, "Maybe this is for the best." That was her inner coward speaking up again. Lilian turned them toward the exit and gave in to it. "You look like you need someone to listen. And as it happens, I have two very capable ears." *Just don't ask me about love. I tend to get that wrong and hurt the ones I love the most.*

"I don't really have anything to say." Caleb walked beside her, his movements and words stiff.

"How about we keep each other company?" Outside, Lilian inhaled the night air and forced herself not to look back. Her son needed her. And the truth was, she needed him. "I'm not quite ready to call it a night and be alone."

He paused and considered her. "Mom. Are you okay?"

I'm a coward. But that was neither here nor there. Just a recently discovered character quirk. She squeezed his arm. "Like you, I'm fine."

A frown formed between his eyebrows. "As it turns out, I have two very capable ears that can listen too."

"But like you, I don't feel much like talking," she said, trying to reassure herself as much as Caleb. She certainly didn't want her son worrying about her. "I appreciate the offer though. And when I'm ready to talk, I know where to find you."

He nodded and tucked her closer to his side as if it was suddenly them against the world. Or perhaps simply them standing united against love. Whatever it was, she welcomed the support.

"You know…" She held on to the last syllable, her high heels clicking on the pavement. "I think I'm in the mood for a nightcap, if you're up for it?"

"I have just the place." Caleb unlocked his truck and helped her inside.

Ten minutes later, Lilian and her youngest son were tucked into a back booth at the All-Day Diner sharing an order of sweet potato fries and sipping on chocolate cookie milkshakes spiked with Irish cream and vanilla vodka. They talked about the last books they'd read and the latest movies they'd enjoyed—and by silent agreement avoided the uncomfortable stuff.

It was their first real mother-son time together. If only it hadn't taken her being a coward to finally experience it, she might have been truly grateful.

CHAPTER TWENTY-THREE

THE FOLLOWING AFTERNOON, Lacey was still searching for that feeling of satisfaction. That triumph that came from doing the right thing. All she kept running into was a gaping emptiness. And a rather unpleasant discontent.

Not that she would let that interfere with her determination to stay on her path. After all, no one ever claimed that doing the right thing was easy.

Take right now, for instance. Lacey parked in her ex-husband's driveway and glanced into the back seat. Willing her smile to look light and easy. "We're here, sweetie."

Aspen plucked at her hospital band around her wrist. "Why can't I stay with you?"

Because it wasn't the right thing. Lacey wanted to remove the beehives on the property to make it as safe as possible for her daughter first. She held on to her smile. "Your dad and Sarah-Beth came home early from their trip. They're worried about you. They want to see you."

"But what about Butterscotch?" Aspen insisted.

"She wants to see me. She likes to sleep with me. She'll be lonely."

Lacey was already lonely. She liked having Aspen at the ranch, sleeping in the next room where she could check on her daughter and the dog anytime she wanted. Where she could soak in her daughter's laughter and wrap herself in her spontaneous hugs. Lacey wanted to reverse out of the driveway and take her daughter back to her house.

Congratulations, you're getting exactly what you wanted. Her cowboy's words snapped through her.

Right. This was all for the best. Lacey grabbed her key fob and opened the car door. "I'll bring Butterscotch over to visit."

"Dad won't let a dog in the house," Aspen grumbled and climbed out of the back seat. "But Caleb lets Butterscotch sit on the couch with us to watch movies. And eat popcorn."

Caleb. That pang in Lacey's chest pulled against her smile, weighing it down. Lacey plucked the stuffed pony from the back seat. "Don't forget this."

Aspen shook her head and pushed the pony away. "Dreamer has gotta go home with you. She's gotta be with Dash. They're partners now."

"Right." Dreamer and Dash, the stuffed animal duo that would keep each other infinitely happy. Lacey clutched the stuffed pony against her stomach. "I will tuck them in tonight."

Aspen pressed a kiss on the stuffed pony's head. "I'll be home soon, Dreamer."

Home. One brief kiss with her cowboy, and Lacey

had almost believed she'd found that. But it was more of a dream. Lacey set the pony on her passenger seat and took Aspen's hand. "Let's get you inside so you can rest and enjoy lots of pampering from Mama-Beth and your dad."

The door opened before Lacey and Aspen reached the porch. Sarah-Beth wrapped them both in a gentle embrace. "I've been so worried."

Jeffrey stepped out onto the porch and kissed Aspen's forehead. "There's my girl."

Lacey released Aspen and tucked her suddenly empty hands at her sides. "I'm sorry you had to cut your vacation short."

"Vacations can be rescheduled. Family is more important." Jeffrey lifted his gaze from Aspen to Lacey, then straightened. Something like concern washed over his face. "Lacey, we need to talk."

"I know. Not now," Lacey said. "I didn't sleep well in the hospital chair." Those sharp pieces of her broken heart had kept her awake. And that emptiness kept trying to consume her. She shifted in her running shoes as if suddenly unsteady. But she'd done the right thing. This too would pass. "I've got to pick up Butterscotch now. And I'm working tomorrow."

"Don't forget to send pictures of Butterscotch." Aspen wrapped her good arm around Lacey's waist and squeezed her. "Remember to give her lots of treats and extra hugs."

Lacey held on to her daughter, stealing one more hug for herself. "I won't forget."

"And you'll bring her over to see me," Aspen ordered.

"Yes, I will," Lacey promised.

"What about my practice?" Aspen spun to face Lacey. "Caleb promised to work with me on trotting. I almost got it."

But Caleb never promised that he'd stick. *And we can't keep falling for him. It hurts now, but it will fade.*

Lacey squatted, putting her at eye level with Aspen and closer to firm ground. "The doctor wants you to rest today. We have to follow the doctor's orders, so we don't end up back at the hospital." Lacey brushed Aspen's hair off her face. "We'll talk about practice tomorrow."

Aspen's lips pulled together. "You won't forget?"

"No." Lacey held out her little finger. "I pinky swear."

Aspen grinned. "That's what Caleb and me do."

Used to do. Lacey blanched and bit back her words. She would have that talk with her daughter soon. When she could think about her cowboy without wanting to cry. "Why don't you grab a blanket and get comfy on the couch? I heard Mama-Beth has special treats and a new movie for you to watch."

Aspen hugged Lacey one more time and headed inside.

"Are you sure you don't want to come in, Lacey?" Sarah-Beth set a comforting hand on Lacey's shoulder. Concern and compassion crossed her face. "I've got hot water for tea."

Jeffrey set an arm around his wife's waist and considered Lacey. "And if you need something stronger, Lace, we've got that too."

"I really should go." Lacey tugged on the ends of her shorts. "The dog is waiting." And her empty house. And her broken heart. She really needed to put those pieces back together.

Sarah-Beth wrapped her in another warm, tight hug. "Well, I'm grateful you were with Aspen. I would've panicked like no one's business."

Lacey had panicked. She still was panicking.

"I've never been good in hospitals," Sarah-Beth confessed.

"I've promised to hold her hand," Jeffrey said, his smile affection filled. "And not leave her side."

Sarah-Beth touched her pregnant belly. "But I could really use some of your courage, Lacey."

Everyone really needed to stop referencing Lacey's courage. They were getting her all wrong. She was simply doing what she had to do.

"Now, you go and get some rest too." Sarah-Beth released her. "Everything will look better in the morning."

"Is that a promise?" Lacey asked. How she really needed that to be true.

UNFORTUNATELY, THINGS LOOKED BLURRY, not better, the following morning. Lacey had returned home to find more care packages and baskets from friends and neighbors. The overwhelming support brought her to tears. The same thing happened when she fell onto the couch, curled up in the blanket, and inhaled her cowboy's lingering cologne. She had cried through her shower and finally cried herself to sleep.

Now her eyes were bloodshot and puffy, and everything that had once seemed so clear was out of focus. Lacey kept her sunglasses in place and headed into the sheriff's department to begin her shift. Work had helped her heal in the past. She would bury herself in it now.

Gertie slowly rose from behind the reception desk, her shrewd gaze fixed on Lacey. She lowered her microphone over her mouth and said, "Attention all units. This is a ten-zero."

Lacey slowed as she passed the end of the reception desk. *Use caution.*

"Repeat. A ten-zero," Gertie stated. "For a ten-four-four-four."

Lacey frowned. "That last one's not even a valid code." Lacey knew that much. She had memorized Gertie's entire code handbook. That one did not exist.

Lacey's stepdad opened his office door and stepped into the lobby.

Gertie tipped her platinum head, that now had lavender streaks running through it, toward Lacey. "We got ourselves a ten-four-four-four, Sheriff."

Lacey exhaled and set her hands on her hips, frustrated. "That's not a legit code."

"It's part of the *special* code list." Gertie opened and closed cabinets underneath her desk as if searching for something. Most likely another codebook.

Lacey ran her hand over her face. She could not take another code list. Not this morning, when she was grumpy, sleep-deprived, and desperate to get her mind off her cowboy. She sighed. "I can take whatever the special call is." A distraction would be more than welcome.

Gertie shook her head. "Sorry, Deputy Nash, this one is above your pay grade."

"I can handle it," Lacey insisted. She was there to serve. To do her job.

"Deputy, code ten-four-four-four is the code for heartbreak," her stepdad said gently, too much compassion swirling in his warm gaze.

Lacey gaped at him.

Gertie closed the last cabinet and set a box of tissues on the counter in front of Lacey. "If you were handling it, you wouldn't be heartbroken."

Lacey slammed her lips together and lifted her gaze to the ceiling, then brought it back to the too-perceptive dispatcher. "Gertie, please tell me you didn't just announce to the entire department that I'm heartbroken."

"No, dear." Gertie's grin was sympathetic.

Lacey exhaled. That was a relief. She certainly didn't need everyone aware of her condition. And besides, she hadn't cried since she'd woken up. She was better now. Dare she say fine, even.

Gertie nudged the box closer to Lacey. "I just announced to the entire department that you were in the building, and they should use caution...considering your heartbreak."

Lacey wasn't sure if she should laugh, but she feared she might sound more hysterical than amused. And that might just dislodge those tears again. Instead, she tapped the tissue box back toward the dispatcher. "I don't need those." One more tap. "And you can cancel that ten-zero. And the ten-four-four-four. I'm fine."

Gertie shared a look with the sheriff.

"Perfectly fine." Lacey stretched her arms out. "I'm going to go in there and do my job. And do you know why?"

Gertie's eyebrows arched. Her stepdad held his silence.

"Because I'm fine." Lacey yanked open the door to the rest of the offices. "Now, when you have a real call, I'll take it. Because I'm fine."

Lacey let the door shut behind her. And if she wanted to tell herself she was fine until the words became an ongoing chant, well, that was her business.

After all, it was up to her to make sure her heart fell in line, and she was determined that would be sooner rather than later. Because she was *fine*.

CHAPTER TWENTY-FOUR

EVERYTHING IN CALEB'S life was back on track, exactly the way he liked it.

His deputy had been kind enough to show him that what he believed about his *so-called feelings* was true all along. *His feelings* were nothing more than a momentary distraction. And best ignored. For the past four days, Caleb had been doing just that. Quite remarkably too, if he did say so himself.

He welcomed back the old squeeze-the-fun-out-of-every-day Caleb with a flourish and much fanfare. He had worked side by side with Georgia and her construction crew every day to finish the renovation on the rackhouse in record time. He had provided breakfasts and lunches and ensured a constant stream of upbeat music and positive energy. The work was physically hard and more rewarding than he'd expected.

With respect to his evenings, well, those he spent behind the bar at The Feisty Owl, delighting customers with new drink recipes and bartending tricks. The laughter and the camaraderie fueled him and crowded out those pesky *feelings* just as he'd intended.

The few hours he gave to sleep, exhaustion kept his dreams dull and uninspiring. And when sleep eluded him, he crocheted. Was he well rested? Hardly. But that wasn't important.

He was back where he started. Where he had always been happy. On his own. And if he couldn't be happy, he could certainly be content. Nothing wrong with content. It was better than hurt.

At the moment, he was standing inside his brand-new office at Misty Grove Distillery, having just officially accepted the position of marketing director. His family surrounded him, their faces full of pride and joy on his behalf.

The dandelion wine tasting event had been a resounding success. Plus, Carter had gotten a private preview of the renovated rackhouse that morning. It was just one day before the wedding weekend would officially kick off with the Friday night rehearsal dinner at the Sloan farmhouse. Carter had shaken Caleb's hand and said simply, "Impressive. Really impressive, little brother."

Caleb had effectively proven his family wrong and completed his career pivot. He was by all accounts a success. It should feel sweeter. Better. He accepted another round of congratulatory hugs from his family.

Soon enough it was only Caleb and his three brothers. His twin, Josh, had left with his fiancée, Vivian, to pick up the thank-you gifts they'd ordered for the wedding party. Caleb pushed more wattage into his smile and said, "There's only one thing left to do now."

"What's that?" Ryan sat in the leather chair behind Caleb's new desk, his boots stacked on the large desk and his hands tucked behind his head.

Caleb sidestepped that dull ache in his chest. "I need to get a date for this weekend."

Grant dropped his hand on Caleb's shoulder and squeezed. Approval flashed across his face. "Finally going to call Lacey then."

"Lacey?" Caleb shook his head. He had given his deputy what she wanted. And he was nothing if not obliging. He rubbed the heel of his hand against his ribs. There was nothing to hurt over after all. "I'm going to ask Georgia."

Carter turned from the wide window overlooking the wheat fields that contributed to their successful bourbon mash recipe and frowned. "Georgia?"

"My contractor." Caleb kept his words as upbeat as his fixed-in-place grin. "The one I've been working with from sunrise until way past sunset to finish the rackhouse on time."

"We know who Georgia is." Ryan lowered his boots, propped his elbows on the desk, and steepled his hands under his bearded chin. Then he considered Caleb as if he was a disruptive nine-year-old in the principal's office. "We just don't understand why you want your contractor to be your date."

"I need to take someone." Caleb shrugged. "I refuse to sit at the singles' table all weekend."

"But—" Ryan started.

"But nothing." Caleb swiped his hand through the air. He had dared to open his heart to his deputy, to take a chance. And he had ended up right where he knew he would. Left behind and alone. He ignored those feelings threatening to rush forward and said, "Georgia and I had fun this week. She's fun to be around. She'll be a fun date." And that was all the old Caleb wanted. Fun, fun, fun. No strings attached. No worries. That was how he remained content. And content was the new goal.

"We get it. Georgia is obviously fun." Carter cast a hooded glance at Grant as if looking for an assist.

Grant jumped right in. "But Georgia is not Lacey."

No. Georgia was definitely not Lacey. No one was his deputy. And if Caleb chanced to linger too long on that thought an unfamiliar fear surfaced. The one that hinted no one would ever be Lacey and his heart would never be the same without her. He set his hands on his hips. "So what's your point?"

"That she's not Lacey," Ryan repeated the obvious, his words flat and insistent.

Caleb understood perfectly fine. He understood the brief kiss he and his deputy had shared would haunt him for the rest of his days. Things between him and Lacey had never really started. Never really finished. It was all just stuck. Right at the beginning, like a misplaced question mark. But he could not—would not—get anywhere focusing on unfinished business. Therefore, he would fold his hand and move on. "You guys misread the situation between Lacey and me." The fates knew he had too. But he was clear now. "I tried to tell you that we were only friends."

Ryan turned the wedding ring on his finger, his eyebrows pulled together. Grant opened and closed his mouth. Carter touched the front of his throat as if working the correct words free.

"Look, I appreciate the concern, even though it's unnecessary. I'm good. Really good." Caleb swept his arm around the room and grinned as wide as he could. Because full smiles were a sure sign that someone was good. "I have exactly what I want. It was always about this job. And look at my office. Who wouldn't want to come to work here every day?"

Carter's jaw clenched as if he crunched down hard on his reply.

Grant didn't hold back. "What about the wager between you and Lacey?"

"We both agreed we were caught up in nostalgia," he hedged. They hadn't actually talked about the wager. But Caleb had conceded, handing over the win to Lacey. At the rate he was going, he would have close to a dozen crocheted scarves to donate to Three Springs's Rodeo Reunion silent auction. Not that it mattered. He shook his head. "But we aren't kids anymore." And the adults they were no longer saw eye to eye.

Grant kept pressing. "But it was different with Lacey. And you know it."

No. It was not different with his deputy. Caleb

would not allow it to be different. Because if it was different, then that would give the whole situation more importance. And it could not be anything significant. Because then that ache in his chest—the one that hadn't let up with every single sunrise that passed—would be something more lasting. Something like a true heartbreak. But Caleb had vowed never to allow that to happen to him.

He clapped his hands together, snapped himself back into the moment. "You all need to leave now. I have to lock up, go find my contractor, and secure my wedding date."

Ryan stood slowly and approached Caleb. His other brothers stepped in behind Ryan as if offering him backup. Ryan seemed to be studying him. "You're sure you want to do that, little brother?"

"Absolutely." Caleb motioned to the door as if eager to find his contractor and start that date immediately. "It's going to be perfect. You'll see."

After all, the venue was perfect. His new position as marketing director and his new office were perfect. He was about to secure a perfect date for the most perfect wedding. And he had it on good authority from his very own deputy herself that his contractor was perfect for him.

And that was how a cowboy saved his heart. What could be more perfect than that?

CHAPTER TWENTY-FIVE

LACEY WALKED ACROSS her backyard to the porch and smiled at the familiar figure sitting in one of the two rocking chairs. Butterscotch took off running toward the new arrival. Lacey and her stepdad had shared dinner together the past five nights, ever since Aspen had been discharged from the hospital.

She was grateful for the company, though slightly concerned about Wells. Whenever she mentioned Lilian Sloan, her stepdad would give her a private smile and tell her that he was still waiting for his doc to figure things out. And then he would deftly change the subject. Same as Lacey deflected whenever the topic of Caleb came up.

Lacey dropped into the rocking chair beside her stepdad and grinned. "The beehive has been successfully relocated."

Thanks to one of Elsie's bee management contacts, Lacey's property was much safer for Aspen. Already, she was anticipating Aspen visiting. The house was too quiet. Fortunately, Lacey had seen Aspen every day.

Elsie and Ryan had insisted that Aspen's practices

continue at their stables. The generous couple had even brought Caleb's Paint, Biscuit, to their stables for Aspen to keep riding. She knew Caleb was behind the horse's relocation. She owed him a thank-you, and in time she hoped she could find her way to expressing her gratitude.

"Your mom and I couldn't keep you out of that orchard behind the stables," Wells mused and shifted a burlap bag from one hand to the other. Then he rubbed Butterscotch's head, resting on his leg. "You called that area your very own secret garden. But your mom worried about snakes and spiders and every sort of woodland creature."

"What did you do?" Lacey smiled and took a handful of roasted pecans when he held the burlap bag out to her—the one she recognized from the care package the Baker sisters had dropped off.

Her stepdad's eyes sparkled. His grin grew. "I taught you to ride horses."

Lacey stilled her rocking chair, and Butterscotch scooted over for attention. Lacey gaped at her stepdad. "Seriously?"

"It's true. Your mom thought if we were riding together, I could keep an eye on you." Wells frowned, yet the delight in his gaze gave him away. "That certainly backfired, didn't it?"

Lacey dropped a few pecans into her mouth, but her silent laughter shook her shoulders.

Butterscotch stretched out between their chairs.

"You quickly became very good," Wells added. Pride flashed across his face before he tossed several pecans into his mouth. "And dare I say I taught you to be a better rider than me. I always took pride in that."

Lacey swallowed her pecans and wiped her hands together. "But Mom worried."

"Even more. She traded one worry for another." He tipped the pecan bag at Lacey and eyed her. "But your mom loved you more than her worries. She knew what made you the happiest."

"Horses." And Caleb. Lacey fixed her gaze on the dusk-filled sky. That was when she had been her happiest. On a horse, her cowboy riding shotgun. It had not mattered what they were doing. As long as Caleb had been with her, her day was better. Back then...and even more so recently. She set her chair rocking again.

"Your mom cried something fierce when we sold your horses. Longer and harder than you. Broke her heart." Her stepdad's rocking chair creaked. "She never forgave herself."

"But it was the right thing to do," Lacey said.

"Didn't make it hurt any less." He chewed on more pecans. His words were casual. "That was why she made me promise not to sell this place."

Lacey slowed again.

"Your mom worked double time before the cancer came back to pay down the mortgage," Wells explained. "She was determined it wouldn't be a burden for either of us."

The depth of her mom's love and sacrifice touched and strengthened her. Lacey wanted Aspen to know that same kind of love from her. "Why would Mom do that?"

"Because your mom always wanted you to have a place to come home to. A place to find yourself again when you needed it." Wells shook his finger at Lacey and lifted his voice an octave higher to mimic her mom's voice. "Mark my words, Wells. My girl will want horses again, and I'm going to be sure she has a place to raise them."

"That sounds like something she would say." Lacey's grin was bittersweet and wistful. "I miss her."

"Me too. Every day," he admitted and pointed to the backyard. "But she's here. You can feel her in this house. On this land. She left her mark."

Lacey inhaled and nodded. She could feel her mom in the memories inside the house and around the property. "I want to make her proud. Honor her memory." And all that her mom had done for her only daughter.

"This place wasn't the same for me without your mom." Wells reached over and took Lacey's hand in his. His gaze was compassionate, his words sincere. "It has always been better suited for a family."

A family. That was one of those dreams from a different time. But then Lacey's marriage had fallen apart, and all Lacey saw was a broken family. One that she had failed to mend. Her deployment had almost been a reprieve from all the things she couldn't fix in her marriage.

Now she was home again. This time, with her cowboy, that dream had returned and felt almost within her reach. Until she lost it again. Lacey blinked at the tears pooling in her eyes.

"You want to honor your mom, Lacey?" Wells squeezed her fingers, drawing her attention back to him. He sounded so earnest. "Fill this house with your family. Fill the stable too. Build your life and live it. Be the happiest you can be."

Her happiest always seemed to circle back to her cowboy. The one she had pushed away.

"Don't settle for anything less than your happiest," her stepdad said, holding her attention and her hand steady in his. "Your mom and I did that. We had no regrets."

Lacey already felt her own regrets building.

"If your mom was here, she would tell you to push past your fear," he continued. "You can't be scared of living and failing, Lacey."

"Mom would say that's only half a life lived," Lacey mused. Her mom had always credited Wells and Lacey for giving her a life that was overflowing. "Mom always told me: *full is the only way to live, Lacey.*"

"Your mom lived her own advice." Wells squeezed Lacey's fingers one last time, released her hand, and sat back with a sigh. "Your mom loved fully and with all her heart. We should all be as fearless as she was in life and love."

Fearless in love. Lacey ran her hands over her jeans. "I wish she was here now to show me how to do that."

"You jumped and trusted those horses all those years ago. Reached new heights with them too." Her stepdad nodded and watched her. "Trust yourself now, Lacey. You might be surprised how far you can go."

"And what if I fall?" That was the fear, wasn't it? Getting it all wrong again. Getting hurt all over again. But she wasn't exactly happy now. And hurting, yeah, she hurt more than she wanted to admit.

Wells scratched his cheek. "What did you do back then?"

Lacey grinned, relaxed at the thought. "Dusted myself off and smarted about it for a few days."

"And then," he pressed.

"Tried again until I got it," she said.

Most often she'd grabbed Caleb and made her cowboy practice jumping or whatever else she was attempting, for however long it took. Then she'd stopped turning to her cowboy, and she'd lost a piece of herself along the way. Until recently. Home again with her cowboy beside her, she had been finding herself. Like her mom had known she would all those years ago.

"Well?" her stepdad drawled.

Her mom had been fearless. It was time to follow her lead. She could keep wallowing inside her fear or get up. Try again. Maybe even get it right this time. Lacey's smile came from deep inside her. "Well, I think I'm done smartin' about it now."

"Now that's good to hear." Approval washed over

her stepdad's words. "What do you intend to do about it then?"

"I'll let you know as soon as I figure it out." She stood, wrapped Wells in a warm hug, and pressed a kiss against his cheek. "Do you mind watching Butterscotch for a bit?" At her stepdad's nod, she added, "There's a conversation I need to have. It's long overdue."

Twenty minutes later, Lacey walked up to her ex-husband's front door and pressed the doorbell.

Jeffrey answered, confusion on his face. "Lacey. Everything okay?"

It wasn't, but it was going to be. "I have some things that need to be said." Lacey inhaled and lifted her chin. "And I'm going to say them now whether you want to hear them or not."

Jeffrey stepped outside and eased the front door closed. He stuck his hands in his pant pockets and looked at her. "I'm listening."

"I'm done apologizing, Jeffrey." Lacey widened her stance and wrapped her courage around her. "For our marriage falling apart. For who I am. For all the parts of me that fell short."

He opened his mouth.

Lacey went on before he could speak. "And I'm tired of carrying the blame for our divorce for both of us. There were two of us in that marriage. It's past time you apologized."

His eyebrow arched at her pause.

Lacey stopped. "I've more to say, but I'm ready to listen to you."

A small smile wavered across his face, but he cut the expression off. "I am sorry, Lacey. Sorry that I ever made you feel less than. That was never my intention. And I'm sorry you've been carrying all the blame. I wasn't the partner you needed or deserved. If anyone fell short, I did."

"Thanks." Lacey exhaled and welcomed the lightness that settled inside her. It was time to pack up the past and set it aside. Finally. "Look, Aspen is the best part of us." Lacey ticked things off on her fingers. "She is well-read, methodical, and intelligent like you. And she's brave, dedicated, and free-spirited like me. We never fully appreciated those qualities in each other. But perhaps we can appreciate them in our daughter."

"What are you saying?" he asked.

"We need to be the parents Aspen needs," she continued. "Her love for horses isn't a whim. It's not a phase. She's good, Jeffrey. And she can win this contest. But she needs our full support."

"I understand," he said simply.

Lacey quit pressing. Her ex-husband would take everything she told him now and think about it. It was enough. It was a start. A step forward. "Perhaps if we'd talked like this all those years ago, things would've been different."

Jeffrey shook his head. "We care about each other, right?"

Lacey nodded and leaned back against the railing. "Always have."

"And that's all it will ever be," Jeffrey said, his

expression sincere. "Lacey, we never worked because we didn't love each other like we needed to." He touched his wedding ring. "We didn't love each other the way I love Sarah-Beth. Or the way our daughter tells me that you love Caleb Sloan."

I love Caleb Sloan. Lacey pulled back, thankful she was propped against the railing for the added support. "Exactly how does Aspen say I love Caleb?"

"Like a cowgirl loves a cowboy." Jeffrey's eyebrows raised. Amusement creased across his forehead. "Your daughter claims you smile so much you glow when you are with Caleb." Jeffrey wiped his hand across his mouth but failed to stall his grin. "Apparently, Caleb glows just the same. Like you both apparently swallowed the sun."

Lacey searched for Aspen's words to Caleb in the hospital. *You hang on until love makes them smile so much they glow.* Lacey glowed. Caleb glowed. Who else had seen it?

She had felt it. The quick pulse. The giddiness. The butterflies. And that warmth that infused her from the inside out. With her cowboy. Or thinking about her cowboy. Her heart was full. So full she glowed.

But then she had gotten scared. Closed those blinders. Closed out her cowboy. And lost her light. She wanted it back, wanted her cowboy back. She wanted to love so much she glowed. Lacey pressed her hands to her cheeks. Lacey loved Caleb. *I. Love. My. Cowboy.*

A PROPOSAL FOR HER COWBOY

Jeffrey considered her. "Aspen is not wrong, is she?"

Lacey lowered her hands, revealing her wide grin. Her cheeks heated. Warmed to what she hoped was a glow. "I think Aspen might just be smarter than both of us."

"That's a given." Jeffrey took Lacey's hand and pulled her in for a quick hug. Then he leaned back to look at her and asked, "Now what are you going to do about it?"

"Mind if I take Aspen for a little bit?" Lacey's smile sank through her like sunshine warming her skin. "I'll have her home by bedtime."

"No need. I promised you three weeks with our daughter." Jeffrey opened the front door and grinned. "By my count, there is still more than a week left."

"Thanks, Jeffrey." Lacey touched his arm before he stepped inside and decided to press her luck. That was the gift of being in love. Insatiable positive vibes. "You will be at Aspen's contest, won't you?"

"Wouldn't miss it." Jeffrey motioned her into the house. "If Sarah-Beth and I can help, please let us know."

"Thanks. That means a lot, but I think I've got this." And she believed it. She turned and walked into the family room where Aspen was stretched out on the couch. "Aspen, I need your help. It's really important."

"Mom." Aspen sprang up and peeked over the back of the couch. "Mom, what is it?"

"I'm going to need my best cowgirl to help me catch a cowboy," Lacey announced.

"Yes!" Aspen thrust her arms over her head, cheered, and danced around the couch. She rushed to Lacey and wrapped her arms around Lacey's waist. "I told you cowgirls belong with cowboys."

Lacey wanted that to be true. For the first time ever, she was going to bet everything on love. And offer her cowboy a proposal he could not refuse.

CHAPTER TWENTY-SIX

THE REHEARSAL DINNER party departed for the Sloan family pond in a flurry of UTVs filled with supplies. Caleb's brothers had already headed over to the pond to light the firepit and prepare for an evening of swimming and water games.

Caleb waved off the last crowded UTV. The tires kicked up dust from the dirt trail, which mixed with the boisterous laughter of the guests. And Caleb realized he was alone for the first time all week. He inhaled and welcomed the sudden silence, broken only by the soft cadence of nature's nighttime choir.

A movement near the stables caught his attention. The stable door opened. A shadowed figure entered and clicked shut the door behind them. But he was supposed to be alone. Caleb frowned and headed for the stable barn.

Just inside the door, he came to a quick halt. "Mom. What are you doing?"

His mother wrestled with a saddle outside Winston's stall. The older brown quarter horse eyed his mother with a mixture of disinterest and boredom.

"I figure there is no time like the present to break in a new saddle."

"Why aren't you at the pond with the rest of the rehearsal party?" Caleb moved to his mother's side and eased the saddle out of her grip.

"Why aren't you?" she countered and propped her hands on her hips.

"Wasn't in the mood," Caleb admitted.

"Me either." Lilian tipped her head toward Winston's stall. "Can you please saddle Winston?"

Caleb never budged. "Mom, how long has it been since you rode a horse?"

"Since before you were born." She swiped her fingers across her forehead and frowned. "About the same amount of time since I was last in love."

Last in love. Caleb let that comment slide. For now.

"But I'm only interested in facing one fear today." She fluttered her hand in the air. "I'm sure it will come back to me. Now, if you won't saddle Winston for me, I'll do it myself."

Caleb walked into Winston's stall and saddled the patient gelding. When he was finished, he stepped out and said, "You're not riding for your first time in over thirty years alone. Give me a minute." Caleb grabbed the bridle outside Whiskey Moon's stall. His horse shook his head and whinnied his pleasure at an evening ride.

Caleb led his Palomino out of his stall, then opened Winston's stall to guide him out.

His mother took Winston's reins and asked, "Don't you need a saddle?"

"Whiskey Moon and I prefer bareback." He opened the wide double barn doors at the end of the stables and walked the horses outside. "He never quite adjusted to the saddle. We have a better connection without it."

"I know something about not adjusting to things." Lilian stroked the Palomino's neck. "We would certainly get along well, I think."

Caleb nodded and wondered again at his mother's peculiar mood. He helped her into her saddle, made quick adjustments to her stirrups, then handed her the reins. Mounted on Whiskey Moon, he led the horses toward the recently harvested wheat fields and the flat roads that cut through them. Slowing his horse, he reined in beside his mom, keeping the pace at an easy walk.

His mom shifted in her saddle and glanced at him. "By the way, where is your date?"

"You mean Georgia?" Caleb shrugged. "She found a better connection with Vivian's cousin tonight."

His mother considered him, her eyebrows arched. "You don't seem all that bothered."

"Not in the least." Caleb frowned and added, "Georgia actually told me I had a broken heart that I needed to fix." That was after the contractor admitted she had agreed to be Caleb's date to see the decorated rackhouse. Apparently, her cousin needed a venue for her engagement party, and Georgia was scouting locations.

His mother pressed her lips together.

Caleb swept his hand over his blue Paisley print

shirt and continued to defend himself. "There's nothing about me that screams broken heart." He was dressed as he always was. Better, even, in his dress jeans, clean boots, and fully ironed button-down dress shirt. "I'm the same as I've always been."

"Your hair is in need of a trim," his mother said lightly.

Caleb drew back. There was something fragile about his mother's grin. As if it was on the verge of collapsing without her full focus. Caleb was more than content to shift the focus away from himself. "Mom, were you serious back in the stables?"

"About not having ridden since before you were born?" His mother adjusted the reins in her hands. A wrinkle formed between her eyebrows. "I thought I wasn't doing too bad. Does it show that much?"

"You look fine. Comfortable in fact," he said. But it was her bruised heart showing that worried Caleb. "I was talking about the last time you were in love. I'm assuming that would have been with my dad."

"You would be correct." There was that fragile movement of her lips again. Just a fleeting lift, then it was gone. "After my divorce, I convinced myself that being in love was more of a hindrance than an asset. So I tucked away my heart."

Caleb knew a little something about convincing himself of things like that. He'd spent the past week convincing himself he had made the right decision. That he did not miss his deputy. That he was better off alone. And he was almost completely convinced. *Almost*. He shifted his weight on his horse's back.

"I've never told anyone this," his mother said, her words measured, her gaze fixed on the horizon. "I panicked after my divorce. I had lost my husband to someone better. Someone who said and did all the right things. I wasn't enough for him. So I couldn't imagine how I would ever be enough for my own kids. Or anyone else for that matter."

This was not the conversation he had been expecting. Caleb flexed his fingers around the reins. "Is that why you went to medical school?"

"I went to medical school to become someone my family could be proud of," she said simply.

"But you never came back to give us the chance to be proud of you," he countered.

"Your grandparents gave you more than I ever could those first few years," she confessed.

"What about later?" Caleb asked.

"I came back." She slanted her gaze toward him. "I watched you play baseball with Josh. You were quite good as the catcher."

He lifted his eyebrows in surprise. She had been there.

"I watched you and your brothers in the rodeo in high school too," she added.

He searched his memory of the ballparks and the arenas. Of the parents crowded on the bleachers. Would he have recognized her? Probably not. He'd been too focused on his brothers, his teammates, and his coaches. And then celebrating his successes with his grandparents. They'd been his world. Yet the image of her alone on those cold bleachers, so close yet so far, bothered him. "Why stick to the bleachers?"

"I sidelined myself," she admitted. "I had already hurt you, but you were thriving. So were your brothers. I didn't want to cause more havoc. And I had a life in New York to return to."

"But what about you?" he asked. "Weren't you hurting?" Just like she seemed to be hurting right now.

She straightened in her saddle. "Nothing I didn't deserve."

"So what was New York then?" he asked. "Some kind of self-imposed penance?"

"I thought the more patients I helped—the more people I saved—the more it would offset the pain I caused within my own family."

"Did it?" he pressed.

"No." Her shoulders lowered. Her words were dry. "I fully realize the irony. A renowned heart surgeon who can't heal her own heart. Tragic, really."

Or lonely. All these years on her own. Alone. But his mother was home with her family again. Still, Lacey had confessed she'd been lonely even in her marriage. But family should be enough. He was counting on it for himself. He rolled his shoulders against the emptiness inside him. The one that had opened up when his deputy had walked out.

But he'd been fine before. Before he'd known what life could be with someone like Lacey beside him. He cleared his throat. "Mom, what happened with Wells?"

"He wanted to love me," she said softly.

Caleb blinked. His deputy had pushed him away, never given him the chance to love her. "And that's a bad thing."

"For someone who hurts those she loves, yes." Her gaze was bleak. "And his words made me panic all over again. Foolish at my age, I know."

"Not so foolish," he said. "But you deserve to be loved and to maybe let yourself love, no matter your age."

"Thank you for that." She reached over and touched his knee. "You deserve the very same."

"Lacey didn't trust that I could love her." He guided the horses down the road that circled back to the stables and added, "Or that I even know how to love."

"I don't believe that." She patted his knee again and returned her grip to her reins. "I've seen you with our family. You know how to love, Caleb, deeply and with everything you have."

"Why do I feel a but in there?"

"But you choose not to love like that," she added. "The same as me."

"I never thought I would say this." Caleb paused and slanted his gaze at his mom, his words wry. "But we are a lot alike. It seems we are both bad at love. And neither of us can seem to get out of our heart's own way."

His mother chuckled. "What should we do about it?"

"Nothing," Caleb stated when she glanced at him. "I think we should stick to things we are good at, and let that be enough." If that emptiness wasn't stretching out endlessly before him, he might have convinced himself.

"I suppose we can't be any more miserable than we are now," his mother sighed.

"That's true," Caleb said and allowed the silence—and that sudden melancholy—to surround them.

They made their way back to the stables and came face-to-horse with an exasperated Grandpa Sam. His arms were crossed over his chest, and his deep frown disappeared into his beard. Worse, he stood in the stable doorway, blocking their entrance. It was clear no one was getting around Sam Sloan tonight. At least not until he had his say.

"Look at the pair of you." Grandpa Sam motioned between them, his movement brusque. "More alike than you want to admit."

Caleb held back from informing his grandfather that he and his mom had only just admitted their similarities. His grandfather was obviously in a mood. *Stirred up*, his gran Claire would've said. Then she would've added, *You'd best hear him out. Every word. After all, you caused it.*

"We went for a ride," Lilian said pleasantly. "Spent a lovely time together."

"You should be happy, Grandpa." Caleb dismounted and helped his mother off her horse. "That's progress for us."

"That's nothing." Grandpa Sam took the reins of Lilian's horse, his disappointment showing. "This was nothing more than two hearts on the run."

"It was a slow walk," Caleb said, purposely mis-understanding his grandfather. "Mom hasn't rid-den in a while."

"Walk or gallop, it's all the same," Grandpa Sam insisted. "I suppose you supported each other's de-cisions too. Came to a mutual agreement that love wasn't worth the trouble."

Caleb avoided looking at his mother, certain his grandpa would catch their guilty stares.

It hardly mattered. His grandfather had already guessed correctly. He would've called it his keen eye for perception. Grandpa Sam rolled right on, "Don't go denying it either. Of course that's what you did. You are two hearts on the run, just like I said."

"Things didn't work out for either of us," Caleb argued, trying to sound reasonable. Same as he had when he'd been a kid and his antics stirred up his grandfather. Besides, things didn't work all the time for lots of folks. "That's just the way it is. We aren't running."

"You sure as heck aren't fighting either." Sam waggled his finger at Caleb, then aimed his frown at Caleb's mother. "And if you aren't fighting, then you're…"

"Running," his mother said simply.

"Now you're catching on, Lily-Bee." Sam's eyebrows hitched higher on his forehead. "And if you keep going, you sure are going to end where you did last time."

"Alone," his mother sighed.

Caleb was fine with alone. Or rather he wanted to be fine with it. He had been fine before his deputy swept back into his life and showed him he might be better off with her.

"When you came back, you told me this time was about doing things different," Sam said to Caleb's mother and smoothed his fingers through his beard. "And yet this looks an awful lot like more of the same from where I'm standing."

"Old habits," his mother said weakly.

Like a locked-down heart. Caleb pressed his hand into his ribs. *You choose not to love.*

"Get a new habit," Sam ordered, but then his face broke out in a grin. "You might find it suits you better."

Caleb was starting to forgive his mother as he began to understand her more. He supposed he was even opening his heart to his mother. That was certainly a point in his favor. He was doing something different. But opening his heart to love? That might be a change too far.

"You mean like running *to* something instead of *away*." His mother's smile blossomed.

His grandfather's gaze sparked. "Now you just might be catching on, Lily-Bee."

"I think I need to go," his mother said, suddenly a flurry of excited movement. "I know what I need to do."

"I'll see to your horse," Sam said and hitched his thumb at Caleb. "There's more work to be done here."

"Thanks, Dad." His mother hugged his grandpa.

Grandpa Sam said, "I put a bottle of bourbon I pinched from Carter's private collection and a dessert from Tess in your car already. Tess and I decided it was all for a good cause."

"I hope it's enough." Caleb's mother laughed, turned, and framed Caleb's face in her hands. "Thank you for giving me this time with you. It was exactly what I needed."

Caleb wrapped his mother in a tight hug. It was the first genuine embrace mother and son had shared. "Maybe we can ride together again soon. I can show you more of the trails."

"I would love that." With a quick wave, his mother fairly ran to her sports car. One honk of her horn, and her taillights disappeared down the driveway.

Grandpa Sam stroked Winston's head, then led the horse to his stall. "Let's get these horses to bed for the night so we can put our feet up."

"I can handle it." Caleb opened the stall door and walked his horse inside. "You can head up to the house."

"We'll do this together," Grandpa Sam insisted, "then we'll sit down together too. You've been running on your own far too long. It's a pace you can't sustain."

But that hardly meant Caleb wasn't going to keep trying. They worked together, brushing down the horses, cleaning the tack, and sweeping the stalls. Once they had fresh water in the buckets and hay on the floor, there was nothing more to do. Minutes later, Grandpa Sam pressed a whiskey glass into Caleb's hand and sat in the chair beside Caleb on the back porch of the farmhouse.

Caleb dragged the coffee table closer and rested his boots on top. He wouldn't deny it felt good to sit down. But he wasn't fooled that his grandfather had nothing more to say to him.

Grandpa Sam sipped his bourbon and rested his boots on the table too. He didn't leave Caleb waiting long before he asked, "Do you know why your grandma always wanted you to sit still? Why it was so important to her?"

"She was tired of chasing me around," Caleb said dryly, adding a tease to his words to lighten the mood.

"She never did complain about that," Sam said. "Always claimed it was the best kind of exercise. She didn't know she was doing it."

Caleb chuckled.

"Your gran wanted you to sit because she worried you were too busy to stop and take stock." Grandpa Sam swirled the single ice cube in his glass. "She worried you weren't checking in to make sure your heart and your head were in alignment."

But Caleb had been too busy on purpose. That was how he outran his heart. Not stopping to take stock kept him from getting hurt. Just look at recent events. He took a deep sip of his bourbon. "My heart and mind haven't ever seen eye to eye." Same as him and his deputy.

"You haven't ever given your heart a proper chance." Grandpa Sam frowned.

That sounded awfully close to what his mother had claimed. "There's nothing wrong with my choices."

"That's your mind speaking for you." Grandpa Sam's laughter was low and knowing. "Listen closer and hear what your heart wants."

His heart wanted his deputy. Wanted a life spent with her. His heart wanted to love and be loved. He cradled his whiskey glass in his hands. "What if love isn't enough?"

"You won't really know if it is or isn't unless you give her your heart," Grandpa Sam mused. "All of it. Not just a piece. Not with conditions. No holding back."

Caleb tipped his head back and stared at the sky. Could he love like that? His heart wanted to try. Lacey deserved nothing less than everything he had to give. "That's quite the risk, isn't it?"

"I've never seen you back away from a risk." Grandpa Sam grinned at him. "Or an adventure. And falling in love just might be the last adventure you need."

He couldn't deny the appeal of taking this adventure with Lacey. He could only imagine what he could accomplish with her next to him. What they might build together.

"Only one question really needs to be answered." His grandpa eyed him over the rim of his glass. "Do you love her or not? Because that's the beginning and the end. The rest is just details."

Love her. Love his deputy. Caleb shifted and rested his elbows on his knees. Closed his eyes and finally took stock. And there, at the core, was the truth. Just waiting for Caleb to accept it. To embrace it. To honor it.

He loved her. It was that simple and that complicated. It was that freeing and that anchoring. And it was everything. Absolutely everything.

He supposed he had always loved Lacey. From the first time he met her. But what had once been affection and admiration was now something deeper. Stronger. Enduring. Oh yes, he loved his deputy.

But his deputy did not know it.

Caleb's eyes snapped open and fixed on his grandpa. "I messed up, Grandpa. Badly."

"It would not be called falling in love if the path was free of potholes." Grandpa Sam's arm draped around Caleb's shoulders. "We all stumbled on our way to love. I can assure you of that."

But Caleb hadn't stumbled. He had not even tried. He had not fought. Instead he had walked away. As if Lacey was not worth the trouble. "I let her down. I'm quite sure I hurt her and…" A different sort of panic simmered inside Caleb. A fear that he might have lost Lacey before he had even fought for her.

314 A PROPOSAL FOR HER COWBOY

"That's the funny thing about love." Grandpa Sam patted Caleb's shoulder. "The ones that truly love you, well, they keep on loving you even when you shut 'em out good and tight."

Please, let my grandfather be right. "Then I can fix this," Caleb said. He could still fight for love. For his heart and Lacey's. "I can still make things right."

"Can't guarantee it will be easy." Grandpa Sam clinked his glass against Caleb's. "But I can guarantee it will be worthwhile."

"Grandpa, I don't think I can do this alone," Caleb admitted. This time the stakes were too high. Lacey mattered too much. And winning her back meant going in with everything he had.

"You haven't been alone." Grandpa Sam beamed at him. "Your family has always been in your corner. We've been waiting for you to turn around and need us."

He was about to take the biggest risk of his life and put his heart on the line. He should be nervous. Scared. Unsure.

Instead, Caleb grinned and decided to double down on his heart and Lacey's, counting on love to win them an adventure of a lifetime.

CHAPTER TWENTY-SEVEN

AND THEN THERE was one. A single Sloan brother left standing. Though if Caleb had his way, he wouldn't be single for long. But that would have to wait for now.

Tonight was about celebrating his twin and his new wife. The ceremony had gone off without a hitch, and now the reception was doing the same. Standing by the bar in the back of the renovated rackhouse, Caleb lifted his champagne glass along with the other guests in a final toast to the ecstatic couple.

Josh twirled his bride around the dance floor under the hundreds of fairy lights Caleb had personally strung from the ceiling. His twin swung his new wife into his arms for a tender kiss, then they bowed to the crowd with a flourish. Thanking their guests for sharing in their special day, the couple encouraged everyone to continue celebrating even though they were heading out. Josh swept Vivian into his arms. The cheers filled the rackhouse as the couple took their leave.

Ryan approached Caleb and quickly swapped Caleb's champagne flute with a tumbler glass. Grant appeared at Caleb's other side and poured bourbon into Caleb's glass with the efficiency of a professional server. Suddenly, Carter, Grandpa Sam, and Uncle Roy were there, holding out their glasses for their own splash of bourbon. And then the glasses clinked together.

"Now that's a proper drink for a toast." Uncle Roy waggled his eyebrows and sipped his bourbon.

"Didn't feel right to be in the rackhouse and not sipping what was made here," Grandpa Sam added, a twinkle in his gaze.

"We're missing someone." Caleb glanced around the tables, found the woman he was looking for, and smiled. He called out, "Lilian Sloan. You're needed near the bar."

Their mother excused herself from her table, where she sat with her date, Sheriff Wells Hopson, and the Baker sisters.

Caleb poured a glass for his mother and handed it to her. He cleared his throat and said, "I'd like to make a toast to family. For always having my back. And believing in me all along."

"If you'd asked us sooner, we would've told you we believed in you." Grandpa Sam clinked his glass against Caleb's. "You just weren't believing in yourself."

"I am now." Caleb raised his glass again. "Thanks to all of you."

"Fine then, I'm going to speak on behalf of your gran Claire and myself," Grandpa Sam said, his words rough, his gaze tender. He reached over and took hold of Lilian's hand. "I don't believe I could be more proud of this family and who you have become. Brothers. Leaders. Fathers. Husbands." He slanted his gaze to Lilian. "Mother. Daughter." He paused and sniffed. "Sure makes an old cowboy like me look back and say: *what a fulfilling journey I've had*. And I owe it all to my family."

Caleb dabbed at his damp eyes, noticing his brothers and mom doing the same. He grinned at his grandfather. "We wouldn't be here without you, Grandpa and Gran Claire. There are no words for the love we have for you."

There was a round of here, here's from his brothers.

"Caleb Sloan, I'm too old to cry," Grandpa Sam said but ruined his statement by tapping the back of his hand against his eye. "And I love you all more."

The Sloan family shared a group hug and another toast to Josh and Vivian, promising to fill Josh in on Grandpa Sam's heartfelt words.

"Now then, this is supposed to be a celebration. We need to be getting to it." Grandpa Sam smoothed his hand over his leather bolo tie. "If you'll excuse me, I'm going to see if Breezy still has a step in her two-step."

"I'll see you out there." Uncle Roy chuckled. "Gayle already promised me a dance."

Caleb's brothers drifted off to find their wives and join the others on the dance floor. Caleb turned to his mother and held out his arm. "Do you think Wells would mind if I borrowed you for a dance?"

His mother smiled and wrapped her arm around his. "I would mind more if we didn't dance."

With that, Caleb guided his mother to the dance floor for a two-step followed by a country swing. When the band shifted into a slow song, Caleb handed his mother off to Wells for a waltz and made his way back to the bar.

Several songs later, Caleb was still leaning against the bar, chatting with the friendly bartender that Chef KC had hired. His back was to the room, but his boot tapped to the beat of the lively music.

Wells stepped up beside Caleb, asked the bartender for a refill, then turned toward Caleb. "I have something for you."

Caleb straightened when Wells extended his arm and placed something in Caleb's hand. Caleb gaped at the white gold diamond ring resting in his open palm. He lifted his startled gaze to the sheriff, now his mother's boyfriend.

"That's the wedding ring Lacey's mom wore." Wells smiled, his expression sincere and open. "I was going to wait to give it to you. But I was talking to Lilian, and well, in case you want it sooner, now you have it."

Caleb ran his fingertip over the solitary diamond. It was heavier than he would've expected. At one time, he would have refused the gesture. Backed away swiftly and steadily. Now he leaned in, curled his fingers around the ring as if to protect it. Because it was everything he wanted now. "I was going to ask for your blessing after I earned your daughter's heart." Caleb had already worked out his approach. He only needed Josh and Vivian's wedding to conclude, and then he would start getting the affairs of his own heart sorted.

Wells grinned. "You have my and Lacey's mom's blessing."

"I'm honored." Caleb hoped Lacey would be too, when he finally put his love-for-the-win plan into play. He tucked the ring safely into his pocket, then reached out and shook the sheriff's hand. "Not that you need it, but you and my mom have my blessing too."

"That means more than you know." Wells pumped Caleb's hand one more time. He tipped his head to the stage and the band who was winding down another set. "I heard a rumor that there's a special request coming up. You won't want to miss it."

LACEY WAS EARLY. And anxious. More anxious than early, really.

Standing on the moonlit grounds of Misty Grove Distillery, she rolled up to the balls of her feet in her new indigo suede cowboy boots and back to her heels. She shook her arms at her sides. Shrugged her shoulders. Rolled her head to one side, then the other. Nothing dislodged the nerves.

She touched her cowboy hat. Smoothed her fingers over her flowy wrap dress and fiddled with the bow resting on her left hip. Still, her pulse only raced faster.

"Mom," Aspen whispered.

Lacey spun around, grateful for her daughter's familiar face. "How do I look?"

"Like the prettiest cowgirl ever." Aspen beamed at her.

Lacey inhaled, felt herself settle slightly. "Is he still inside?"

Aspen's grin grew wider. "Yup. And now it's time to catch a cowboy, Mom."

"I don't know if I can." Lacey's boots felt stuck in the gravel and dirt.

Her win-back-her-cowboy strategy had seemed like an excellent one when she first came up with it. She had garnered the support of her family and her cowboy's family, and that had only emboldened her. What wasn't to like? It would be surprising, heartfelt, and romantic. Except if Lacey couldn't go through with it, the entire thing would be nothing more than an almost-good idea that didn't win her anything.

Suddenly, a pair of thin arms wound around Lacey, and she found herself wrapped in her daughter's version of a bear hug. "Just hold on, Mom. I'll squeeze you until you glow."

Tears pooled in Lacey's eyes. She embraced Aspen and held on, grateful for the blessing of her daughter and her constant love. Mother and daughter stayed like that for another minute before Lacey kissed Aspen's head. "That was exactly what I needed."

"You feel better, right?" Aspen peered up at her.

"Immensely." The fullness in her chest steadied Lacey like nothing ever had. She reached down and took Aspen's hand. "But if it's okay with you, I could really use your support to walk out on that stage."

"I won't let go, Mom. I promise." Aspen clutched Lacey's hand tighter and studied her. "Do you want my glasses to read the words, Mom?"

"No, but thanks." Lacey laughed. "I have the lyrics memorized. I just need my voice to remember to sing the correct words."

"Grandpa Swells says it doesn't matter if you get the words right." Aspen swung their arms forward and back between them. "So long as you sing from your heart."

"I think that's the best advice I've heard." She would lead with her heart and convince her cowboy to follow.

Lacey walked with Aspen toward the side door of the renovated rackhouse. The one glowing with soft dim light and filled with the Sloan family and their guests.

Aspen pressed her ear against the door. "The music is slowing, Mom." Aspen clapped her hands and shimmied in place. "Wait till they hear you sing. They're gonna be so surprised."

The side door creaked open before Lacey's nerves could sweep through her again. Elsie popped her head out, her smile brighter than the full moon, and motioned to them. "Come on. Ryan is already onstage. It's time."

Aspen's hand was back inside Lacey's, and her daughter was tugging her through the door before Lacey's second thoughts could snag her. She was on the stage with the band, a microphone pressed into her free hand and being introduced by Ryan Sloan before her reservations could catch her. Aspen never left her side. Never loosened her grip.

And all of a sudden, the entire rackhouse quieted. Ryan nodded to Lacey and picked up his own microphone. And Lacey turned.

All eyes were on her. But she had eyes for only one. She scanned the crowd, searching until… There. Near the back. *My cowboy.*

And just like that, everything else fell away around her. The onlookers. Her nerves. Her doubts.

Her cowboy had her in his sights. He was moving forward, his gaze locked on hers. Lacey squeezed Aspen's hand to let her know she was alright. Aspen squeezed back, then slipped her hand free and headed off the stage.

Lacey lifted the microphone in both hands and, with her cowboy her only view, said, "Caleb Sloan. This one is for you."

That half grin—the one reserved only for her—dipped into his cheek. He kept coming toward her as if he had no intention of stopping until he got her.

The band started playing behind her. Ryan filled in the harmony. The music swirled around her, through her, and when Lacey opened her mouth, she sang from her heart. A country love song about being better than she was, stronger than ever, and who she wanted to be because of his love.

Her cowboy never lost track of her. She never lost him. When he finally reached her, her hand found his. And still Lacey sang, her love for her cowboy spilling into every lyric.

He raised her arm, pressed the gentlest, most perfect kiss against her fingers. Then he flattened her palm over his heart and covered her hand with his. His gaze had a certain sheen. She was sure hers did too. And if someone wanted to know what love looked like, Lacey would've said her cowboy. Right there. In that moment. The one she imprinted on her heart.

Lacey finished the song. Applause swelled toward the ceiling. Someone took the microphone from Lacey's hand. But her attention was on her cowboy, her only focus getting closer to him. He was of the same mind as his arm came around her waist and he gathered her to him.

Her gaze traveled over his face. Finally, she managed a breathless, "Caleb."

"Speechless," he finally whispered. His tone was raw and honest. "You leave me speechless." There was an intensity to his gaze. "Beautiful. Your voice. You. You're so beautiful. Inside. Out."

A tear slipped free and slid down her cheek. "You've always seen me. Always accepted me just as I am."

"My cowgirl." He caught her tear with his thumb.

His expression was achingly tender. "I don't deserve you."

Lacey curved her arms around him and held on. "You should know, cowboy, that I have no intention of letting go this time."

"There will be a fight if you do," he promised. "I'm holding on too. I'm going to be the cowboy you deserve."

His words lightened her. Encouraged her. She tangled her fingers in his hair and playfully asked, "Out of curiosity, how do you plan to do that?"

"By loving you like you've never been loved before," he said, his words serious.

But his touch was gentle and steady on her cheek. And the affection in his gaze was more than she had anticipated. Her pulse jumped.

"I love you, Lacey Nash," he said, simply and effortlessly. "You're my reason. The start and the ending. It's you. It's always been you."

Lacey's heart soared. She would have joined it if Caleb's arms weren't anchoring her to him. Right where she wanted to be. And suddenly, speaking from her heart came naturally. Easily. "You should know I love you too, Caleb Sloan. And I have plans to love you like you've never been loved before."

"I do believe that's the first time I've ever been swept off my boots. I think I like it." Caleb dropped his head back and shouted his love for her to the entire venue, then pinned his gaze on her again. "I had a strategy to win you back. I organized it all."

"But I got to you first." Lacey smiled, feeling herself glow.

Caleb released her and patted the pockets of his dress pants. "I was going to do this... Well, it doesn't matter when because I don't want to wait any longer. I can't wait."

"Caleb." Lacey searched his face, wanted back into his arms where the world felt right.

He dropped to one knee. Right there in the middle of the dance floor, with his family and friends watching, with her daughter and stepdad looking on. Then he reached into his pocket and held out a ring to her.

Lacey gasped. She knew that ring. Her tears fell in earnest then.

"Lacey, I'm tired of sitting back and hearing about everyone being in love," he started, his gaze searching hers. "I'm ready to experience love. With you."

Lacey was already nodding. She was ready too. With him.

Caleb's grin spread, and his face glowed. "Lacey Nash, will you marry me?"

This time it was Lacey shouting a resounding yes to the crowd and launching herself into her cowboy's arms. Amid the claps and congratulations from their friends and family, their lips collided for a kiss that opened hearts and promised a love that spanned a lifetime.

Lacey pulled away long enough for Caleb to slide the ring onto her finger. She framed his face and spoke through her tears. "I love you, Caleb."

Caleb kissed her again and linked their hands together. "Ready for an adventure like you've never seen, cowgirl?"

Lacey pulled him closer and said, "Always, but only if it's with my favorite cowboy."

EPILOGUE

Two weeks later...

LILIAN SLOAN RUBBED her palms on her jeans and shifted on the metal bench in the Three Springs Rodeo arena. "I don't believe I've ever been this nervous before."

"Doc, you're a heart surgeon. Steady hands are required. You couldn't afford nerves on the job." Wells leaned closer and took her hand in his.

"But now I'm retired," Lilian said and linked their hands until they were palm to palm. "And it seems all those nerves I ignored for so many years are coming out now."

"How about we keep each other steady?" Wells chuckled and covered their joined hands with his other. Just the way Lilian liked. Wells added, "I'm a bit nervous too."

Lilian gaped at him.

"What? It's my granddaughter, riding a horse on her own in an arena with a crowd watching," Wells confessed. "This is her first ever Junior Royal Rodeo court parade."

Pride was clear on her sheriff's face. And Lilian admitted to feeling a bit of it too. After all, she had been assisting Aspen with her preparations for her two-minute speech in the competition. Lilian wanted to believe her support and guidance had helped Aspen secure her spot on the Royal Rodeo Court as a first-time entrant.

"Okay. Okay." Lacey slid onto the bench beside Lilian and rubbed her hands together. "It's almost time for the parade to start. I'm so nervous."

Caleb joined them, wrapped his arm around Lacey's waist, and pulled her close. "Aspen is going to be great. She's riding Biscuit. They both have matching ribbons in their braids. And they make a stunning pair."

"You can say that because you got to be back there with Aspen while she prepared for the parade." Lacey kissed Caleb, then frowned at him. "I'm still not pleased about that."

"The rules of the royal court explicitly state one adult chaperone is allowed backstage." Caleb kissed Lacey back, then chuckled. "I can't help it that Aspen chose me as her one person."

"She chose you as her chaperone," Lacey corrected. "And she already told me I could be there with her next time."

"Actually, dear, she promised me." Lilian fought to keep her grin in place. "I have a text right here from Aspen."

Lacey read the text on Lilian's phone screen and

shook her head. "She did. Aspen invited Nan Lily to be her chaperone for tomorrow's parade."

Lilian had helped Aspen prepare for the competition, and in turn, Aspen had helped Lilian finally choose her name. From here on out, the grandkids would call her Nan Lily. Lilian thought it had a nice ring to it, especially when Aspen used it right before she greeted Lilian with one of her all-encompassing hugs.

"I'm sure you will get a turn." Lilian tucked her phone away and nudged Wells. "Right, Wells? Lacey will get a turn to be chaperone, won't she?"

"Not likely," Wells admitted but then laughed at Lacey's stunned expression. "Aspen told me that her mom makes her too nervous, so she can't be around her beforehand."

Caleb chuckled. "Aspen told me that too."

"What do I do?" Lacey crossed her arms over her chest.

"Apparently you worry too much, dear." Lilian placed a gentle hand on Lacey's leg. "And you fuss with Aspen and the horse and every little thing."

"Now I know exactly how my mom felt all those years ago." Lacey buried her face in her hands and her shoulders suddenly shook. "How did she handle this?"

Wells leaned around Lilian and said, "She shared it."

Lacey lifted her head and grinned. She linked one hand with Caleb's and her other with Lilian's and said with a new confidence, "Then that's exactly what I'm going to do. Share my worries with my family because we are stronger together."

Family. The word filled Lilian and warmed her. She was home. With family. And stronger for it. Finally, she was right where she belonged.

* * * * *

For more great romances
from Cari Lynn Webb and
Harlequin Heartwarming,
visit www.Harlequin.com today!

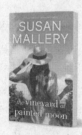